The Carpenter's Son

DEDICATION

To my parents for bringing God and faith into my life.

Special thanks to the priests and nuns of St. Joseph's Church and the Christian Brothers of LaSalle Institute in Troy, New York, for their religious instruction, patience, and guidance. And, as always, to my wife, Courtney, who is my northern star, forever leading me to be a better man.

The Carpenter's Son

A Novel

John Gray

PARACLETE PRESS
BREWSTER, MASSACHUSETTS

2025 Second Printing
2025 First Printing

The Carpenter's Son: A Novel

ISBN 978-1-64060-966-2

Library of Congress Cataloging-in-Publication Data
Names: Gray, John (John Joseph), 1962- author.
Title: The carpenter's son : a novel / John Gray.
Description: Brewster, Massachusetts : Paraclete Press, 2025. | Summary: "This novel gives you a chance to walk with Christ and see the world through his eyes. Most importantly, it will renew your faith in God and each other"—Provided by publisher.
Identifiers: LCCN 2024044091 (print) | LCCN 2024044092 (ebook) | ISBN 9781640609662 (trade paperback) | ISBN 9781640609679 (epub)
Subjects: LCGFT: Christian fiction. | Novels.
Classification: LCC PS3607.R3948 C37 2025 (print) | LCC PS3607.R3948 (ebook) | DDC 813/.6—dc23/eng/20241011
LC record available at https://lccn.loc.gov/2024044091
LC ebook record available at https://lccn.loc.gov/2024044092

10 9 8 7 6 5 4 3 2

Published by Paraclete Press
Brewster, Massachusetts
www.paracletepress.com

Printed in the United States of America

CHAPTER 1

Cork in a Blender

"Get back in your car."

The state trooper's tone sounded more like a threat than a suggestion to Brooklyn Sterling's ears. His deep voice cut through the sharp wind high atop the Rip Van Winkle Bridge. Locals referred to the mile-long span over the Hudson River as *The Rip*, and on this bitter March evening, traffic in both directions was at a standstill. Brooklyn shifted her eyes to the right, just beyond the trooper, to where a woman dressed in little more than a housecoat was standing on the outside of the railing in her bare feet, her hands white-knuckled as she gripped metal supports. As a breeze flipped the hair up on the woman's shoulders, Brooklyn thought, *My God, she's barely hanging on.*

"Have you tried talking to her?" she asked the trooper.

"Of course. She told me to back away or she'd jump." Before Brooklyn could reply, he said, "And I told you to stay in your car."

The officer, six foot four if he were even an inch, had the name MILLS sewn in purple thread on his jacket. He craned his neck right and left as if looking for someone.

"Is help coming?" Brooklyn asked.

"Not soon enough."

As Brooklyn looked at the dozens of cars stopped in gridlock, the trooper added, "Supposed to be a crisis counselor from Columbia Memorial on the way, but I don't know."

"Trooper Mills," she continued, "I know this is going to sound strange, but I was sent to this bridge tonight to help that woman."

"Sent by whom?" he asked.

Brooklyn hesitated, uncertain how to answer.

"'Well?" Mills asked again.

"You wouldn't believe me."

"The night I'm having, I'd believe anything," Mills quipped.

"True enough," Brooklyn said. "But . . ."

"What?" he asked. "Speak."

"Alright, then. God sent me," she said.

The trooper stifled a laugh. "God?"

"He's a personal friend," she answered. "Long story."

Trooper Mills engaged the button on his handheld radio, asking when the crisis counselor would arrive.

"ETA, twenty minutes," a voice replied.

Mills turned his head toward the woman hanging onto the bridge and muttered, "I don't have that long."

Brooklyn inched closer. "May I speak to her?"

"Why? You some kind of shrink?"

"No," she answered. "A journalist and a woman who's been on the ledge before."

As the cop gave her an odd look, Brooklyn said, "Metaphorically."

He took in a deep breath, clearly uncertain of how to proceed.

"Let me try. Please."

The trooper looked at her for a hard ten seconds, sighed, and said, "I guess it can't hurt."

The last thing Brooklyn wanted to do was startle the woman, so she raised her hand, like a fourth grader waiting to be called on in class, and said, "Excuse me, can I speak to you?"

The woman looked and nodded, so Brooklyn moved closer.

As she got close, the woman revealed sad eyes that were wet with tears.

"Is that from crying or the wind?" Brooklyn asked.

"A bit of both," she answered. Brooklyn then asked, "Can I get you a blanket? It's freezing up here."

The woman replied, "I don't plan on being here long."

When Trooper Mills turned his head sharply, Brooklyn raised both her hands. "It's alright. We're just talking. Nothing more. Right?" She turned her attention back to the woman. "You have a moment to talk, yes?"

The woman gave a slight nod.

"I'm Brooklyn, like the bridge."

"I'm Sandy, like the beach."

The comparison caused Brooklyn to smile.

As the woman turned her face to the river below, Brooklyn tried to pull her attention back.

"Why are you here, Sandy?"

She didn't respond.

"I mean, I know why," Brooklyn continued. "That's obvious . . . what I'm asking is *why?*"

Sandy said, "Do you have a blender at home, the kind you make shakes with?"

"Yes."

"Can you imagine if you were the size of a wine cork? Can you picture that?"

"I can."

Sandy let out a mocking laugh. "Well, imagine you're that cork and someone drops you into the blender and turns it on."

Brooklyn conjured the image in her mind.

"And as the sharp blades are spinning," Sandy said, "you're jumping and ducking, trying not to get hit. Only it's impossible not to get hit. It's like every single blade is an accusation or judgment."

Brooklyn said, "And that's your life right now? You're the cork in the blender?"

"Yeah. I am."

Brooklyn took one step closer. "Would it surprise you to know, I've been in that blender myself?"

Sandy looked away from the dark abyss below and into Brooklyn's eyes.

"And there is a way out, Sandy. I can show you the way out."

Sandy shook her head. "There's nothing you can say that will change the mess I'm in."

"I'm here because of the mess you're in," Brooklyn said. "A friend sent me."

"What friend?"

Brooklyn tilted her head. "I promise we'll get to that."

Sandy asked again, "Who sent you?"

Brooklyn took a deep breath. "Someone I never believed in, but now I do. People question my sanity because of the things I've seen and written, but I promise he's as real as that freezing water down there."

"I'm not moving until you answer my question," Sandy said.

Brooklyn took one more deep breath. "God sent me, Sandy. Jesus himself."

"Oh, so this is a faith thing?" Sandy shot back. "Let me stop you right there. Because I lost my faith a long time ago."

"I understand," Brooklyn said. "You're talking to someone who had no use for God. Who didn't believe."

"And now you do?"

"Yes."

"Why?"

Brooklyn replied, "Because of what happened to me last fall. Because of Edward."

Sandy turned away again. "This is all nonsense. I came here to do this, and we're wasting time."

Trooper Mills moved closer. He was evidently ready to intervene, perhaps make a grab at her. *That would be way too risky.*

"Sandy, I don't think it's in your heart to hurt yourself this way. You've been up here awhile with plenty of chances to jump, and now you're talking to me."

"You don't know me."

"You're right, Sandy, I don't. But I'd like to."

The woman on the edge looked back again at Brooklyn.

"Come sit with me a moment in my car to talk. Trooper Mills won't mind—will you, sir?"

Mills answered, "If it gets her off that railing, I'm fine with it."

Brooklyn inched closer to Sandy.

"Let me help get you home."

"That's just it," Sandy said. "I can't go home. I've hurt too many people."

Brooklyn edged closer and slowly extended her open palm over the railing. "Take my hand and give me a chance to show you there is always forgiveness. There is always redemption. There is always a way home to him."

Sandy's face dropped as if she were lowering her weapon and surrendering. She gingerly released her grip on the metal railing of the bridge and locked fingers with Brooklyn.

"I've got you now," Brooklyn whispered. "God has you now."

Sandy slowly brought her leg over the railing and back to safety, never letting go of Brooklyn's firm grip. As their eyes met, the woman who'd just been standing on the edge of the world asked one question. "Who is Edward?"

CHAPTER 2
Catch Evi

SIX MONTHS EARLIER

"We need a ladder," Evi called out to her parents.

Brooklyn's husband, Connor, wearing a red and black checkered flannel shirt and faded Wrangler jeans, was already ahead of their daughter, marching between a row of trees with a fifteen-foot ladder in tow. Even though they'd been together more than a decade, Connor still gave Brooklyn butterflies, especially when the sunlight caught his chiseled features and deep blue eyes. And when he doted on their daughter, displaying a father's love, Brooklyn was reduced to a marshmallow on a stick over an open flame.

The two of them had met at an Irish bar in Boston called *The Black Rose.* He was sitting by himself, while his friend from college played bass guitar in a band entertaining the happy hour crowd.

Sitting at the bar with a few of her co-workers from the *Boston Globe*, Brooklyn was unable to take her eyes off him. She smiled when she realized he was mouthing the words to every song.

After downing something called a "lemon drop" shot, she pushed her hair back into a ponytail, popped up from the stool, and announced loudly, "Audaces fortuna juvat."

"What did you say?" one of her friends asked.

Brooklyn replied, "Fortune favors the bold."

As she made a beeline for her quarry, she overheard one of her friends say, "I guess *we* should have studied Latin at Bard like her."

The closer she got, the better-looking this man appeared, wearing a black button-down shirt, dark slacks, and tassel loafers. His thick hair, somehow organized and messy at the same time, matched perfectly with the light stubble on his face.

Brooklyn hadn't fussed getting ready that night but was happy with her choice of jeans and a white blouse with a red silk scarf looped neatly around her neck. Her green eyes danced in the candlelight illuminating the tables she weaved through to reach him.

"Can you teach me the words to an Irish song?" she asked, visibly startling him.

Recovering quickly, Connor pushed out the chair across from him with his foot. "How about *Galway Shawl*? It's a love story."

Brooklyn accepted his invitation to sit. "Just tell me, do they live happily ever after?"

Answering in a ridiculous Irish brogue he clearly didn't possess, he replied, "It's an Irish song, me love. Those never do."

Her laugh echoed across the bar.

They sat and talked for the next three hours. When Connor asked Brooklyn to describe herself with one word, she answered *tenacious*. As he kissed her goodnight, she added, "Brave. I'm also brave."

Today everyone at the apple orchard would have a front-row seat to Brooklyn's bravery.

Their nine-year-old daughter, Evi, was standing on the top rung of the ladder, trying to reach a shiny red prize. Standing directly behind her on the ladder, Brooklyn spied a branch above and decided it was thick enough to hold her weight. She stepped carefully around Evi, using a smaller branch to take her up to the branch where she could grab a large, juicy apple.

"Can you reach it, Mommy?" Evi asked.

With one hand on the tree for safety, Brooklyn reached out with the other to grab the biggest apple in the orchard.

Even though it was eight inches around, Brooklyn's weight, pressing down in one spot, produced a bloodcurdling crack, loud enough to turn every head within twenty feet of the tree.

"Jesus!" Connor called out. Evi was at the top of the ladder, and Brooklyn was a few feet higher still when the branch she was on snapped clean away. As she fell, she instinctively clutched the top of the ladder, causing it to shift and tip over. Now both of them were falling toward the ground.

Brooklyn wanted to scream, "CATCH EVI," but there wasn't time for the words to form.

Fortunately, Connor was way ahead of her, extending his arms as if carrying a stack of laundry, and positioning himself directly under their daughter. Evi was plunging straight down, feet first, when the cuff of her pants caught a small branch hanging from the tree. This was a stroke of luck because the branch yanked Evi's leg, causing her body to shift and complete her fall horizontally.

With a *thud,* Connor caught her safely in his waiting arms. The only injury to either of them was a fat lip Connor received when Evi's elbow clipped him in the face on the landing.

Brooklyn was another story altogether. Because of where she was positioned on the tree, she did not fall freely to the earth but banged off several branches on the way down, like a painful game of human pinball. Since it was late in the apple picking season, there were rotting and half-eaten apples in the soft grass beneath the tree, softening the blow at the bottom.

The worst came when her head snapped back against the ground. She was hit with a flash of white light, what many call *seeing stars.*

A crowd had gathered. As Brooklyn lay there, the only voice she could hear was her daughter's.

"Mommy, are you okay? Mommy?"

Brooklyn blinked hard, trying to clear her head. "I'm okay, honey."

Connor let out a huge sigh. "Oh, thank Christ."

Brooklyn raised her hand to take Connor's. As he slowly eased her up from the ground, she said, "You crack me up. You really do."

Connor waved the crowd of onlookers away. "Me? What did I do that was funny?"

Brooklyn hugged her daughter and looked up at the broken branch. "You thank God that I'm okay from the fall but don't blame him for the branch snapping."

Connor enfolded both of them. "I'm not having this argument. Not today. You're both safe. Let's leave it there."

A few people were still gathered around, gawking at the woman who had just fallen from the sky. Brooklyn was just now noticing them. Off on the edge of the crowd was a familiar face. For a moment they locked eyes, and then a man in a black and gold jacket nodded as if acknowledging a connection before disappearing into the crowd.

"I know him," Brooklyn said.

"Who?" Connor asked.

She strained her eyes, scanning the onlookers. "He's gone."

Evi looked up. "Are you sure you're okay, Mommy?"

Brooklyn gave her daughter another tight squeeze. "I'm fine, my sweet. I just hit my head."

A man approached and introduced himself as Norm Sebastian, the owner of the orchard. "I called an ambulance," he said. "I think you should sit down, miss."

Brooklyn rubbed the back of her skull. "No one has called me 'miss' in a while," she joked. "I'm fine, sir. Really. Cancel the ambulance."

Connor put his hand on her cheek. "Why don't we let the medics decide if you're okay, hon."

"What happened?" Norm asked.

"It's my fault, I left the ladder putting all my weight on a branch."

"Normally it would have held, but we had so much rain this summer, those old limbs are waterlogged and weak."

Brooklyn started scanning the crowd again. "The face, the jacket. I'm telling you, I know that guy."

"What's she talking about?" Norm asked Connor.

"I don't really know," he replied. "Brooke, what are you going on about? Who do you know?"

She dusted her hands off on her jeans. "Oh, geez, I'm covered in smooshed apples." She looked at her husband. "What did you ask me?"

Evi replied, "You said you saw someone."

Brooklyn looked around again. "I did, but he's gone. Something odd about it."

"What do you mean, odd?" Norm asked.

Brooklyn patted the older gentleman on the shoulder. "Sorry, sir, just my Spidey Sense going off."

The man looked confused. "Spidey?"

"She's a journalist with the *Boston Globe*," Connor explained. "Sometimes she gets hunches, for stories."

"I see."

Brooklyn touched her head, which was now throbbing. "It's nothing, and I don't need the ambulance. Probably just a couple of Advil, and I'll be good."

Just then, two EMTs arrived. At Norm's urging, they looked Brooklyn over and checked her vitals. Besides a slight bump on her head, she appeared fine, and they cleared her to go.

Connor asked, "Are you sure you're okay, sweetie?"

Brooklyn took a deep breath and picked up Evi. "Fit as a fiddle. Now, who wants Chick-fil-A on the way home?"

Evi called out, "ME."

Brooklyn gave a soft kiss to Connor's lips. "I'm okay. Let's go."

She gave one last look around the orchard, searching for that familiar face, but he was gone.

Exactly twenty-two miles away from the orchard in Danvers sat the upscale Boston neighborhood known as Beacon Hill. A white work van with a company logo—*The Carpenter's Son Woodwork*—was parked in front of a pristine two-story brownstone.

One flight up, Gabriel Matthews stood in awe at the hand-carved angels his new worker had just completed on a piece of crown molding above the fireplace. Gabriel was in his sixties, but years of standing on ladders and crawling on floors had given the carpenter the posture of someone much older. Despite his infirmities, Gabriel still provided top-shelf custom woodwork.

Rich people bragged to their friends, and there was now a list of Boston's upper crust waiting on *The Carpenter's Son* to visit them. Having an assistant that could match his quality work would be a godsend. Gabriel stared at the perfect angels, now etched in the wood. "You weren't kidding, Edward," he said. "You really do know what you're doing with a chisel and mallet."

Edward turned to face him. He was of average height and build, early thirties, with brown shoulder-length hair, deep brown eyes, and a neatly trimmed beard. "Glad you're pleased." He quietly returned his tools to a wooden box, then went to the window.

"Whatcha looking at?" Gabriel asked.

"The sunset," he answered in a gentle tone.

"Is it a good one?"

"They're all good in my book," he replied.

"It occurs to me," Gabriel said. "I don't even know your last name."

Edward continued looking out the window.

"I'll need it to pay you. Your last name . . ."

Without turning around, Edward said, "It's Manuel, but no payment is necessary, Gabriel. The room you've promised above your garage and food at your table is recompense enough."

"Hogwash." Gabriel looked again at the hand-carved angels Edward had just created. "I have to pay you something for this fine work."

Still no reply.

Gabriel inched closer. "You okay?"

"The branch couldn't hold her," he whispered.

"What branch?"

"Too much rain," Edward said. "It weakened the limb."

Gabriel drew even closer. "What did you say?"

Edward turned, smiled, and placed both hands on Gabriel's shoulders. "You're a good man. Let's go home."

CHAPTER 3

The Wicked Borrow

Connor and Evi were sitting together on the couch, looking for something to watch together on television.

As Evi quickly skipped through the channels, her father said, "Wait. STOP. Go back."

"*Who Ha*," Connor called out. "*The Scent of a Woman*. Love this."

"Is that the actor who always plays the gangsters? she asked.

"Al Pacino, yes."

"So I can't watch it then."

"No, no, this one you can. He's a grumpy old blind man who turns out to be a nice guy and helps a kid in trouble."

Evi asked, "Is it good?"

"Oh yeah, wait until you see him do the tango."

"The *what oh?*"

Her father laughed, "It's a dance—let's watch."

In the kitchen, Brooklyn opened a bottle of water, so she could take the four extra-strength Tylenol in her hand. Her head had been thumping like a bass drum since she dropped like an apple out of that tree.

Connor called to the kitchen, "Did you see the package for you on the counter?"

Brooklyn didn't answer. Instead, she was looking at the granite countertops, the stone backsplash, the open archway that revealed a beautiful dining room, thinking, *I love this house.*

The 1,800-square-foot colonial, in the small town of Wakefield just outside of Boston, caught their eye a year after Evi was born. Brooklyn and Connor were paying $2,800 a month for a cramped one-bedroom apartment in Brookline. It was convenient for work but money out the door for a couple with a newborn.

"Hon? Did you hear me?"

Brooklyn snapped out of her daydream and saw a brown bag with handles resting on the counter. "Got it."

Inside was a small square box with the words "Massachusetts Publishers Association" stamped on the top. And in the box was an award with the words *Columnist of the Year* etched in glass. Between the apple picking, her fall from the tree, and twenty minutes in line at Chick-fil-A, Brooklyn had forgotten all about the awards ceremony she had skipped at the Marriott earlier that day in Boston. This was the third time in five years that she'd won this award for her weekly *Gotcha* column at the Globe, exposing crooked politicians and their ilk.

She read the etching and called to her husband and daughter, "I won."

When there was no response, Brooklyn grabbed the statue and entered the living room, only to find the two of them engrossed in the movie.

When neither looked over from the large flat-screen TV, Brooklyn cleared her throat and posed with the award like a model holding a prize on a game show.

Still no response. "Really, you two. Really?"

Both looked away from the movie and saw the statue in her hands, prompting them to jump up and run to Brooklyn.

"You won, Mommy!"

"I did, sweetie. How do you like them apples?"

"Apples?" Evi asked.

"Just an expression, hon."

Connor looked proudly at his wife. "Well done, young lady."

Brooklyn glanced down at the statue. "I'll bet there are a few politicians in Boston who'd like to throw *it* and *me* into the harbor."

Evi said, "Like they did with the tea."

Brooklyn gave her a confused look.

"The patriots in the harbor," Evi added.

"The Boston Tea Party," Connor said. "Very good."

Brooklyn chuckled at her daughter's comparison, then in her best *pirate's voice*, said, "Arr, exactly, headfirst into the slimy deep, me matey."

Evi laughed.

"I'm going to go make popcorn," Connor said. "Come finish the movie with us. We'll celebrate your victory with extra melted butter."

Before Brooklyn could answer, Connor was already off to the kitchen. She sat down on the couch, Evi to her left side, the child's feet now draped across her lap. As a car commercial blared from the television, she looked at Evi, then down at the statue. *I should be happier,* she thought. *Why am I not happier?*

Two towns away in Woburn, Massachusetts, Piper Matthews was setting the dishes out for supper. She and her father, Gabriel, normally only needed two place settings, since she'd lost her mother to cancer and her brother to a war in a place most people couldn't find on a map.

Now in her early twenties, Piper would have been fine taking the plates into the living room to eat and watch TV on the couch, but her father wouldn't hear of it.

"Dinner is the one meal a day to be treated with respect," he'd insist.

That meant dining at a table together. No cell phones.

At first, Piper resisted this quiet time with her father, but after the death of her brother, Paul, in Afghanistan, she grew fond of it. Sometimes the only conversation between them was the clicking and clacking of the silverware or a smile one shared with the other in silence. A loving glance could say a lot, Piper always thought.

Tonight, however, she was setting the table for three because her dad had invited a stranger into their home. Just as she was folding napkins and placing them under the silverware, she heard a gentle tap at the back door.

"Come in," Gabriel called out.

Piper said sharply, "Don't you think you should ask who it is first?"

"Why?"

"Oh, I don't know, Dad. 'Cause it could be a serial killer or something."

Edward, her dad's new worker, opened the door slightly and peeked around the corner. "I'm not a killer but I do like cereal."

Gabriel laughed. "Never mind her, Edward, come in, please."

As Edward rinsed his hands off in the kitchen sink, Piper grabbed three bottles of water from the refrigerator and placed them down on the counter a bit harder than required.

Gabriel looked at her. "Do we have a problem?"

Piper nodded her head toward the other room and walked off, Gabriel following closely behind. "Excuse us a moment, Edward."

The second the door swung shut and the two were alone, Piper said, "Explain to me again who this guy is and why he's living in our house."

Gabriel glanced at the door, a look of anxiety on his face.

"He can't hear us," she said.

"First of all, keep your voice down, and while we're at it, lose the tone."

Piper adored her father and hated to see him even remotely upset with her. "I'm sorry. I'm just trying to understand."

Gabriel said, "You know I've had three men work as my assistant since your brother left us—"

"Died, Dad. He died. He didn't leave us. Paul put on a uniform, served his country, and died."

Gabriel matched her tone. "I know that, Piper. You don't have to throw it at me like a rock every time we mention his name."

Piper could see the pain in his eyes. "You're right. I'm sorry, Daddy. What were you saying about the men who worked for you?"

"I started to say that the last one, Barclay what's his name, walked off in the middle of the job I'm doing right now."

"I know. And?"

"And . . . Edward said he saw the work truck in front of the house on Beacon Hill and literally walked in, just as Barclay was walking out."

Piper lowered her voice. "So you hire a stranger with no experience, on the spot."

"I have experience," a gentle voice said from the slightly opened doorway. "I'm sorry to interrupt, but I do have experience."

Piper sized the man up, convinced she should not trust him. "Trade school? An apprenticeship?"

Edward pushed the long brown hair from his eyes. "No. I learned the old way."

Piper furrowed her brows.

"My father was a Tekton," he said. "That's a carpenter of sorts."

"Where? Not around here?" She heard the accusation in her tone.

"No," Edward said with a disarming smile. "A long way from here."

She scoffed. "So you just happened upon my father the moment his worker quit? That's a bit convenient, don't you think?"

Edward reached over and put his hand on Gabriel's shoulder. "I saw the work van and the name, *The Carpenter's Son,* and seeing I am a carpenter's son, I wanted to meet the man who owned it."

Gabriel jumped in. "And we got to talking, I had an opening, and here we are."

"Wait," Piper said, "not so fast. Your workers get paychecks and have homes. Why is it, I'm sorry, I forgot your name—"

"Edward."

"Why is *Edward* living above the garage and sitting at our kitchen table?"

"Well . . .," Gabriel began.

Edward intervened. "Because that is all I need. Food and a warm place to stay for a short time."

Piper perked up. "So this isn't permanent?"

"No," Edward said. "Just a short visit."

Gabriel rubbed his calloused hands together. "I'm sorry to hear that. You're a good worker and good company.

Edward grinned. "And as I said earlier today, you're a good man, Gabriel. The wicked borrow but don't pay back, while the righteous give generously. You give generously."

"Is that Tony Robbins?" Piper asked wryly. "I think I heard him say that on TikTok."

Edward looked confused. "Tick tock? Like a clock?"

Piper glared at this stranger in her home. *Is this guy for real?*

After an awkward pause, Gabriel said, "Dinner is getting cold."

Piper ignored her father's comment. "So, this arrangement, you above the garage—"

"A short visit, I promise," Edward said. "I'm just here to help."

"Did I mention it's meatloaf?" Gabriel said.

Edward turned toward him. "That sounds wonderful. Let's eat."

With that, the three of them convened in the dining room for supper. Piper had more questions for this stranger, but for now, they could wait.

A short drive away, it took three bags of microwave popcorn to fill the large bowl that Brooklyn, Connor, and Evi were dipping their hands into as they watched the end of the movie. Al Pacino was ready to rise from his chair and deliver his big over-the-top speech to save the day.

Just as Pacino banged his cane on the table at the school tribunal, Brooklyn stood up and said, "He's blind."

Evi giggled. "You're just figuring that out?"

Before Brooklyn could answer, Connor said, "You've seen this movie before, hon."

"I'm not talking about the movie."

Now it was Connor who seemed confused. "Are you okay?"

The noise from the television was distracting. Brooklyn grabbed the remote and paused the DVR. "The guy at the apple orchard," she said. "He's blind."

Connor looked at Evi, then back to Brooklyn. "What guy?"

Brooklyn paced back and forth, trying to work it out in her head, whispering under her breath as she tried to put all the pieces together.

"You're scaring me, Brooke."

She looked up, confronted by concerned looks on their faces. "I'm sorry, I don't mean to . . ." She sat back down on the couch. "After I fell from the tree, I saw a face in the crowd. The man looked right at me, and I could tell he knew me, and he knew that I knew him."

Connor shrugged. "Okay. So?"

"So, he's blind. The guy is blind."

"I don't understand, Mommy."

Brooklyn grabbed Evi's hand. "What I'm trying to say is I've seen that man many times outside of Faneuil Hall in Boston."

She looked at Connor. "He's blind and sells pencils for a dollar."

"But you said he looked at you at the orchard like he knew you."

"Exactly! He did."

"I'm still confused," Evi said.

"He's not blind, hon, he's pretending."

"Why would he do that?" she asked.

"To trick people into giving him money, so they'd feel sorry for him."

"Well, that's not very nice," Evi said.

"No, sweetie, it's not." Brooklyn squeezed her daughter's hand.

"Are you sure it's the same guy?" Connor asked.

"Positive. He even had the same jacket on that he always wears when he's selling pencils. Black with gold sleeves and a big gold P on the chest."

Connor took out his phone and started typing something into the screen. Then he showed her an image. "Like this?"

"That's it."

"It's a Pirates jacket."

"He's a pirate?" Evi asked, wide-eyed.

"No, sweetie," Connor said with a smile. "It's a baseball team. The Pittsburgh Pirates. He's probably just a fan."

Brooklyn hurried to the desk in the corner of the room, opened a drawer, and took out a notepad from work. "He's not the only one scamming tourists outside Quincy Market."

Connor joined her near the desk. "What do you mean?"

"Hang on." She thumbed through the pages.

Anyone who knew Brooklyn had seen her like this before, many times. It's the way she acted when her journalistic nose was sniffing out a great story.

She slapped a page on her notebook. "There it is. Father and daughter violin players."

"What?" Connor asked.

"Someone told me months ago that I need to investigate this father and daughter team pretending to play music outside Quincy Market and taking donations."

"They're pretending?" Evi asked, wide-eyed again.

"Yes, pretending. I was told they have a machine playing the music while they put this whole act on, making it look like they can both play their violins perfectly."

"Oh, so they're fake too?" Evi asked.

"Yes, they are."

Connor said, "Do you see a connection between these two things? The violin people and the guy from the orchard?"

"Not yet," Brooklyn said. "But this could make a nice little series for the newspaper, exposing the frauds who bilk tourists of their hard-earned cash."

Evi went over and picked up her mother's glass award. "Uh oh, get ready for another trophy."

Connor smiled. "You should pitch it at the paper tomorrow."

Brooklyn returned to the couch, picked up the TV remote, and hit "play." "I will, but first let's watch your boy Pacino tear the roof off this school."

Back in the home of Gabriel and Piper Matthews, dinner was done, and their new houseguest had retired to his room above the garage. It was a barren space, offering little more than a bed, a bathroom, and a single chair by the small solitary window that looked down on the driveway. There was no television or shelves full of books. Gabriel wondered what Edward did to occupy his time and mind before sleep. Come to think of it, Edward didn't even carry a cell phone. No matter. He seemed as happy as a man could be, so Gabriel let it alone.

As he made his way down the hallway toward his bedroom, Gabriel noticed Piper's door was slightly ajar, a sliver of light escaping into the hallway.

He took hold of the doorknob. "Did you want this closed all the way?"

Piper, sitting at a small desk to the side of her bed, did not respond.

"Piper?" Gabriel called, louder this time.

Piper jumped. "Oh, hey, Dad."

"You okay?" he asked.

"I'm fine, just thinking of something our new tenant said earlier."

"What's that?"

She rose from the chair and hugged her father. "It doesn't matter. Good night, Dad."

Gabriel held his daughter extra tight, his mind wandering to the heartache she'd felt when her only brother died in the war. He'd never forget the moment when Piper answered the door to find two uniformed men standing at attention on the front steps.

"Dad, there are Marines outside," she'd called to him, not understanding the horrible significance attached to such a visit.

Gabriel had known the sad truth in that instant, having served in Vietnam and having heard too many stories of Marines and door knocks and terrible news that was always delivered in person.

"Are you okay, Dad?" Piper broke their embrace, concern etched on her brow.

Gabriel kissed her on the cheek. "I'm great. Sweet dreams."

After Gabriel shut Piper's bedroom door, she immediately went back to the seat at her desk and opened Google on the computer screen. She looked toward the ceiling, a habit she had when trying to remember something, and then her gaze fell back on the screen and the blinking cursor in the search box.

With little more than a whisper, Piper said as she typed, "The wicked borrow but don't give back, while the righteous give . . ."

She paused, asking herself, "While the righteous give what? What did he say?"

Then it hit her, "Generously."

She typed the missing word and read it one more time.

The wicked borrow but don't give back, while the righteous give generously.

Piper hit the "enter" key and waited no more than a second before a dozen hits popped on her screen. They all offered various interpretations of the expression that came from Edward's lips before they all sat down for dinner. The search responses also had one thing in common and it *wasn't* Tony Robbins.

Piper was not a religious person by any means. She had gone to church at St. Anthony's on Main Street in Woburn with her dad and brother back when she was young but lost her way completely after Paul's death. In fact, Piper rarely went to church even when she went to church.

Gabriel insisted his two children go each Sunday, but Piper and Paul learned they could pop into St. Anthony's five minutes before mass, grab a bulletin, then skip out and do something fun. That church bulletin was proof that they had gone.

Following the death of his beloved wife, attending church gave Gabriel a small measure of comfort. Sadly, her death had the opposite effect on his children, causing them, especially Piper, to question God and the fairness of it all, losing her mother so young. Piper treated God like a cactus full of thorns. She knew he existed but stayed clear of him.

Her eyes locked on the computer screen and the relevance of Edward's quote.

Every article the search retrieved mentioned Psalm 37:21. The word *Psalm* sounded familiar, but she wasn't certain of the context. Clicking through several of the passages, she soon realized Edward's quote was from the Old Testament.

Piper stood and went to her bedroom window now, glancing up to the lone porthole that was lit up above the garage. As if on cue, the moment she noticed the light, it went out.

She whispered a question, impossible for him to hear. "Whatcha doing quoting the Bible, Edward?"

She wasn't close to being finished with her inquisition of one Edward Manuel.

CHAPTER 4
Lexington It Is

Boston Globe editor Rex Ryerson had a firm policy at the newspaper: you were either early for a meeting or late. There was no such thing as *on time*, so the conference room at the *Globe* was filled by 8:53 for the 9:00 a.m. staff meeting.

Brooklyn came in with half a bagel hanging from her mouth, a venti coffee in one hand, and a Starbucks goodie bag in the other. One of her colleagues stood up and performed a slow clap in praise of her having won the publishing award the day before. Others joined in, giving a standing ovation that felt to Brooklyn like one part praise, two parts teasing.

She was about to give them a mock bow when Rex bolted into the room. "ENOUGH, ENOUGH, she didn't even bother to show up for the darn thing."

Her coworker Alice, who wrote for the business section, said, "You blew off the awards lunch?"

Brooklyn took a bite of her bagel. "We took Evi apple picking instead."

She could tell from her co-worker's reaction that they would have chosen being honored at a podium over spending a morning with a child. What most didn't realize was Brooklyn had been adopted at birth and had made a vow at a young age to never take time with a child for granted. How her birth mother could have abandoned her haunted her to this day.

"Ideas?" Rex said, officially starting the meeting and ending Brooklyn's moment of praise.

"There's a rash of con artists bilking the tourists in Quincy Market," Brooklyn said.

"Define *rash*?" he shot back.

"A father-daughter pretending to play the violin when they can't and a blind guy selling pencils who is not. Blind, that is."

"That sounds like two, not a rash," he commented.

"I'm sure I'll find more."

"You see this as a series?"

"Yes. And if I can scare up a couple more scams, it could be a good draw for us with the readers."

"Sounds good," he said. "Go ahead and get started."

Brooklyn smiled, prompting him to say, "You already did, didn't you?"

"Yeah. Remember the story I did three years ago on the Boston Symphony?"

"Vaguely."

"Well, I called the PR lady over there, she gave me the number of their first chair violinist, and she's meeting me outside Quincy Market at ten-thirty."

Rex said, "I don't know what that means, *first chair*, but it sounds like you're hitting the ground running."

"Yes, I am. In fact, if the fake blind guy is out with his pencils, I'll nail him too."

"Two in one day," Rex said. "That's a bit aggressive."

Well, she thought, *you know me.* "I need quality pictures and someone who isn't afraid of confrontation. Can you give me Vars?"

Vars was Matt Vars, the *Globe*'s top photographer, and winner of a Pulitzer Prize for the pictures he took at the Boston Marathon bombing. He was older and slower than the others but a true artist. He also had seniority and could veto Brooklyn's request for him.

"He's been pretty surly lately," Rex said. "Are you sure you want to ask him?"

She shook the Starbucks bag in her hand. "That's what this is for."

Rex grinned. "Let me guess. A blueberry scone, extra dry."

Brooklyn laughed. "So dry he'll choke on it."

Rex waved her off. "Go get me a story."

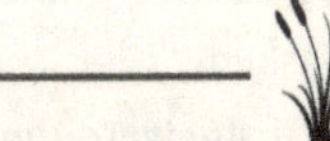

Back at the Matthews' home, Piper was standing by the kitchen window, which looked out onto a backyard covering nearly a half-acre.

There was lush grass, a stone walkway, and a bench situated beneath a pear tree that Piper had planted in her mother's memory. Every time it bloomed white flowers in the spring, Piper thought it was her mom saying hello.

There was no fence around the yard, so wild animals made daily visits, scarfing up the corn and seed that Gabriel was kind enough to scatter on the ground for the birds.

He came into the kitchen and saw Piper standing motionless, mug with hot coffee in hand by the window. "Whatcha looking at, hon?"

Without breaking her stare, she answered sarcastically, "Oh, nothing. Just our new houseguest talking to a deer."

"Talking to a what?" He joined her at the window.

Edward was sitting on the bench in front of a small fawn. You couldn't hear what he was saying, but he was clearly talking to the animal.

"It's not even afraid of him," Piper observed.

"I'm going out," Gabriel said.

The moment he turned the doorknob it made a clicking noise. The fawn darted off into the woods.

"Sorry," Gabriel said as he approached Edward. "Didn't mean to scare him."

Edward rose to his feet. "Do I smell bacon?"

"You do. Come in and eat with us."

Edward started toward the door, giving Gabriel a friendly wink as he passed by.

Once inside, all three were at the kitchen table for no more than thirty seconds when Piper blurted out, "Oh, come on, am I the one who has to say it?"

Edward took a bite of bacon and raised his eyebrows.

"The deer," she said. "The freaking deer."

"What about the deer?" Edward asked.

She threw her hands in the air as if she were the only one not in on a joke, looked at her father, and let out a loud sigh.

"I think what Piper is wondering, Edward, is what did you say to it?"

Edward rose and took orange juice from the refrigerator. "Well, *it* is actually a *she.* And *she* got separated from her mother and was just looking for something to eat."

Piper scoffed. "And you just said, come on in, miss deer, the buffet is open."

Edward shrugged slightly. "Hmm . . . something like that."

Piper was lost for words again.

Gabriel cleared his throat. "I guess what we're wondering is why wasn't she afraid of you? Most deer don't act that way."

Edward poured the carton of juice into a glass, then sat down again at the table. "Well, when she poked her head through the tree line looking for breakfast, I told her she was welcome here."

"And that's when she spoke to you and told you about her mother?" Gabriel asked.

Edward nearly choked on the juice he was drinking. "No, Gabriel. Deer can't talk."

Gabriel smiled sheepishly. "So . . ."

Edward picked up a piece of toast. "Isn't it obvious that she lost her mom?"

At this, Piper bolted up from the table, then grabbed her jacket off a coat rack. "Doctor Doolittle. That's who we have living with us."

"I've never been to medical school," Edward said. "I'm a carpenter's son, remember?"

"What?" she asked.

"I'm not a doctor," Edward answered. "Carpenter."

Piper rolled her eyes, picked up her car keys, and started toward the door.

"Try to have a good day at work, hon," Gabriel said.

'We both know that's not going to happen," she called over her shoulder.

"Why not?" Edward asked.

Piper turned to face this odd stranger. "Because I process claims for an insurance company, Edward."

"And this is not rewarding?"

"No, it is not. Any other questions before I go?"

"Aren't there other jobs?" he asked.

"Why, yes, there are, Edward, but not for people who drop out of college."

She went silent, collecting her thoughts and slowing her breath.

What was with this guy and the twenty questions?

Gabriel said, "She dropped out to help me with the bills after her brother died in Afghanistan."

"That's selfless of you," Edward said. "Those who humble themselves will be exalted." He went back to eating his breakfast, crunching loudly on a piece of burnt toast.

Piper looked at her father. "None of this is strange to you?"

"What?" he asked.

She pointed at Edward gorging himself at their kitchen table. "He pops up out of thin air, doesn't want money, speaks in riddles, and now he's talking to Bambi."

Edward wiped his chin with a napkin. "I met your father in Boston, and there's nothing wrong with money. When I talk, I speak the truth, and Bambi, as you called her, didn't talk. I just said hello."

Both Edward and Gabriel smiled at Piper, who shook her head in exasperation. "You two have a nice day together."

As the sound of Piper's car revving away, Gabriel said, "We have a busy day. We must finish the job in Brookline, and at some point later today, I need to make a quick stop in Lexington."

"Lexington?"

"Yes. I have to pick up a check from a job I did last week."

Edward crossed the kitchen to the window above the sink and looked out. "Sunny day," he said.

Gabriel put his dirty dish in the sink. "Yes, it's a beautiful morning."

"You have to watch the sun glare today," Edward said.

"What's that?"

"Too much glare can be dangerous."

Gabriel grabbed his jacket. "What are you talking about?

Edward approached Gabriel and firmly placed his hands on both shoulders. "We should go to Lexington now, this morning, not later."

Gabriel replied, "It would be easier to circle back after lunch to get that check—"

"Now," Edward repeated. "Right now."

Gabriel scanned his new friend's eyes. "Everything okay?"

"It will be."

There was an awkward pause. "Alright, Edward, Lexington it is."

CHAPTER 5

Behind the Drawer

Photographer Matt Vars wore the same faded Boston Red Sox sweatshirt to work three days a week. This morning it was covered in crumbs from the bribe Brooklyn had given him to work with her.

Vars was 63 and walked with a noticeable limp. Normally Brooklyn wouldn't ask him to shoot a story that involved a lot of walking, but she needed someone who wouldn't miss the shot, especially if the person being photographed decided to run off.

"Thanks for the scone," he said.

Brooklyn noticed the crumbs on his shirt. "Did any of it make it into your mouth?"

"Keep it up, and I'll drop you at the aquarium with the seals."

"Do it," she said. "I love seals."

As Vars drove, he asked, "We're meeting her outside the Salty Dog, correct?"

"Affirmative. West end of Quincy Market."

Traffic was heavy, but with forty years of experience navigating the streets of Boston, Vars weaved through it like an Olympic skier.

When they arrived at the location, Ha-Joon Kim, a Korean national who had come to America on a music scholarship to Berklee, was waiting for them, violin case in hand. "Hurry up," she said. "I spotted them by the Gucci store."

"Ha-Joon, this is my photographer, Vars. Vars, this is Ha-Joon, the best violinist this side of the Mississippi."

"Good for you," Vars curtly replied. "Let's go."

As much as Vars could come off as rude, Brooklyn liked it when he had his game face on. She had a feeling they'd need it.

As the three walked east outside Faneuil Hall, Ha-Joon said, "I got here early and saw them playing, and you were right, Brooklyn, they're total fakes. They move their fingers around the violin, putting on a show, but the music from the speaker is a recording, not them."

Hearing this only quickened their steps toward the frauds.

Ten miles away in Lexington, Gabriel and Edward arrived in a beautiful neighborhood called Meriam Hill. A mixture of families and young professionals called this area home. Gabriel parked on Oakmont Circle, aptly named because the road formed a circle around a small body of water known as Granny Pond. Gabriel had built custom-made cabinets in a two-story Federal-style house that faced the pond and was here to pick up his final payment.

"Come up with me," Gabriel said. "I want to show you my finished product."

Edward got out of the van and looked around. He had an uneasy expression on his face.

"Everything okay?" Gabriel asked.

"Sure."

Both men headed up the stairs just as a boy exited a front door, two houses down, throwing them a wave.

Jayden Lancaster was an eleven-year-old who spent nearly all his free time fishing in Granny Pond. While catching any fish would be fine, his true goal was landing a huge carp he called *Jumbo.*

The short trip from his front steps to the pond on his bicycle was not dangerous, so Jayden's mother never worried when he lit out with his fishing pole. She also knew he understood the rules and followed them to the letter. *Never ride in the road.*

Jayden hopped onto his bike and headed off.

Upstairs in the home, Edward ran his fingers along the custom-made cabinets Gabriel had built. "Fine work, Gabriel. Beautiful."

A well-heeled woman in a Versace dress, with matching earrings and belt, came around the corner, waving a check so Gabriel could see it.

"Paid in full." She handed him the money.

"Thank you so much, ma'am," Gabriel replied.

The woman winced. "Ouch! Did you just ma'am me?"

Gabriel tried to mend the error. "Miss, I meant to say."

"Just teasing. Who's your friend?"

"You can call me Edward." He crossed the kitchen to an antique hutch standing watch in the corner and touched the faded brass latches on its front. "Your grandmother's," he said, more a statement than a question.

The woman's eyes went wide. "It is! How did you guess?"

Edward didn't respond, instead touching the latch. "May I?"

The woman nodded.

He picked up a white Pfaltzgraff salad plate with blue flowers along the edge and said, "Forget special occasions. Every time family is over, it's special."

Gabriel was only half paying attention, but the woman's face froze as if she'd just seen a ghost. There was silence as Edward carefully placed the dish back in the hutch and closed the delicate glass door.

"We should get going, Gabriel," he said.

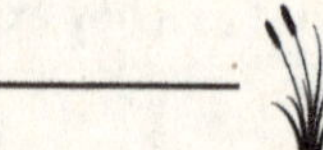

Despite ten minutes of casting and reeling at the pond, none of the fish were biting this morning. Jayden hadn't eaten breakfast, and his stomach was starting to sound like a tiny marching band was in there.

The boy looked toward the murky water and called out, "Until next time, Jumbo." Then he grabbed his pole and hopped aboard his red Schwinn bike.

The ride from the far end of Granny Pond to his house took less than two minutes, especially when he was hungry and pedaling fast. In all that haste, he'd forgotten his mother's rules somewhere.

Jayden was told to always ride on the sidewalk. The only time he should be *in* the road was when he walked his bike across to reach his house. She was crystal clear on that point: he would *walk*, not ride across the street. Walk.

As he pedaled along the sidewalk and inched closer to his home, Jayden joked to himself. "Why did the chicken cross the road? I haven't a clue. Why did Jayden cross the road? To eat pancakes."

Maybe it was the thought of a hot breakfast that made him do it, or he knew his parents weren't home to catch him breaking the rules, but this morning Jayden did not stop and get off the bike to walk it across the street. This morning, he would hop the curb and shoot straight across Oakmont Circle.

Cassandra Marshall was the daytime manager at the Crafty Yankee gift shop in Lexington. It was her responsibility to open at ten a.m. sharp, with no exceptions. A small wireless camera was installed behind the counter so the owner could keep tabs on her tardiness. Cassandra knew if she was late one more time, she'd lose her job.

The drive from her home in Winchester to Lexington was only six miles, but on days when Cassandra was running late, she used the Meriam Hill neighborhood as a shortcut. The speed limit at Oakmont Circle was 30, but today Cassandra was doing nearly double that. Making matters worse, as she came around the bend near Granny Pond, the morning sun caught her windshield at a dangerous angle, the glare blinding her completely.

Upstairs in the home where Gabriel had just collected his check, he and Edward entered the hallway to leave.

"Goodbye now, and thanks again," Gabriel said, heading for the staircase.

Edward, standing right behind him, placed his foot on the top step.

"Wait. Please," the homeowner said.

Edward turned toward her. "Do you know me, sir?" she asked, a resolute expression on her face.

Edward replied, "We were just introduced."

"My name is Emily Johnson."

"It's nice to meet you, Emily. Again."

As he turned to leave, she repeated, "Do you know me?" Her eyes brimmed with tears. "I ask because you knew that was my Nana's hutch and more important is what you said."

Edward looked as if he were about to reply, then stopped himself, like someone struggling to keep a secret.

Emily touched his arm. "My nana has been dead, must be thirty years now. When we were little, my parents would drop me and my brothers at her house to visit."

Edward engaged her eyes, seeming unsurprised by what she was sharing.

Emily continued, "She had cheap everyday plates, but whenever we grandkids would visit, it didn't matter if we were having grilled cheese or peanut butter and jelly . . ."

Edward smiled gently. "She'd say, 'Forget special occasions, every time family is over it's special. Use the good dishes.'"

The woman's eyes were an ocean of water now, streaks of tears coming down her cheeks. "That's right. How did you know that, sir?"

"Edward!" Gabriel shouted from the bottom of the stairs. "Come quick! Something has happened outside!"

Edward looked back to Emily and said, "I have to go." Then he reached out, took her hand, and squeezed it. "Look at me. She's happy, and she's proud of you."

Emily stared at him. He looked as if he were listening to someone who wasn't there. "You didn't lose it," he said. "Look *behind* the drawer."

With that he let go of her hand and dashed down the long, circular staircase, vanishing from her sight.

At the same moment, back at Quincy Market, Brooklyn approached an older man performing with a teenage girl. They were outside a busy store, appearing to play their violins perfectly. The music echoed across the courtyard from a portable speaker on the ground.

A badly made cardboard sign lying on the cobblestone read, *Family in Need*, the message printed in red ink. Next to the sign was an open violin case, with what had to be at least fifty dollars in coins, singles, and fives strewn about inside. *They're having a good day,* Brooklyn thought. *Let's end that right now.*

She looked at Ha-Joon, who was watching them intently.

"So?" Brooklyn asked.

"Not even close," Ha-Joon answered.

Brooklyn approached them, Vars furiously snapping photos with each step.

"Stop, stop, stop," Brooklyn said, waving her hand dismissively at the performers.

The crowd of tourists began rumbling, clearly confused as to why she would interrupt such perfection.

The older man, still moving his bow across the strings of his violin, took on a panicked look and nodded to his daughter.

The young girl bent down and flipped a nob on the speaker, causing the music to stop abruptly. The noise from the crowd was growing.

"My name is Brooklyn Sterling, with the *Boston Globe*. This is Ha-Joon, a *real* violinist with the Boston Symphony Orchestra, and you two are fakes."

The young girl appeared on the verge of tears as she bent down quickly to slam shut the violin case full of money, moving with such haste that several bills fell onto the sidewalk.

"Don't you want the money you scammed?" Brooklyn pointed at the errant cash.

The girl looked at Brooklyn, and instantly something felt off. Brooklyn had confronted many people before in her *gotcha* moments and always got one of three reactions—denial, anger, or guilt. This teenage girl was different. She wore an expression of intense shame.

Vars kept snapping photographs of the pair, causing Ha-Joon to say, "Okay, okay, I think you got it."

Vars barked back, "I shoot until she tells me enough."

"Enough," Brooklyn said. "That's enough."

She took a second look at the man and his daughter, now standing together with their heads hung low. His left shoe had split open from wear, exposing his sock. The girl, a slip of a thing, had a stain on her blouse.

If this is an act, Brooklyn thought, *they're certainly playing it all the way.*

The man cast his eyes toward the ground and fidgeted nervously with his hands. "This will be in the newspaper?"

She answered, "Afraid so."

The man picked up the speaker, held it close to his chest with the violin, and said, "May we leave now? We won't come back."

Vars spoke for everyone when he said, "Just go."

The duo skulked away. As the small crowd of onlookers dispersed, Brooklyn noticed several dollar bills still on the ground.

Ha-Joon picked up her violin case. "I don't want to do anything like this again," she said. "And keep my name out of your article." Then she walked away.

Brooklyn looked at Vars. "I'm sorry to do that to them, but they're scamming people out of their money."

Vars nodded. "Hey, you're preaching to the choir. Are we done?"

Brooklyn was going to go and look for the man pretending to be blind and selling pencils in the plaza, but this encounter was enough for one morning. "We'll get the other guy tomorrow."

As they walked away, a menacing eastern wind came off the bay and blew through Quincy Market, scattering the discarded money on the cobblestones in every direction. One of the dirty and crumpled dollar bills seemed to be chasing Brooklyn and Vars back to their car, as if judging them each step of the way.

Gabriel was the first one to reach Jayden. He'd watched with helpless horror through a downstairs window as the car hit the little boy's bike at high speed. His crumpled body landed twenty feet from where he was hit, skidding across the sidewalk like a rag doll and coming to rest at the foot of a driveway. The impact was so great, the boy came out of his sneakers.

Gabriel knelt beside him. There wasn't as much blood as one might expect. He figured the damage must be internal from such a violent event. He could see the boy was unconscious but still breathing, his tiny chest laboring up and down.

In the center of the street, Cassandra Marshall exited her wrecked car, sobbing. She had only lost sight of the road for an instant, she cried out to the crowd of witnesses who had already gathered. The glare of the sun had blinded her, she said. It had hit the windshield at just the right angle. Gabriel looked up long enough to see her collapse to her knees in the street.

"An ambulance is on the way," a UPS driver called out. He looked over at Cassandra and added, "The cops too."

Gabriel kept his eyes on the boy, watching his chest rise and fall, slower each time. When the child exhaled, Gabriel waited, praying he would draw in another breath. The two seconds between breaths felt like two hours. Gabriel couldn't draw oxygen into his own lungs until the boy did.

As people gathered in a half circle around the boy, a woman who lived across the street bent down in front of Jayden and started praying. *Our Father, who art in heaven . . .*

Others joined in, saying the Lord's Prayer with her. It was a communal act of love that would have been beautiful if the situation weren't so tragic.

As Cassandra continued to sob uncontrollably, Gabriel looked toward the center of the road and the bicycle the child had been riding only moments before. The frame was bent into a V, the front wheel destroyed, and the gears and chain spread out on the pavement like some grotesque yard sale. The boy's broken fishing pole rested next to the debris.

Off in the distance came the harrowing call of approaching sirens. It sounded like more than one emergency vehicle coming. *Send everything you've got,* Gabriel thought. Even if they did, he feared it wouldn't be enough. There weren't enough doctors in all of Boston to fix this. The boy was dying right in front of him.

Just then, Edward approached, using his outstretched arms to separate the crowd and ease himself closer to the stricken child. "Excuse me, sister," he said to the woman praying over Jayden.

She rose and gave him a pathway to the boy.

Edward kneeled next to Jayden. Gabriel had a good view of Edward's face, and he looked almost serene. His expression sure didn't match the gravity of this situation.

The street fell dead silent, the only sound the sirens growing closer.

Then, as if he was leaning in to hug a friend, Edward bent down and put his right hand on Jayden's chest.

"Is he still breathing?" Gabriel asked.

Ignoring the question, Edward leaned in and put his mouth next to Jayden's right ear. Gabriel couldn't make it out, but Edward was whispering something to the dying boy.

In that instant, the child's eyes fluttered open for a moment. Edward rose and shifted his eyes, seeming to take in the crowd that was holding vigil only steps behind him.

An ambulance screeched to a halt directly in front of the driveway where Jayden Lancaster still lay motionless.

"What did you say to him?" Gabriel asked.

Edward answered, "We should go."

Gabriel and the others were told to step back to allow the first responders to attend to the boy. Gabriel didn't know the child, but his heart was broken over how this would undoubtedly end.

As Gabriel and Edward boarded their work van, a small satellite truck from one of the Boston television stations pulled up to the corner. Gabriel recognized the female reporter who leaped from the vehicle, the call letters of the TV station, WCVB, stamped in black letters on the microphone already in her hand.

Veronica something was her name, he thought. It didn't matter. His hands were trembling. He felt sick. He pictured his own son dying at war and now this boy at his feet. Too much death, too few miracles.

"We're not working today," he said. "I want to go home."

"It's going to be alright." Edward rested his hand on Gabriel's shoulder. "Everything's going to be okay."

Emily Johnson couldn't bear to watch any more. As the paramedics knelt beside the boy, she turned away from her upstairs window and tried to distract herself by thinking about that man's cryptic words.

You didn't lose it. Look behind the drawer.

She retired to her bedroom at the back of the house. In it was a large dresser with two small drawers at the top. In one drawer she kept important papers. The other was reserved for jewelry.

Emily's nana had a ruby pin she wore on the outside of her jacket. Emily loved it, and her nana knew it.

After her grandmother's death, Emily's mother surprised her when she handed her the pin, saying simply, "She'd want you to have it."

She was careful with the heirloom, only wearing it twice a year when she attended Christmas and Easter mass.

Several years ago, she opened the drawer and found it missing. She tossed everything out of both drawers, but the pin was gone. Her heart sank. She couldn't help but feel a piece of her nana had died all over again.

Now this strange man had arrived and knew the story about the hutch and the good plates and her grandmother.

You didn't lose it. Look behind the drawer.

Was he talking about? It couldn't be.

She took hold of the dresser drawer with the jewelry inside and pulled it out as far as it would go. She then lifted and gave it a hard tug, causing the small drawer to release from its tracks and come apart from the dresser.

Emily couldn't see into the dark space where the drawer was, but she reached her hand into the void and felt around. Sure enough, her fingers closed around something round and smooth.

She pulled the prize into the light. Nana's ruby pin! She closed her hand around it, her mind picturing Edward's face, and said, "Thank you."

Down on the street, a small crowd remained around Jayden Lancaster. A police officer arrived and saw the car with significant front edge damage and the mangled bike in the street.

Jesus, Mary, and Joseph, he thought.

"Has anyone seen the driver?" he called out. No one answered.

Cassandra Marshall was gone.

Later that evening, Brooklyn plopped down on the couch and let out a tired sigh.

"You never said how today went," Connor said.

When she failed to answer, Evi asked, "Did you catch the fakers?"

Brooklyn looked over to the award she'd won two days before, sitting proudly on the shelf. "Sometimes I wonder who the fakers are."

Connor touched her hand. "You wanna talk?"

"Not tonight. I just want to sit."

He nodded. "Well, I'm getting ice cream. Any takers?"

"ME, ME," Evi called out.

Brooklyn said, "I'd take a hug instead."

Connor put his arms around her. Brooklyn locked her fingers behind his back and squeezed him extra tight. *This is better than mint chocolate chip,* she thought.

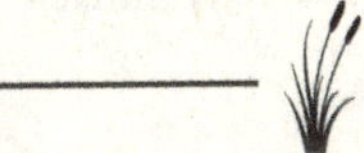

A short drive away, in the home of Gabriel and Piper, dinner was a quiet affair. Edward excused himself immediately after and went up to his room above the garage.

Gabriel grabbed the TV remote and turned on the six p.m. news on WCVB. The lead story would have to be the death of that boy on the bike in Meriam Hill. If he wasn't dead, at best he was clinging to life.

Instead, the top story on the news was about incoming rain and the possibility of flooding. That was followed by crime stories and political news from the state capital. The tragedy on Oakmont Circle should have been there, yet there was no mention of it.

"I don't get it," he said.

"Get what?" Piper asked.

He turned off the television, grabbed his smartphone, and started typing on the tiny screen.

"What is it, Dad?"

He hit the *call* button on his phone, then put the iPhone on speaker.

"WCVB newsroom, how can I help you?"

"Yes," Gabriel began, "I saw your news crew in Meriam Hill this morning for a boy hit by a car. I thought I'd see it on the news but there was no mention."

"Please hold," the male voice said.

After a brief pause a woman came on the line. "The boy is fine."

Gabriel shot up from his chair. "Excuse me?"

"The boy is fine. That's why it wasn't in the show."

"Wait a minute. Meriam Hill, Oakmont Circle. Are we talking about the same thing?"

"Yes, sir, this is Veronica Snow. I was the reporter on the scene. The kid is fine. Anything else?"

Gabriel almost dropped the phone.

"Sir? You still there?"

He gripped the top of the chair to steady himself. "Ummm, yes. Thank you for the information."

With that, the call went dead.

Piper stared at him. "What's going on?"

"Nothing."

"Daddy. You didn't say two words at supper and now this phone call."

Gabriel raised his hand and nodded, acknowledging her concern as he slowly crossed the room to look out the window. Through the half-open curtains, he peered up to the room above the garage, where his new house guest was staying.

"Are you okay, Daddy?"

He took a deep breath. "I think you might be right about Edward." He turned to meet her eyes. "There's more to him than we know."

CHAPTER 6

Those Who Mourn

Brooklyn took the near-empty bottle of ibuprofen from the medicine cabinet above her bathroom sink and shook it.

I need four. Does that sound like four?

It turned out there were three. As she swallowed them with a glass of water, a knock came on the door. It opened slightly, and Connor's face appeared around the edge.

"Headache again?"

"Just a little one." She gave him a quick peck on the lips and brushed past, heading toward the kitchen.

"What's your day look like?" he asked.

"I need to stop at the *Globe* to talk to the boss about this story I pitched."

"The scam artists working the tourists? Is there a problem?"

Brooklyn grabbed a carton of cream from the fridge, put a coffee pod in the Keurig, and turned it on. "Not a problem, really. It didn't go as planned, and I want to take Rex's temperature on it."

Connor took a seat at the kitchen table. "I didn't push, but I could see you were off last night."

She stirred a packet of Splenda and cream into her morning elixir. "Vars and I confronted the father and daughter, if that's what they even are. I mean, who knows, right? They were faking on the violin, and we caught them red-handed."

"That's what you wanted, right?"

"Yes, but it bothered me."

"Bothered you how?"

She joined him at the table. "When people get caught cheating or lying, they usually deny it or get defensive."

"And this time?"

"Shame. Nothing but shame in their eyes."

Connor paused, then said, "Well, you caught them scamming people. They should be ashamed, right?"

Brooklyn pictured the sad look on that young girl's face. *Why can't I shake that girl's face?*

"Brooke?"

She turned her attention back to Connor. "Yes, you're right, but I felt like I was confronting someone taking food out of a dumpster."

He reached across the table. "No matter what, I'm sure you'll figure it out."

Brooklyn shrugged. "Yeah, we'll see."

She hesitated, then said, "Wouldn't it be funny if the tough-as-nails journalist lost her nerve? How do you like them apples?"

Connor remained silent on her rhetorical question.

She glanced at her watch. "Geez, gotta go." As she grabbed her jacket from a hook by the door, she looked back at her husband. "Thank you."

"For what?"

"Just listening. Sometimes you just want someone to listen."

Connor answered with a warm smile.

She opened the door. "Kiss Evi for me."

"Count on it."

As the sound of her car roared to life, Evi emerged from her bedroom rubbing the sleep out of her eyes.

"Did I miss Mommy?"

"Just."

He rose and opened the cabinet, revealing a shelf full of cereal boxes. "Raisin Bran, Frosted Flakes, or Rice Krispies?"

Evi sat in the chair her mother had just vacated. "Hmm . . . Let's go with snap, crackle, and pop."

Connor grabbed the box. "You got it, kiddo."

As he poured milk into the bowl of Rice Krispies, he said, "Hey, Ev. Did you notice if mommy was taking any medicine yesterday, for a headache?"

Evi scooped a healthy amount into her mouth and, with milk dripping from the corners, answered, "I think so. After dinner."

Connor took his cup of coffee over to the window and looked out at the birdhouse hanging from the maple tree in the yard.

That's three days in a row she's been taking medicine.

Her headaches never last this long.

"Daddy?"

Connor turned. "Did you call me, hon?"

"Yes. I asked if Mommy is okay?"

He crossed the kitchen to hug his daughter. "You bet. Healthy as a horse."

"A horse?"

"A very pretty horse," he added.

Evi pulled back from the hug and looked into his eyes, searching.

"I promise you, honey. She's fine."

A few miles away, Gabriel and Piper were arguing during breakfast.

"Go if you want, but leave me out of it," she barked.

Gabriel took a butter knife out of the drawer, slamming it shut just as Edward entered from outside.

"I'm sorry if I interrupted." His kind brown eyes went back and forth between father and daughter.

"It's fine," Gabriel said. "We have hard rolls, eggs, and cereal. Help yourself, Edward."

"Cereal sounds good." Edward took a dish, a spoon, and a box of Cap'n Crunch from the cabinet.

The silence between father and daughter haunted the room as Edward poured milk into the bowl. "Do you think he's really a captain in the Navy?" he asked.

Piper gave him a hard stare. "Who?"

Edward held up a spoonful of the cereal. "Captain Crunch."

After an awkward pause, Gabriel burst out laughing.

Piper pushed her chair back. "I have to go."

"Piper, please," Gabriel said. "I thought we could, you know, finish our talk."

She grabbed her keys from the counter. "I don't hate God, Dad. I don't. I'm just not in the mood to praise him after what happened to Paul."

Gabriel sighed a weary sigh and slowly rubbed his brow.

"Paul is the son you told me about?" Edward asked gently. "The Marine?"

Gabriel looked up into eyes full of compassion. "Yes, my only son. Died in combat."

Piper planted her hand on her hip. "My father wanted me to join him at church on Sunday, and I'm taking a pass."

"I see," Edward said.

"That's the argument you walked in on," she added.

"Got it."

"It's fine, Piper," Gabriel said. "It was just an idea." He turned to Edward. "We're taking the morning off. I have an errand to run and then I'll pick you up at eleven."

"Alright, Gabriel."

Gabriel hesitated, then said, "And I'd like to talk about what happened yesterday, with the boy."

Piper looked at Edward, waiting for a response.

He answered, "Sure. We can talk later."

Gabriel paused on his way out of the kitchen. "I'm sorry we fought, Piper. I find comfort at church, but . . . I understand your feelings. Your anger."

When she didn't answer, he left the room.

Piper watched Edward push soggy orange nuggets around with his spoon.

"Angry with God?" he asked.

"Not really your business."

Edward smiled. "You think so, huh?"

"I know so," she shot back.

Without warning, Edward tipped the box of cereal over, spilling nuggets onto the kitchen table. He then started moving them around with his finger.

"Playing with our food now?" Piper asked.

"Not really your business." He gave her a playful wink.

She let out an exaggerated sigh before walking out the door.

A few moments later, Edward called to Gabriel in the other room. "I'm heading out for a walk."

"Have fun," Gabriel answered back.

Showered and dressed, Gabriel returned to the kitchen to clean up and was brought to a halt by what he found. The milk was back in the fridge, the dirty bowl and spoon in the dishwasher, and the countertops wiped down. Everything was spotless, except for some cereal scattered across the table.

Gabriel wet a cloth at the sink and was about to wipe the discarded breakfast into the trash when he saw it. The cereal nuggets were not tossed about as haphazardly as they first appeared. On closer inspection, he saw that they spelled a seven-letter word and two numbers: Matthew 5 4.

"Piper? You still here?" he called out. "Edward?"

No response.

Without touching the cereal, Gabriel went to his den and a large bookcase. He strained his eyes scanning the dozens of titles, some being his wife's old favorites, dating back decades. He was searching for one specific book he thought might help solve this puzzle.

"There you are," he said when he spotted it.

He pulled down a black leather book, turning it on its side to reveal the words KING JAMES BIBLE along the spine. Next to it on the shelf was a framed photo of his wife taken at one of their favorite places on Cape Cod: Chatham. They went on a whale watch out of Provincetown not long after they met, ending the day in Chatham eating fresh lobster by a bonfire on the beach.

Gabriel tried to smile, but the pain from missing her weighed too much. He could spend days in this room just visiting with the ghosts and memories of what used to be.

He snapped out of it, saying to himself, "What did it say again, Matthew 5 4? So that's Matthew chapter 5, verse 4."

He began thumbing through the old Bible, eventually finding the Gospel of Mathew and the appropriate passage.

Blessed are those who mourn, for they shall be comforted.

With the Bible still in his hand, Gabriel returned to the kitchen and stood for several moments staring at the cereal on his table.

Edward did this, right? It had to be Edward.

He took his cell phone off the charger, went to the contact list, and scrolled down to the letter E.

Wait. He doesn't have a phone.

Gabriel grabbed a handful of the cereal and ate it, brushed the rest off the table and into the trash, then took up his phone again to call Piper.

"Yes, Daddy?"

"I'm sorry to bother you at work."

"No worries, what's up?"

"Your job at the insurance company. Do you have access to DMV records?"

"Yes, we have special access to DMV, Social Security, and criminal background checks, but we're only supposed to use it for work-related things. Why?"

"Oh, I see. Alrighty, then. Never mind." He'd have to figure out another way.

"Daddy. What's going on?"

He didn't reply.

"You want me to run Edward's name?" Piper asked.

"I don't want you getting into trouble."

She lowered her voice. "Daddy, if you're worried about Edward, just ask him to leave."

Gabriel smiled. "It's quite the opposite, honey. I think he's here to help us."

There was silence on the phone.

"Piper?"

"I'll run his name, but what makes you say that?"

"What?"

"That he's here to help us," Piper replied.

Gabriel looked at the table. "You know the saying *the writing was on the wall*?"

"Of course. Why?"

"Let's just say the writing was on the kitchen table."

CHAPTER 7

Fit as a Fiddle

When you're the editor of the *Boston Globe*, you get a special parking spot outside the main entrance. A small white sign with black type announces whose car belongs there.

Brooklyn was sitting on the pavement beneath Rex's sign, hoping to intercept him before he went in. Vars waited with her.

"This must be good," Rex said through his open window as he pulled in.

"Everything is fine," she said.

Rex burst into laughter as he got out of the car. "Let me tell you something. Never in the history of human conversation has everything been fine when someone begins a conversation with the words *everything is fine.*"

"We found the scam artists," she said. "The ones with the violins."

"Good."

"But, exposing them in front of a crowd made me feel . . ."

"Satisfied?" he asked.

"Like crap."

Rex just stared.

"What I'm saying is, something was off, exposing this father-daughter."

He punched the key fob to lock his car. "When did you become so sensitive?"

"I know, I know. This just felt different."

"Listen, Brooklyn. This is the job. Sometimes you have to get into the dirt to go after dirty people."

She stared at the ground.

Rex said, "I'm not talking to a 22-year-old working her first job out of college, am I?"

Brooklyn looked up. "No, sir."

"Tell me your resume again."

She squared her shoulders. "Bachelor's degree from Bard. *Whitehall Times*, *Berkshire Eagle*, and then here."

"So, not your first rodeo?"

"No, sir."

He turned his attention to Vars, standing mute as a mule. "Where are you on this?"

Vars looked at Brooklyn, then back to his boss. "Brooke is right. They didn't strike you as scam artists. It was hard not to feel sorry for them when we dropped the hammer."

Rex folded his arms. "Did it ever occur to you two Einsteins that *THAT* is part of the scam? Turning on the waterworks whenever they get caught?"

Brooklyn imagined them again, hiding their shame. She understood what Rex meant but this felt different.

"Vars?" he said. "I asked you a question."

"I suppose so."

"Alright, then," Rex said. "One down, a couple more to go. Who's next on the hit list?"

Brooklyn was silent.

Do I have the stomach for this? Is this even a good story?

"Who's next, I asked."

Vars answered, "The blind guy who isn't really blind, right, Brooklyn?"

She snapped out of it. "Yes, the phony-baloney selling pencils."

Rex glanced at his watch. "I'm late. Tell ya what. You two go talk to this blind fraud and if you tell me after, this *isn't* a story, we'll drop it. Fair?"

Brooklyn nodded. "You got it, boss."

At the same moment, in the Meriam Hill neighborhood of Boston, Emily Johnson came down her front steps on the way to run errands.

"Mrs. Johnson," a voice called.

She turned and saw Gabriel leaning against his white work van with the words *The Carpenter's Son* across the side.

"I thought the job was finished," she said.

Gabriel approached. "It is, Mrs. Johnson, I came back to inquire about the boy from yesterday."

Emily was silent, her expression confused.

"On the bike," Gabriel said. "The kid hit by the car."

She lit up. "Isn't that amazing? All that fuss over a few scrapes and bruises."

Gabriel couldn't believe his ears. "So, he's okay?"

"He seemed fine."

"Fine?" he echoed.

"Yes. I saw him talking to the paramedics out my window."

Gabriel rubbed his forehead, trying to make sense of it all. "Is he around? Have you seen him?"

Emily looked down the quiet block. "This time of day, I'd imagine he's in school."

Right. If he wasn't hurt, he would be at school. That made sense. But . . . "You said he's not hurt. You saw this with your own eyes?"

"I did. He's very lucky."

Gabriel said under his breath, "I'm not sure luck had anything to do with it."

"I'm sorry, what?" she asked.

"Nothing. Sorry. I won't hold you up. Thank you." He headed back to his van. With the turn of a key the engine roared to life, but he just sat, his mind racing.

He's really okay? She said he was, and she saw him. Unless she's lying. Why would she lie? She wouldn't. So, he must be fine.

"TAP, TAP, TAP."

Gabriel jumped. Emily was slapping the car window with her fingernails to get his attention.

He rolled down the glass.

"Sorry if I startled you. Do me a favor and thank that helper of yours, Edward."

"For what?"

"Tell him I found my Nana's pin. He'll understand."

Gabriel had no clue what that meant, but answered, "Your Nana's pin. Got it."

As she turned to go, he said, "Mrs. Johnson?"

"Yes?"

"I'm sorry to keep asking this but, the boy hit by the car is *really, truly* okay?"

"Fit as a fiddle."

Gabriel shook his head in disbelief. "Fair enough."

Meanwhile, at Quincy Market, Vars and Brooklyn parked in their usual spot and made their way to the north end of the open-air plaza. This was where Brooklyn had seen the blind man selling pencils many times before.

As they inched closer, Brooklyn spied a couple dozen people who had formed a crescent moon around someone in the square, a sure sign a performance was happening. When she heard the crowd laughing, she knew who it was.

Presto was a street magician who charmed people with his sleight of hand and silly gags. He performed a magic act every quarter-hour, then ducked into the nearby coffee shop to either cool off or warm up, depending on the date on the calendar. His act only lasted six minutes, so when the nearby church bells chimed on the quarter hour, he knew it was time to get back on stage.

Brooklyn and Vars waited for the crowd to disperse before making their approach. Presto was tall and thin, in his mid-forties, with dirty blonde hair poking out of a floppy hat. Brooklyn thought he looked like a wayward scarecrow lost from his field.

As he packed his cards and tricks into a brown leather satchel, he said, "You just missed the show, but if you can wait, I'm back on in . . ." He looked at his watch. "Eight minutes and seventeen seconds."

"I'm not here for the show," she said. "I wanted to ask you a question."

The magician looked at Brooklyn and Vars. "Cops?"

"Not even close," Vars said. "Nobody is looking to hassle you."

Presto walked toward the *Uncommon Grounds* coffee shop adjacent to the plaza. "Buy me a cappuccino and you can ask whatever you want."

Outside Boston, Gabriel stopped at the McDonald's drive-thru for his morning favorite: a sausage, egg, and biscuit sandwich. He was on cholesterol medication and the golden arches were a big *no-no*, especially in his daughter's eyes.

What she doesn't know can't get me in trouble.

He was only two bites in when his phone lit up with Piper's name. He swallowed fast to hide the crime. "Hello?"

"Are you sitting down?" she began.

Gabriel looked around his empty car and replied gleefully, "I'm as sitting as sitting can be."

"Okay, good. So here's the thing. I ran the name Edward Manuel through the DMV, Social Security, corrections records, everything."

"And?"

"He doesn't exist."

Gabriel put the sandwich down on the console. "Doesn't exist *here* you mean? In Massachusetts."

"Anywhere, Daddy."

He scratched the stubble on his chin. "That's strange."

"How do you pay him? Did he give you any personal info or a bank account number? Something?"

"No. His compensation is the room above the garage and the food at our table. I never asked for ID."

"So, he just appeared in our lives like that fawn in the backyard," she said.

"Oh, you don't know the half of it."

"What now, Dad? Is he talking to the squirrels?"

Gabriel considered whether to share what had happened.

"Dad?"

"Piper, talking to wildlife would be easier to understand than what I saw yesterday."

There was silence. Then she said, "What did you see?"

Gabriel completed his short drive home and pulled in front of the house.

He shifted in his seat. "I didn't tell you, but at a job site in Boston, a boy got hit by a car."

"Oh, my God! Is that why you were glued to the news last night?"

"Yes. I'm telling you, Piper, this kid was down for the count. Really bad shape."

"That's terrible," she said.

Gabriel took a tiny bite of his sandwich. "Actually, not so much."

"What do you mean?"

"I stopped by there this morning, and the kid is fine. I didn't see him, but everyone says he didn't get hurt."

"So, he was lucky," she said.

"Nobody is that lucky, sweetheart."

There was silence again. Then she said, "What does the boy have to do with Edward?"

Just as she said it, Gabriel saw Edward returning from his morning walk, waving hello with such joy on his face.

"Dad? You still there?"

Gabriel took a larger bite of the sandwich and said with his mouth full, "Gotta go."

"Hey, wait! What are you eating? Is that drive-thru? That had better not be Mc-"

Before she could say it, Gabriel hung up.

"I think she's on to you," Edward said as Gabriel got out of the car.

"Huh?"

Edward patted Gabriel's shoulder. "Never mind. Should we get to work?"

Gabriel scanned Edward's eyes, and the man looking back at him seemed different. For the first time, Gabriel saw something he'd missed before. A calm reassurance. If life was one big pop quiz, it felt like Edward knew all the answers in advance.

Whether it was courage or just plain curiosity, Gabriel held his gaze with Edward and asked the question that had been lingering on the fringes of his mind for days. "Why are you here, Edward?"

"We'll get to all of that. I promise."

Gabriel frowned.

"You're not happy with my answer?"

"It's not a complicated question," Gabriel replied.

"How's this?" Edward said. "I'm here for the same reason I pick up my woodworking tools. To fix what's broken. To create something beautiful."

Gabriel pondered such an esoteric response, then said, "My daughter thinks you talk to squirrels."

Edward laughed. "Only if they talk to me first."

As the two drove off to work, Gabriel thought, *I'm not sure he's kidding.*

CHAPTER 8

Keep Your Word

"Watch this, watch this," Presto told Brooklyn and Vars.

The three were standing at the counter of the coffee shop in Quincy Market, waiting for a drink to be prepared.

"I just have a couple of questions," she said.

"Questions second, *real* magic first," he answered.

Vars rolled his eyes at Brooklyn.

"There she is," Presto said, pointing at a young woman behind the counter. "A true artist."

The barista handed the magician his mug with a perfectly drawn rose in the white foam on top.

"Now, THAT is magic," he said.

The three grabbed a table in the corner. Presto placed the hot drink down, then glanced at his watch. "You have six minutes and fifty-one seconds until my next show. Go!"

Brooklyn said, "I won't need a minute. On this plaza, there's a blind man who sells pencils. Do you know him?"

Presto took a sip. "Hot."

"Do you?" Vars asked more firmly.

The magician shot him a snide look. "I'm not a fan of your tone. Do you know what could lighten the mood?" He reached behind Vars' ear. "A big red ball." With that, he produced a plastic ball out of thin air.

Vars went to snatch it from his hand, and Presto pulled it away. "Ah, ah, ah. Nobody touches my props."

Vars shook his head. "I'm done with this goofball. I'll be outside." He zipped up his coat and left the coffee shop.

"Presto?" Brooklyn said.

"Five minutes and twenty-nine seconds."

"It's a simple question," she said. "You know him or you don't."

He pointed at his cappuccino. "Isn't it amazing how they draw the rose on top."

"Okay." She rose from her chair and started for the door. "Enjoy your drink."

"Hey, hey, hey," he called after her. "I'm sorry. Sit, please."

"You're running out of time, Presto."

"Ezra."

"What?"

"My name. It's Ezra. Ezra Prentiss." His tone had shifted toward humble.

"Nice to meet you, Ezra." She extended her hand to shake his, then sat down again. "I'm Brooklyn, like the bridge, and I'm trying to track down the blind guy with the pencils."

Ezra took a sip. "Yes, I know him. His name is Stew."

"Stew? Like the stuff you cook on the stove with potatoes, carrots, and beef?"

The magician laughed, "I never thought of it that way, but yeah."

"Can you tell me how I can find him?"

Ezra paused. "Why do you want to talk to him?"

"Because I'm a journalist with the *Boston Globe* and I just—"

Ezra abruptly looked at his watch. "I'm up in four minutes, so I'd better get back." He rose from the chair, downed the rest of his drink in one big gulp, and called out to the barista, "Perfect as always, my dear. Until next time."

The woman, wearing a badly stained green apron, waved goodbye.

Brooklyn followed the magician out the front door. As Presto walked past her photographer, she announced, "You were right, Vars. He's a waste of time and money."

Ezra stopped on a dime, turned, and gave Brooklyn an angry look. "I don't want to help you because Stew is my friend, and I don't want you hurting him."

"Why would I hurt him?"

Ezra looked at his watch more emphatically now. "I'm gonna be late. The whole key to performing is you can *never* be late."

Brooklyn stepped toward Ezra, lightly touched his arm, and said, "Hey, look at me."

He glanced up from his cheap timepiece.

"Why would I hurt him?" she whispered. "Because he's pretending?"

Ezra laughed and shook his head. "You two don't know, do you?"

Vars said, "We know he pretended to be blind, and he's not."

"*Really*?" Ezra fired back.

"Yes," Brooklyn said. "We also know we busted a father and daughter who were pretending to play the violin for money."

"Good for you," Ezra said sarcastically.

"Let me guess," Vars pressed on. "Word got around that we were doing a story on fakes begging for change, and suddenly your pal with the pencils is hiding."

Ezra answered sharply. "*I'm* the fake, okay? Me."

"What do you mean?" Brooklyn asked.

"I'm the one with loaded dice, marked cards, and boxes with false bottoms. But nobody gets ripped off. The audience knows none of it is real. It's just a silly show."

"And your friend Stew?" Brooklyn asked. "Is he just a silly show?"

"You wouldn't believe me if I told you."

"Try us," Vars said.

"Okay," Ezra replied. "Here's the truth. My friend Stew was blind and now he's not. And I don't need you two messing that up for him."

"How would we do that?" Brooklyn asked.

The church bells began to chime, indicating it was time for *Presto* to perform. "Listen to what I'm saying to you. Stew was blind. A man helped him, and now he sees. That's why he doesn't sell pencils anymore. He can see. And now, I really do have to go."

"What man?" she asked. "Who helped him?"

"I honestly don't know. People are waiting. Please."

"What did you mean, you don't want us messing that up?" Vars asked.

Ezra eyed the waiting crowd, then said, "In a world of fakes, Stew's case is a true miracle. And when a miracle happens, you don't question it. You don't investigate it, write about it, or judge it. You just say thank you."

With that, the magician dashed away to begin his next show.

As he climbed up on a small stage, Brooklyn called out, "I won't hurt your friend, but I do need to talk to him."

Ezra called back, "Try the Charlestown shelter. He hangs out there."

Brooklyn moved closer to the stage. Then she and Ezra locked eyes.

"Thank you for the drink," he said. "Now . . . keep your word."

She answered with a nod of her head.

Vars sidled up next to her. "What's going on with this story?"

"Honestly?" Brooklyn replied. "I don't know."

Back at the home of Gabriel and Piper, Edward was mixing tuna fish in a bowl by the sink.

"Can I make you some?" he asked Gabriel.

"No, thanks. I broke my diet with a trip to McDonald's."

As Edward tended to his tuna, Gabriel said, "Interesting note you left me with the cereal earlier."

"I hope it helped."

"Tell you something?" Gabriel said.

"Sure." Edward stopped mixing.

"Since my son Paul's death, I feel like there are heavy chains wrapped around my heart. And every day they tighten a little more to remind me of my loss."

Edward looked at him with deep compassion. "Thank you for telling me that, friend."

Gabriel crossed the kitchen and squeezed Edward's hand. "That Bible passage you directed me to did help."

Edward returned the squeeze with a carpenter's grip. Then he finished making his tuna sandwich and took half of it with him to the window. A steady October breeze made the branches sway on a pair of trees.

"They look like they're dancing," Edward said. "The trees."

Gabriel joined him by the window. "I met my wife at a dance."

Edward put the sandwich down on a small table near the window. "Tell me about that day."

Gabriel could see it all again, for the first time in years. "It was sponsored by the church, in a large hall next to the Catholic school. They called it a Sadie Hawkins dance."

"Who is Sadie Hawkins?" Edward asked.

"Beats me. What that means, though, a Sadie Hawkins dance, is that the girls ask the boys to dance."

"You were young?" Edward asked.

"God, no. We were all adults, you know, just getting together to have some fun."

"And she was there? Your future wife?"

Gabriel nodded. "She came with a girlfriend. Something to do on a Saturday night."

Edward smiled. "She asked you to dance, and the rest is history."

"Yeah, I guess so."

Edward closed his eyes. "She wore a mauve-colored dress with polka dots and white lace piping around her neckline."

Gabriel gasped in astonishment. "My gosh! I think that's exactly what she was wearing that night." He paused. "How'd you know that?"

Edward smiled, not answering. He took his sandwich back to the kitchen table to sit.

"I forgot to tell you," Gabriel said. "I saw Emily Johnson this morning. She said to tell you she found her nana's pin. Said you'd know what that meant."

Edward took a bite of his sandwich. "Good."

Gabriel waited for something more. But evidently, the man of mystery wasn't going to elaborate on that either.

As he finished his lunch, Edward said, "Before we get busy with the day's work, can I ask a favor?"

"Sure."

"This business with your son, Paul, and Piper's anger over losing him."

"What about it?" Gabriel asked.

"I think I can help her."

Gabriel rubbed his chin as if searching for the right words. He liked Edward and didn't want to hurt his feelings. But . . .

"I know you mean well, Edward, but this isn't something you can fix with Cap'n Crunch and a passage from the Bible."

"I agree," Edward said. "Could you ask her to take a drive with me tomorrow? I promise it's going to help."

Gabriel considered the request, then said, "Two things."

"Okay."

"First, I can't promise she'll go, but I'll ask."

"And second?"

"Before you spend that kind of time with Piper, you should know that she's pretty angry," Gabriel said. "Well, I mean, you've seen it. Heard it."

Edward nodded. "Who is she angry with?"

Gabriel threw his hands in the air. "Oh, geez, you name it. The Marines, the war, Paul for signing up, me for agreeing, herself for letting him go. And God, let's not forget him. If there's a list, God is at the top."

Edward sat quietly, listening. Then he said, "Piper thought Paul's life would have a purpose. Then he joins the Marines and dies alone on a mountainside in a place far from home. A tragic, meaningless ending."

"That's right. That's exactly how she views it."

"But it's not true."

"Which part?"

"All of it," Edward said. "His life had great purpose. And when he drew his last breath he was most certainly *not* alone."

Gabriel stared at his friend. "How would you know that, Edward?"

Edward remained silent.

"How would you know that, or what my wife wore to the dance 30 years ago, or what a fawn that wandered into my yard was thinking? What happened with that boy hit by the car, Edward?"

Edward met his gaze. "Important questions."

"Yes, they are."

"A conversation for another day," he answered, and rose from the table.

That was it, then. At least for now. Gabriel fought hard to conceal his frustration. "Well, guess we should get to work, then." He rose from the table too. "If you think you can help Piper, I'll talk to her about taking a drive."

"Thank you."

"Can I ask where you're going? Or is that a mystery too?"

Edward placed the dirty dish in the sink. "Gloucester."

Gabriel grabbed his jacket and keys and headed toward the door. As his hand touched the brass doorknob, he paused.

"Can I ask what she'll find in Gloucester?"

"Oh, that's an easy one, Gabriel. She'll find the truth."

CHAPTER 9

Turn or Two in the Road

Monday was grilled cheese day at the Charlestown Rescue Shelter in Boston. Today guests even got a bonus: hot tomato soup to dip their sandwiches in.

"I'm guessing by that dress and his belly, you two aren't homeless," a man said.

Vars and Brooklyn turned to face an older gentleman in such great shape that if you saw him from a distance, you'd swear he was in his twenties.

Vars patted his stomach. "I'd smack you for that insult if it weren't true. Plus, I like your shirt."

The man looked down at his t-shirt. "Journey. Yes. Got this in 1982 at a concert in Dallas."

"I bet it was a great show," Vars replied.

"It was. The opening act was, um, give me a minute."

Brooklyn said, "It's not important, sir. We're looking for the manager."

"Hold up, it's coming," he replied. "Blue Oyster Cult."

Brooklyn tried again. "Is the person in charge around?"

The man began singing, "*I'm burning, I'm burning for you*. Remember that one?"

"I do," Vars said. "Great song. So, hey, I'm Vars, this is Brooklyn, we're with the *Globe*."

"The *Boston Globe*? You broke the church scandal story a few years back."

Brooklyn nodded. "We did, sir."

"Good for you. It had to be done." He paused. "So, you want the shelter manager, huh? That would be the handsome priest, Father Calhoun."

"Can we talk to him?" Brooklyn asked.

The man wiggled his eyebrows playfully. "You already are."

"You're the priest?" Vars asked with a slight grin.

"In the flesh, as Jesus might say." With that, he wiped off his right hand on his faded jeans and extended it. "I'm Rip. Father Rip Calhoun. Welcome."

Brooklyn shook his hand. "Rip? Interesting name."

The priest became animated. "My real name is Jack, but first year out of seminary I'm celebrating mass before the Bishop and I wanted to look sharp, 'cause you know, it's the Bishop. So, I washed my good pants on the hot rinse cycle instead of the cold, and you'll never guess what happened."

"They shrank," Brooklyn said.

"Bingo," he replied. "I get to the part in the mass where I have to do this very deep bow—"

"And the pants went *RIP*," Vars said.

The priest laughed heartily. "You could hear it in the back row of the church."

"That's a great story, Father," Brooklyn said. "Now, the reason we came—"

"Hey, you wanna hear a joke?" the priest said.

"Not that lame joke again, *Fah-tha*," one of the guests said in a thick Boston accent as she passed by holding a plate of food."

He smiled at her. "Shush. They haven't heard it."

Father Calhoun turned to Brooklyn. "Why do people go to church early?"

Brooklyn played along. "I don't know, Father. Why?"

He grinned broadly. "To get a seat in the last row."

Nobody laughed. "Told ya, *Fah-tha*," the woman said. "Lame."

He looked at his fresh audience of two. "Don't you get it? Nobody wants to sit down front at church, so you have to get there early to . . . oh, never mind."

Vars said, "Anyway, padre, we're trying to track down a homeless man named Stew."

Brooklyn added, "He was pretending to be blind."

The moment she said it, the friendly expression on Father Calhoun's face took a serious turn. He motioned Brooklyn and Vars away from the busy food line. "Follow me, please." He took them to a door, then to an empty alley outside the shelter. "Pretending?" His voice had turned aggressive. "Stewart was *not* pretending."

Brooklyn raised her hands, palms facing the priest in a show of contrition. "Okay, relax. I meant no offense."

"Sorry," the priest said. "I just get worked up when people mock the divine."

Vars looked from Brooklyn over to the priest. "What do you mean, divine?"

Before he could respond, Brooklyn said, "You called him Stewart. Are we talking about the same person?"

The priest nodded. "Yes, Stewart. Everyone called him Stew. He sold pencils around town and came here for years until he got his sight back."

Vars nodded along. "Oh, so he *was* blind and had an operation and could see after that?"

"Half right," the priest said.

"Which half, father?" Brooklyn asked.

"Yes, he was blind, but there was no operation."

"Then how did he suddenly see?"

The side door to the shelter flew open with a bang, and a young woman with long red locks tucked under a hairnet said, "Are you coming in to help us, Father? We're swamped. They always come for the grilled cheese."

"Yes, coming now, Molly," the priest said. "I have to go."

"Wait . . . Father . . . How did he suddenly see?" Brooklyn asked a second time.

The priest grabbed the doorknob, then said, "I honestly don't know. He called it a miracle."

Vars whispered to Brooklyn, "We're doing a story on scams, not miracles."

She shot him a *Yeah, no kidding!* look.

Before Father Calhoun left, he said, "You should talk to Dr. Foster. Devon Foster. She works out of the urgent care on High Street, a few blocks away."

"Why?" Vars asked.

"She comes in here twice a month to do pro bono work on my flock."

Brooklyn asked, "And she treated Stew?"

"Yes, indeed," Father Calhoun said. "Anything else?"

She looked at the clergyman's messy hair, muscles, and vintage rock t-shirt. "No offense," she said, smiling, "but I never would have pegged you for a priest."

He answered, "Jesus never judged a follower by how they looked. Besides, he told us to go where we're needed most."

"And that's this shelter?" Brooklyn asked.

"Don't knock it," Father Calhoun replied. "A turn or two in the road and any one of us could be in that food line inside."

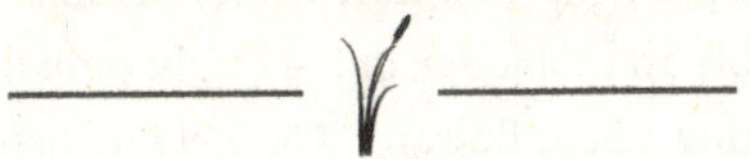

On the other side of Boston, Gabriel and Edward were busy bidding on a job to build bookcases for a well-heeled lawyer from Cambridge. Gabriel was impressed as he stood in the man's study and saw photos of him posing with members of the Kennedy family. Ever since the sacrifices of John and Bobby, the Kennedy name was royalty in Massachusetts.

When Gabriel showed the lawyer photographs of his previous work and was hired on the spot, he promised to start the new bookcases in a few days. As the two of them drove through Boston, Gabriel slowed the van down.

"Are we stopping?" Edward asked.

Gabriel let out a large yawn. "I need a jolt of caffeine." He glanced at his friend. "Can I tell you something personal?"

Edward's silent, patient demeanor told him to proceed.

"Every time I argue with Piper about church or losing her brother, Paul, it takes something out of me."

"And you lie awake at night, thinking about it," Edward said.

"I do."

Edward said, "Ever read the book of Isaiah?"

"Not recently, why?"

"He gives strength to those who are tired, power to the weak," Edward said.

Gabriel smiled. "And for the times in between, there's coffee."

He continued driving. A few moments later, he pulled the van in front of a Starbucks on Boylston Street. Even though Edward said he didn't want a coffee, he got out of the vehicle anyway.

A small card table, 3 by 6 feet in diameter, was set up in front of the coffee shop, with two women in matching sweatshirts sitting behind it. The shirts had a picture of kittens with the word *Whiskers* underneath.

When customers walked by, the women called out, "*Whiskers Animal Shelter. All adoption fees waived this Saturday.*"

As Gabriel reached for the store's door handle to go in, Edward lingered by the table and took one of the bright pink fliers.

"We're not getting a dog, Edward," Gabriel said firmly.

"I know."

"Or a cat, either."

"Got it. No animals."

Gabriel joked, "You can talk to the deer all you like, as long as I don't see them at the dinner table."

"Go get your drink," Edward said, signaling that this great adoption debate was over.

Once Gabriel was inside the shop, Edward folded one of the pink fliers, placed it in his jacket pocket, and returned to the van. Gabriel, drink in hand, joined him a few minutes later.

As they continued their drive home, they noticed a small ice cream shop on the right side of the road, with what looked like a father and daughter sitting alone at a table with their frozen treat.

School was in session, so it struck Gabriel as odd that a girl her age, seven or eight, would be counting scoops of vanilla instead of numbers on a blackboard.

Edward tapped Gabriel's arm. "Pull over, please."

"You hungry?" he asked, as he stopped the van.

"Only to help someone. I won't be long. I promise."

With one effortless motion, Edward opened the van door and hopped out. He walked across a patch of grass that separated the street from the stamped concrete that surrounded the ice cream shop. His long brown hair bounced on his shoulders with each step.

With the van windows up, Gabriel couldn't hear what they were saying, but he watched as Edward approached the father and daughter and took a seat at their table.

The father sat silent as Edward engaged in dialogue with the child, his hands moving about in the air as if he were spinning a yarn for the girl. Occasionally, he saw the young girl smile and nod her head in agreement.

After a couple of minutes, Edward reached into his pocket and produced a pink flier like the ones Gabriel had seen on the animal shelter display. He gave it to the little girl, stood up, and shook her father's hand. The man's face revealed immense gratitude.

Edward looked down at the little girl, gently placed his hand on her head, then returned to the van.

Once he shut the door, he turned to Gabriel. "Thank you for stopping. We can go now."

Gabriel turned off the ignition. "Nah ah, pal. We're not leaving until you tell me what that was about."

Edward said, "Her name is Anna, and her father took her out of school today and got her ice cream because her cat died a few weeks ago and she's been sad."

"Aw, I'm sorry to hear that."

Edward said, "The cat was already eight years old when Anna was born, so she's never known life without him."

"Wait. Can I ask? Do you know these people?"

"I just met them today," Edward said. "But to truthfully answer your question, yes, I've known them their whole lives."

Gabriel paused a moment. "I don't understand what that means."

"I promise you, Gabriel, eventually—"

"I know, I know, we'll talk about it later."

Edward answered softly, "We will."

Gabriel sighed. "Okay. Go on with your story."

Edward continued, "I told Anna that Sylvester is fine, he's with God in heaven, and someday, a very long time from now, she'll see him again."

Gabriel chuckled. "Because all dogs go to heaven, right?"

Edward replied seriously, "Sylvester is a cat, but yes, our pets go to heaven."

"Even goldfish?" Gabriel asked. "I mean, is there even water up there?"

Edward laughed. "God created the universe, Gabriel. Don't you think he can conjure up a fishbowl?"

Gabriel thought about that, then said, "And the pink paper you handed her? Was that the flier from the table outside Starbucks?"

"Yes. And here's the best part. An orange tabby kitten is at the shelter right now. So, when Anna goes on Saturday—"

"He's free." Gabriel looked over at the little girl, still eating her frozen treat. Her whole demeanor seemed brighter since her brief visit from Edward.

He started the van and continued their drive home. "Quite a coincidence, how you grab a flier from the animal shelter with a sale on kittens, five minutes before you meet a little girl who is heartbroken over the loss of her cat."

As usual, Edward didn't answer.

Gabriel's mind was racing. *How did he know about the cat? The girl? Any of it?*

"Ever play the lottery?" Gabriel said in jest.

Edward glanced out his window, where the red and orange trees were showing off their autumn colors.

"Did you hear me?"

"I'm rich enough already, Gabriel. We all are."

Gabriel didn't probe any further. Something in his heart told him Edward was right.

As his house came into view, he said, "I forgot to tell you. Piper is reluctant to take a drive with you tomorrow. I'm not sure she trusts you. Sorry."

Edward let out a laugh, which seemed an odd response to the news Gabriel had just shared.

"Did I say something funny?"

Edward replied, "If she were a boy, we could call her Thomas. Always filled with doubt."

Gabriel pulled into the driveway. "She's taking that road trip with you, isn't she?"

"Yes. Even if I have to show her the wounds in my hands."

"What wounds?"

Edward silently got out of the van.

"You are a mystery, my friend," Gabriel said.

Edward answered, "A truer statement never told."

CHAPTER 10

What If It's True?

The next morning, Piper emerged from the bathroom to find her father waiting with his arms folded and a look on his face.

"What?"

"Edward," he answered. "He's sitting outside and wants to speak to you about taking this drive with him."

"Why is this so important?"

"I think he wants to help you."

Piper brushed by her father. "I wasn't aware I needed help."

She glanced out the kitchen window and saw Edward fiddling with an orange leaf that had drifted down from a nearby tree. As much as she wanted to be suspicious of Edward, watching him now, there was an undeniable grace about him.

"He gets two minutes, Dad. No more."

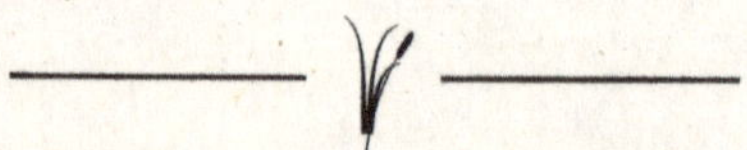

Two towns over, Brooklyn was on the way to her kitchen when she paused to look in Evi's room. The bed was messy, the blankets kicked about, an errant pillow on the floor.

As she collected the wayward pillow, she looked at a beautiful photograph of Mount Everest on the wall. It was fitting for a child named after the world's highest peak to have this poster near her bed.

Tell it again, tell it again, Evi would say to her parents, wanting to hear the story of how she got her name.

Ten years ago, only days after their wedding, Brooklyn and Connor decided to check off one of their *bucket list* items. While many newlyweds dream of a honeymoon in Paris or Rome, they dreamt of hiking to *base camp* at Mount Everest.

The roundtrip journey to the camp and back to Kathmandu took fifteen days, and by the time it was over, two things were true: Connor's camera was filled with breathtaking photographs, and Brooklyn's belly was home to a tiny hiker just starting her own adventure.

Brooklyn closed the bedroom door and headed to the kitchen to grab a toasted bagel and her car keys. Her next stop would be Urgent Care in South Boston and a conversation with Dr. Devon Foster. No doubt a woman of science would share the truth about Stew's eyesight and chase away this silly talk of miracles.

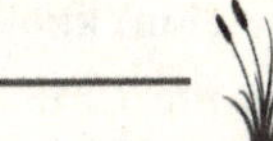

The screen door slammed hard behind Piper as she stepped outside to talk to Edward in the yard. Somehow the *BANG* didn't startle him as he sat alone on the bench, still staring at the orange leaf in his hand.

"You don't want to go with me," he said.

Piper took a seat next to him. "Nothing personal," she said. "I just don't know you."

Edward let the leaf float to the grass, then looked into her eyes. "I think you do; you just choose not to."

Piper shook her head and pointed at him. "*That!* That right there is why I won't go with you. These vague, strange answers . . . these constant riddles coming out of your mouth, since the moment you got here."

Edward seemed unfazed. "Your brother, Paul . . ."

"What about him?" Piper fired back.

"You're so angry at him. Why?"

She bristled. *How dare he?* She wanted to tell this strange man, *You're wrong!* But somewhere deep in her heart his words rang true. And they cut like a jagged stone.

"Why do you blame him?" he asked.

She let her unspoken thoughts race through her mind. She *did* blame Paul. Why did he insist on signing up for the Marines? Why leave his family and put his life in jeopardy in some stupid war? Why did he waste his life that way?

"But he didn't, Piper," Edward said.

"What?"

"Waste his life. Quite the opposite."

Piper looked at him, dumbstruck. "How do you know my mind?"

"We'll get to all of that soon," he said gently. "I promise."

Much as she wanted to go back in the house, something about this man, the truth in his eyes, the kindness in his voice, left her frozen in place. It was like his whole being was compelling. Like a fishing net that drew you in. Not in a romantic way. This was something different. Like being welcomed home to a place you didn't know you'd left.

And then he said, "Why don't you pray?"

She laughed wryly. "Seriously? 'Cause prayer doesn't work, Edward."

"Why do you say that?"

"If it did, my brother would be sitting on that bench. Not you."

He looked up. Piper followed his gaze, taking in the beautiful October sky. Large, puffy white clouds were being pushed across the cobalt-blue canvas by a stiff wind sweeping down from the north.

It will get cold soon. Then winter. Things change, whether we want them to or not.

Edward broke the silence. "Have you heard the story about the woman who wanted the perfect job?"

"No. Am I about to?"

He laughed. "God certainly gave you a sharp tongue."

She ignored the backhanded compliment. "Your story?"

Edward said, "A woman waited years for the perfect job, and it finally became available."

"Let me guess," Piper interrupted. "She said a prayer and got the job. Proving that prayer works. The end."

Edward chuckled again. "No, that's not what happened. May I finish?"

She crossed her arms. "I can't wait."

"On the day of the interview," he continued, "the woman left an hour early, making certain that she wouldn't be late. Then, all along the way, she was delayed. A car accident, red lights, everything was working against her."

Piper interrupted again. "So she didn't make it or get the job. What does this have to do with my brother or prayer?"

"I'm getting there," Edward said. "She got to the building with one minute to spare, but there were no parking spaces, and she was going to be late. So, for the first time in many years, she prayed. She said, 'Dear God, if you can help me make this meeting on time, I'll be a good woman and never sin and dedicate my life to being a better person.'"

"And?"

"And at that very moment, in the middle of this beautiful prayer, a car right in front of the building pulled out. At which point she stopped praying and said, 'Hey, God, never mind. I don't need ya, a spot just opened up.'"

Piper sat in silence, then asked, "Are you saying God answers our prayers and we don't realize it?"

"I'm saying, Piper, people question the existence of God, heaven, and faith even when it's standing right in front of them, even when the prayers are answered."

She listened to the wind singing a song as it shook the tree branches above. "So, where do you want to take me this morning?"

"Gloucester," he answered. "There's someone I want you to see and someone I want you to meet."

For the first time since he'd arrived, she smiled at him. "You're not trying to fix me up with a guy, are you?"

"Heavens, no, but you never know what you'll find when you're not looking."

"Another riddle for an answer, Edward. You're good at that, you know?"

"I promise one thing," he said. "Today will be good for you."

Urgent Care on High Street in Boston opened at 8:00 a.m. Dr. Devon Foster was everyone's favorite because she talked and worked fast. A child in need of stitches could be in and out in less than ten minutes.

The waiting room was already busy. One man had his leg elevated, an older woman had a cut on her hand, and a college-aged boy was pressing a bloodied white towel to his face.

A woman with glasses dangling off her nose looked up from the computer and waved Brooklyn over to a small window.

"I feel like I'm at the bank," Brooklyn joked. "Maybe I should make a deposit."

The receptionist pushed a clipboard toward her. "Fill it out, front and back. If you don't know an answer, skip it. I'll need your insurance card if you have one."

Brooklyn slid the clipboard back. "I don't need a doctor. I mean, I do, but just to talk."

As if on cue, an attractive blonde in a white coat pushed through the swinging door with a sense of urgency, calling out, "Michael Phelps!"

Every head turned, but none rose to answer the doctor's call. Brooklyn saw the words *Dr. Foster* stitched across her chest.

The doctor looked down at the file in her hand. "Let's try this. Mark?" With that, the college boy holding the towel to his nose answered, "That's me."

Dr. Foster said to no one in particular, "Nobody gets my sense of humor."

As Mark made his way toward an examination room, Brooklyn said, "Dr. Foster, a quick word, please."

"Wait your turn."

Brooklyn stepped closer. "I'm not sick. I just need to ask you about Stew the homeless guy who pretended to be blind."

The doctor spun around. "*Pretended?*" she echoed. "Who are you?"

"My name is Brooklyn Sterling. I'm a journalist from the *Boston Globe*."

Devon Foster sized her up. "Do you believe in miracles, Brooklyn from the *Boston Globe*?"

"No."

"Me neither," Devon said.

"Doc, this really hurts," Mark interrupted, still holding the towel to his face.

Dr. Foster turned toward him. "Would you mind if I talk to this woman while I fix your face?"

"Sure, no problem."

"Both of you, then, exam room three." She followed them down the hall. After shutting the door behind them, she said, "You on the table, you in the chair."

Both did as they were told.

"Why did you call me Marty Phelps?" Mark asked.

"Michael Phelps," she answered. "*Michael.* He's a famous swimmer. Won gold at the Olympics."

"I don't get it."

"Me neither," Brooklyn said.

Dr. Foster looked down at the sheet. "It says you split your nose open diving into a pool."

His face lit up. "Oh! I get it now." He looked at Brooklyn. "The guys in my fraternity bet I couldn't jump from the balcony and reach the water."

"How'd that turn out?" Brooklyn asked with a smile.

As the doctor cleaned the wound, she said to Brooklyn, "Hand me that tube of SurgiSeal."

Brooklyn turned to the shelf next to her, spotted it, and handed it over.

"Because you got a clean cut, Mark, I'm able to glue your nose back together."

"Seriously?" he replied.

She squeezed the concoction into the wound. "This will sting, but if you hold still, it will be over in a snap."

"Should I bite down on something?"

Dr. Foster winked and said, "That's only in the movies, kid." With one quick motion, she pinched the boy's skin together tight. While she held it, she watched a clock on the wall. "This is the tough part, Mark," she said as a tear rolled down his cheek. "Just hold still. Almost done."

The room was dead quiet for the next minute, then the doctor slowly released her grip. "Voila!"

His face looked as good as new. Dr. Foster held up a small mirror so he could see.

"Holy cow!" Mark said. "It worked."

She shook his hand. "No more swan dives into the pool."

He gave her an exaggerated handshake back. "Deal."

As he opened the door to go, the doctor said, "One last thing, Mark. Very important."

He waited.

"Do. Not. Sneeze."

"*Ever?*"

Dr. Foster and Brooklyn both laughed. "For the next few days."

Once Mark was out of sight, Devon said, "There goes the future president."

Brooklyn took out her pen and notepad. She'd be quick. "So? About Stew and his eyesight."

"Hold up," Devon said. "Some ground rules first. I'm sure you've heard of HIPAA."

"Of course."

"I'm not losing my medical license talking out of school about a patient."

"Understood. Can I ask you some general questions, then?"

"Depends," she answered. "Try me."

Brooklyn clicked her pen. "Stew can see?"

"Yes."

"But, there was a time when he couldn't?"

"Yes."

Brooklyn tapped the pen on her knee as she tried to come up with questions that didn't break the rules. "Did a doctor fix his eyes?"

"Not according to him."

"So . . ."

"How did he get his sight back?" Devon asked. "I can tell you this part because it has nothing to do with medicine."

"Okay. Great. Thanks."

"Stewart, the man you call *Stew,* used to be a respected engineer here in Boston."

"Used to be?"

"Yes. He had a wife, a life, the whole package."

Brooklyn leaned forward in her seat. "What happened?"

"Some kind of industrial accident that cost him his eyesight."

"What caused it? Was anyone else hurt?"

"I'm not getting into all that. HIPAA, remember." She hooked a chair with her foot and sat down across from Brooklyn. "He lost his sight, went away for a while, and ended up on the street."

"I used to see him selling pencils in Quincy Market," Brooklyn said.

"That's right. I met him at the shelter."

"That's who sent me here, Father Rip."

Devon laughed. "Now *there's* a character!" As her laugh faded away, the room became as quiet as a church. "He was blind for several years," she finally said. "And then . . ." She paused as if measuring the weight of each word.

"Then what?" Brooklyn urged.

"Then one day he walked into this office and could see."

"How?"

"How? Yeah. There's the million-dollar question."

Silence again.

"What aren't you telling me, Dr. Foster?"

She shifted in her chair. "At the risk of brushing up against HIPAA, let's just say the damage to Stew's eyes was not fixable by medical means."

"So, how then?" When the doctor didn't immediately reply, Brooklyn said, "I'm not out to hurt him or you. I promise. I just want the truth."

Devon exhaled slowly. "The truth, according to Stew, is that he met a man who took him down to the river, splashed water in his eyes, and gave him his sight back."

Brooklyn's mouth dropped open. How was she supposed to make sense of this?

Knock, knock, knock. A nurse opened the examining room door. "I'm sorry, doctor, but they're asking for you."

"I have to go," Devon said, rising from the chair.

"Wait. Please. Is this why you asked me earlier about miracles?"

"You said you don't believe in them," Devon said.

"Correct. And you said *you* don't believe in them either."

The doctor shrugged and smiled.

"Did you lie? Are you calling this a miracle, doctor?"

"I'm not calling it anything," she replied.

"Then what am I missing?"

Dr. Foster paused at the door. "He said the man who touched his eyes and gave him sight was God."

Brooklyn was dumbstruck again.

"You won't find that procedure in any medical book," Devon said. "Although, I *can* think of one book where you see miracles like that."

Right, Brooklyn thought. "What are you saying, Dr. Foster? It's a *real* miracle? If I write a story about this, can I quote you on that?"

Devon grinned. "I'd like to be able to go to a cocktail party on Martha's Vineyard next summer without being mocked by my atheist friends, so, no, you may *not* quote me."

As the doctor opened the door wider, Brooklyn said, "Can I ask for one more favor?"

"You're running up quite the tab," she replied wryly.

"I need to talk to this guy. Do you have a number or address?"

Devon let out an exaggerated sigh, then went into her pocket to retrieve her iPhone. She scrolled, then started typing.

"I'm asking him if he'd like to meet you," she said. A moment later, her phone dinged. She held it up so Brooklyn could see the screen.

It was an emoji of a happy face with an address in Boston. Brooklyn scribbled it in her notebook.

As the two of them walked down the hallway together toward the waiting room, Brooklyn said, "Can I ask one more question?"

"You really are pressing your luck," she answered.

"I know. But if there's no medical explanation, is it possible something divine happened here?"

"I'm afraid to answer that."

"Why?"

Devon smiled at her. "Do you remember that song, *What If God Was One of Us?*"

"Sure. Joan Osborne. It was a big hit years ago."

"Right. There's a line in there about how, if you believe in God then you have to believe in *all* of it, heaven, hell, Jesus, and the saints."

Brooklyn considered what she was implying. "You're a woman of science?"

"Yes."

"And everything has an explanation?"

"I always thought so," Devon responded.

"But this case?"

There was a long pause. "Cards on the table?" Devon asked.

"Sure."

The doctor said, "It scares me."

"Why?"

She answered, "What if it's true?"

Brooklyn paused, considering the question.

Devon met her eyes. "Let's be honest. Life is a lot easier to live when there are no consequences for your actions. No *judgment day*."

Brooklyn said, "But, if there's a God . . ."

Devon offered up half a grin and said, "Exactly."

"Thank you for your honesty, Dr. Foster."

"Sure."

Brooklyn paused at the waiting room door.

"Something else?" the doctor asked.

"Nah," Brooklyn said, smiling. "I was just thinking, with all the horrible things we both see in our jobs, you a doctor and me a journalist . . . Maybe the world could use a few miracles about now."

Dr. Foster shook Brooklyn's hand. "Amen to that."

CHAPTER 11

He Was at Peace

The drive from Piper's home in Woburn up to Gloucester was not far. Edward gave her the address for St. Anne's Catholic Elementary School, and away they went. As Adele sang about heartache over the car's speakers, Piper noticed Edward quietly staring out the window at the beautiful fall colors.

He's at peace. He's always at peace. I can't imagine what that's like, strolling through life seemingly without a care. How does he do it? What's his secret? she wondered. Her rage over Paul, losing her mother when she was a toddler—life had been especially cruel, and there were so many restless nights staring at the ceiling asking "Why?" If there was a road to that kind of peace, Piper had lost it years ago. Maybe Edward could help her find it again.

An hour later, they arrived, parking on the street under the shade of a chestnut tree, away from the entrance but close enough to see. "Here we are," Piper said. "St. Anne's school."

Edward looked at the long red brick building. "They should be out any moment."

"Who?"

As if on cue, a school bell rang, and a set of double doors were flung open. Dozens of children in school uniforms ran to the playground.

Next to a swing set and slide was a patch of asphalt where someone had drawn white chalk boxes with numbers inside. Piper watched children jump from one box to the next. "Hopscotch? I didn't know kids still played that."

Edward pointed toward a group of girls. "See that little girl with the brown hair? The one patiently waiting her turn?"

Piper spotted the child. "What about her?"

"Her name is Maya, and your brother is the reason she's alive right now."

The statement hit Piper like a thunderbolt.

What in God's name is he talking about? Paul died before this little girl was born.

Edward said, "Look at her neck, on the left side."

"Why?"

"Look closely. It's hard to see, but it's there."

"What do you mean my brother is the reason she's—"

"Look, please," Edward said.

Piper fixed her eyes on a little girl who was no older than seven or eight. She wore shiny black shoes and a blue skirt with a white top. She looked closer at the child's neck.

"Do you see it?"

"No."

Just then a breeze blew, and the little girl's hair was lifted away from her face, revealing her neckline.

"I see something, but can't make out what it is, Edward."

"It's a scar, stretching from her jaw, down to her neck," he said.

"Okay. What does that have to do with Paul?

Edward reached into his pocket and produced a small piece of white paper. "Drive to this address."

"Can you answer my question first?"

"Can you trust me?" he replied. His expression was placid. As usual. "I promise, all your answers are at this destination."

"Listen, Edward, I've tried to be a good sport with you, but—"

"If we don't hurry, we'll miss him."

"Who?" she asked. "Enough of the cloak and dagger."

Edward pointed at the piece of paper in her hand. With a sigh, she typed the address into the GPS and drove to the destination three miles away: a large oval building with a sign out front that read, *Gloucester Ice Rink.*

Edward exited the vehicle first. "All your answers are inside."

Except that the front doors were locked, and a decal on the window revealed the rink wouldn't be open for several hours.

"So much for that," Piper said. She never should have agreed to come.

"You of little faith," he said, chuckling. "Follow me." He walked around the side of the building, with Piper trailing behind. They came upon a rusted metal door being held open by a large white stone. Rock and roll music blasted from inside.

With a firm tug from both of them, the door groaned open like an old man getting out of a chair.

"Carry On Wayward Son" instantly filled their ears. "An appropriate song for the task at hand," Edward said with a grin.

Piper shook her head. Out on the rink a man was driving a Zamboni and cleaning the ice. As he made a turn, she caught a glimpse of his face. She could tell he was handsome, even from afar.

Spotting his unexpected guests, he turned off the machine, picked up a small remote, and stopped the music. "Rink's closed," he called out.

"We know," Edward called back. "We aren't here to skate."

The twentysomething guy maneuvered down from the Zamboni and carefully slid his way across the ice to a small door that led him off the rink. "How can I help you?" he asked as he climbed the stairs two at a time.

As soon as he was in front of them, Piper saw him do a double-take. People often said she was attractive, but she never liked the attention. So she deliberately toned down her makeup and clothing. She figured baggy was always better for keeping the wolves away. Despite her best efforts, though, this young man seemed to see right through her subterfuge. He was silent. Staring at her.

Piper looked down, embarrassed by the attention. Then, surprising herself, she looked up and stared back at him. He had dark hair with bright blue eyes and was fit in the way a man is when he does real labor. In brown boots, weathered jeans, and a Carhart jacket, he was, what her father might call, *a guy's guy*. You didn't need to look at his hands to know you'd find calluses there.

Edward said, "I am going to step away and let you two talk."

Piper spun toward him. "About what? We don't know each other."

The man from the Zamboni asked, "What's going on, sir?"

Edward smiled. "Sir? Very respectful. You got that from the military." He turned to Piper. "Tell him who you are, and then tell him what I showed you at the school." He started walking away. "I'll be right outside," he called over his shoulder. With that, he disappeared behind the door they'd just come in.

The good-looking stranger gestured for her to take a seat, leaving an empty one between them when he sat down. "So? Who are you?" he asked politely.

Piper looked toward the closed door. No sign of Edward.

Why did he bring me here? What is this about?

"Miss?" he said. "I don't mean to be rude, but I have work to do."

"Am I keeping you? I'm sorry."

"It's fine. But you know what they say."

Piper scanned his face. "No, I don't. What do they say?"

He flashed a broad smile. "The quicker you get to it, the quicker you get through it."

Piper laughed. "I like that."

"How 'bout we start with your name?" he began again.

"What?" She felt her face flush.

"You have a name, don't you?"

Piper giggled. She never giggled.

Am I flirting? No way, impossible. Answer the handsome man. Did I just call him handsome?

"Piper. Piper Matthews," she managed to reply.

"You local? From Gloucester, I mean?"

"No, I'm from Woburn, a small town outside of Boston."

His face froze.

"Piper *Matthews*?"

"Yes."

"Matthews?"

"Yes."

"From Woburn?"

"Correct."

He visibly choked up, his lips starting to tremble.

"Are you okay?" Piper asked.

He stared at the floor for a moment. When he raised his eyes, they were damp with tears. "Did you have a brother Paul, who was a Marine?"

She gasped. "How did you know that?"

"Did he die in Afghanistan?"

She didn't need to answer. The overwhelming sadness on her face confirmed it.

"My name is Luke Delaney, Piper. Your brother saved my life."

She was speechless, trying to comprehend what she had just heard. Finally, she spoke. "When? How?"

Luke said, "Your brother and I met in the two eight."

"The two eight?"

"Sorry. Second battalion, eighth Marines, out of Camp LeJeune, North Carolina. We met in basic and deployed to Afghanistan together."

Piper thought a moment. "Wait, your name is Luke Delaney. *L.D.* Did he call you L.D.?"

He smiled. "Yes, they all called me L.D. Your brother was my best friend."

"He wrote about you in his emails," Piper said. "And mentioned you when he called."

Luke smiled again. "Yeah, my folks heard all about your brother from me too."

Piper adjusted her position in her seat. "What did you mean, he saved your life?"

"You don't know what happened?"

"No. Only what the government told us, which wasn't much."

He nodded slowly. "We were in Afghanistan on a humanitarian mission, giving escort to a medical group trying to reach the village of Nusay. Two Humvees were providing cover along a road that in truth was more of a goat path." He paused, his expression changing, as if he were reliving a bad memory.

"We hit an IED," he said. "Improvised explosive device." Beads of sweat started to appear on his brow. "The guys in the first vehicle were gone in that instant. Our Humvee flipped over with three of us getting hurt. Your brother included."

Piper took a deep breath and tried to catch it on the exhale.

"I'm sorry. We don't need to talk about this."

"No, please. I want to know."

Luke lightly touched her hand. "Your brother took shrapnel to his right shoulder and side, but could still move, a little."

"Okay," she said, bracing herself for the details.

"It was an ambush, first the IED, then a dozen or so Taliban coming over the hill to finish off what was left."

Piper urged him forward. "What happened then?"

"Paul took hold of the M2 50 Cal machine gun and mounted it on the side of our overturned truck. I was on the ground with a concussion, my ears ringing, smoke everywhere. I wasn't sure what was happening. And then Paul shouted, 'Luke!' Which shook me awake because your brother *never* used my first name like that."

Piper was hanging on every word.

"He said, 'Luke, get the wounded on the medical truck and go back. I'll keep them off you.'"

Luke clasped his hands together. "There's no way I was going to leave his side, but the look on Paul's face. My God, he was so brave."

Piper fought back tears. "Yes, he was. Always."

Luke said, "His expression in that moment—"

Piper put her hand on top of his. "Please tell me."

"It may sound crazy, Piper, but I could see in his eyes that he loved me, and he needed me to go, to save the others." He paused. "I did as I was told, and we raced away from the danger. The whole time I heard that 50-cal with your brother at the trigger, keeping them away."

"The Marines won't tell you this, but Paul took a half-dozen bullets, before . . ."

"He died," she said.

"And when we went back, to get him," he said, his voice cracking, "we found Paul sitting on the ground in front of the Humvee, his eyes closed. I'd have sworn he was sleeping."

Her eyes burned with tears. "Do you think he suffered?" she asked.

He shook his head. "That's the thing. Your brother had this grin he'd get when he was about to tell a joke or if he thought of a nice memory."

She could see it. That smile they'd all loved. "I know that grin well."

"That was the expression on his face, Piper. Whatever went through his mind, when he drew that last breath, I think he was at peace."

She brushed away the tears.

"I'll tell you this for certain," Luke said. "He saved a dozen lives that day, including mine."

Piper was starting to feel a chill from the ice rink and rubbed her hands a bit to generate heat. Luke immediately took off his heavy jacket and wrapped it gently around her shoulders.

"Thank you."

After an awkward silence, he said, "Can I ask how you found me?"

She gestured toward the door. "The man I came with, Edward. He brought me here."

"I don't know him."

Piper chuckled. "Neither do I, not really."

"Why would he bring you here?"

She thought a moment, then said, "I guess he wanted me to know my brother died a hero." She stole a glance at her watch, then looked down at the ice. "Well, you've got work to do, and I've taken up enough of your time."

"It's no trouble," he said.

"It was so nice to meet you, Luke. Thank you so much for telling me the story. It means a lot to me to hear it."

She was just about to stand when he said, "Hold up. What was the other thing he told you to ask me about? Something about a school."

"Oh, right! He wanted me to ask you about a little girl from a school near here. Maya."

"Maya Patal? From St. Anne's? About eight years old?"

Piper lit up. "Yes, he took me by the school as the children came outside to play. For some reason he wanted me to see a wound on her neck."

Luke looked as if he'd seen a ghost. "What's going on?"

"I don't know what you mean."

"Maya's neck," Luke said. "That happened right here, last January."

"What do you mean, *happened*?"

He pointed toward the ice. "We have free skating every Sunday, and she was here with her family learning to skate. She'd been pushing around an orange cone so she could stay on her feet, but decided to try skating without it."

When he hesitated, Piper asked, "What happened?"

"She fell. Then another boy who was skating by her tripped and the blade of his skate caught her on the side of her neck. It was a one-in-a-million accident."

"Oh, my God," Piper murmured.

"It was terrible," Luke said. "It severed her jugular vein."

Piper tried to blot the image from her mind. "I'm normally not here on Sundays, but I had paperwork and was in that office upstairs." He pointed to a door above them. "I'm not an EMT, but they taught us basic triage for the battlefield in Afghanistan, and I was able to get to her quick and tie a t-shirt around the open vein."

Something Edward said earlier was now echoing through Piper's mind. He'd told her that Paul's life and sacrifice were not in vain. She felt ashamed.

"Are you okay?" Luke asked.

"All these years I've been angry with him."

"Who?"

Piper looked up at the ceiling. "Stupid. So stupid."

"I'm not following," he said.

She glanced toward the closed door Edward was likely standing behind. "I understand now, why he brought me to Gloucester." She reached over and gently took Luke's hand in hers. "Paul saved you so you could save that little girl."

Luke stared at their clasped hands. "I never connected the two events, but I guess you're right."

"There's no guessing about it. If you hadn't come home from the war . . ."

He finished her thought. "Maya wouldn't be here."

The side door to the ice rink opened, and Edward's kind face peeked around. "Now you understand," he said.

She let go of Luke's hand. "Who are you, Edward? Really?"

The carpenter's son ran his hand over his neatly trimmed beard and said, "We'll get to that soon." He smiled at the two of them. "I'll wait by the car."

Piper took off the jacket Luke had loaned her. "Thank you so much, Luke. For everything."

He tossed it onto a chair and gave Piper a warm, firm hug. "That was from Paul," he whispered in her ear.

She whispered back, "You're making me cry again."

He released her from the embrace and wiped a tear from her cheek. "Can I have your number? In case you want to talk some more about your brother. Nice memories, I mean."

Piper felt herself blush. "I'd like that."

As she turned to go, Luke blurted out, "Can I tell you something and you not think me weird?"

"Of course."

"I think you're beautiful," he said.

Piper blushed again. "And I think you're . . . worth the drive to Gloucester.

As she made her way to the door, she only had one thought.

I should have kissed him.

Edward was wearing a goofy grin when she met him outside.

"What?" she asked.

"You should have kissed him."

CHAPTER 12
Time to Forgive

A half-hour after leaving the urgent care facility and her visit with Dr. Foster, Brooklyn pulled her car in front of 111 Public Alley, Boston.

Is this right? Who names a street 'Public Alley'? Boston, apparently.

Smiling at the notion, she got out of her car. The man she was looking for was already sitting on the front steps, reading a book.

"Stewart Phillips?"

He looked up from the hardcover. "Guilty as charged."

"Whatcha reading?"

Stew held it up to display the cover.

She read it aloud. "*The Pioneers*, by David McCullough. Any good?"

"Very. He did that HBO series on John Adams. I'm assuming you're Brooklyn, the reporter the doc texted me about?"

"I am."

Stew clapped the book shut and laughed. "I know you."

"Yeah?"

"Yeah. The apple orchard. You're the one who fell the other day."

"Very good," Brooklyn said. "And where else do you know me?"

Stew answered, "Let me close my eyes first." He closed them. "Now, you say, *Here you go, sir*."

"I don't understand."

He opened his eyes again. "Humor me. Say, *Here you go, sir*."

When he closed his eyes a second time, Brooklyn chuckled to herself and said it.

Stew opened his eyes. "That's what you always said when you bought one of my pencils in Quincy Market."

"You recognize my voice?"

"When you live in darkness," he said, "your other senses grow sharp."

Brooklyn said, "So at the orchard . . ."

He nodded. "I walked over when all the commotion happened and heard you talking to your family."

"Suddenly you had a face to match the voice," Brooklyn said.

"Bingo. I'm glad you didn't get hurt."

"Me too. May I sit?"

"Of course. Call me Stew."

She took a seat on the beige stone steps.

"So, why is a reporter with the *Globe* looking for me?"

She hesitated, "Well . . ."

"How much did the doc tell you?" he asked.

"Not much. Only that you had your sight and lost it in an accident, then got it back."

"She tell you I was once an engineer with a wife?"

"Yes."

"She tell you I lost everything that mattered to me?"

Brooklyn said, "Sort of. She was being cautious, because of HIPAA . . . the rules."

Stew set the book down next to him. "I hurt my back and got hooked on opioids. One day, I was on a job site, high on oxy, and made a mistake on a machine setting." He looked away.

"It's alright if you don't want to go into it," Brooklyn said.

"No. You should hear this, to understand my story."

She waited patiently for him to continue.

He rubbed his forehead slowly. "A valve blew because of my incompetence, and two men got hurt, one pretty bad."

"What about you?"

"I got it the worst. A blow to the head that gave me a brain injury and something called *traumatic optic neuropathy*."

"In layman's terms?" she asked.

"Damage to the optic nerve, so pronounced, I would be blind the rest of my life."

"So you were blind, then?"

"Yes."

Brooklyn searched for what to ask next. "The doctor said you '*went away for a while*,' I think were her exact words."

"Jail," he replied. "A year in county lockup for criminal negligence. I should have gotten more, but they felt sorry for me, being blind."

"And when you got out?"

"Wife, job, life, home, all gone," he said.

"I'm so sorry, Stewart."

"Thank you. And Stew, please." He smiled at her. "You were always kind to me. Asking how my pencil sales were going, sometimes buying one for a buck when I'm sure you didn't need it."

"I remember." She paused. "Which raises the million-dollar question."

"If I was blind then, how can I see now?"

A small black crow on the power lines above them started squawking and making a fuss about something. They both looked up, taking notice.

"I think he's telling me to skip the truth because you'd never believe it," Stew said.

"This is the God part?" Brooklyn replied. "Some fantastical story about water from the river and miracles?"

"You don't believe in miracles?"

"Not in the way you told the doctor."

"I don't know what that means," he said.

Brooklyn shifted on the stoop so she could face him. "The day my daughter, Evi, was born, and I saw her face for the first time, *THAT* was a miracle. The Red Sox winning the World Series in '04, ending the 88-year drought, anybody in this town will tell you *THAT* was a miracle, but this . . ."

Stew chuckled. "So, God healing me seems less plausible than the Sox sweeping the Cardinals in four, is what you're saying?"

"Can you blame me?"

He shrugged. "You never answered my earlier question. What does a reporter from the *Globe* want with me?"

It was a straightforward question. She'd give a straightforward answer. "I'm working on a series for the newspaper about scam artists.

I confronted a father-daughter duo who fake playing the violin for tips."

"Ah, okay," he said. "I have it now. You thought you'd unmask the fake blind man in the square."

She was surprised he didn't sound accusatory or defensive. "Honestly, I'm not sure what story I'm writing anymore. I'm willing to believe almost all of it—addiction, the accident, jail, losing your sight . . ."

Stew nodded. "But not the miracle part."

"No," Brooklyn said. "I can't go back to my editor with a Jack and the Beanstalk yarn about magic beans. He'd laugh me out of his office."

"You don't believe in God, then?" Stew asked bluntly.

She rubbed her brow, searching for an answer that wouldn't offend him. "I don't know what I don't know," she said. "But if there is a God, he'd have some explaining to do about wars and famine and kids with cancer, ya know?"

"I get it," Stew replied. "And I agree with you."

Brooklyn thought, *He does seem to get it. He's so reasonable and normal. Not the type she imagined wandered around the city speaking of miracles.*

"Let's talk about when you got your sight back."

"Okay."

"You say God healed you?"

"It was Jesus, actually. But same thing."

"I don't suppose you asked Jesus about any of those terrible things I just brought up and what an awful world he created?"

Stew matched her salty tone. "*No*. I was too busy saying thank you." He stood up. "You know what's funny about you?"

"No. Tell me."

"You've already decided you won't write this story because of your prejudices against people of faith."

"Oh, please. Not true."

"Then why don't you let me tell you what exactly happened before you dismiss it?"

Brooklyn saw sincerity in his eyes. "Okay. Sure." She patted the step beside her, inviting him to sit again. "I'm sorry. I'm listening."

He searched her face a moment, then sat. "One day, *when I was blind*, I was selling pencils in my usual spot, and it was getting late. Some men approached me and demanded my money."

"How many?" she asked.

"Going by their voices, at least four. I tried to reason with them. Told them to take half but leave me enough to eat."

"What did they do?"

"Hit me," he said. "From all sides, all at once, until they had me on the ground. They took everything and broke my pencils. One gave me a kick in the face as they left."

She pictured him prone and injured on the cold cobblestone. "I'm so sorry," she said.

"I lay there a good ten minutes, trying not to swallow the blood in my mouth. And then a hand reached down and took me by the elbow. I said, 'If you're here to beat or rob me, you're late.'" He looked at Brooklyn. "This voice in the darkness told me, 'I'm not here to hurt you. I'm here to heal you. But first, you must answer one question.'"

"What question?" she asked.

"He helped me sit up, put his hand on my shoulder, and asked, 'Do you want to be healed?' I mean, here I was, broke and broken and bleeding and living in never-ending darkness, and this man is asking such a question."

"So, what did you do?"

Stew smirked. "I wiped the blood from my mouth and said, 'If you're here to mock me, please, just go.'"

"I'm guessing he didn't leave."

Stew shook his head. "No. He called me by my name and told me that the drugs, the accident, losing my wife, and going to jail were all terrible things. But . . ."

Brooklyn was riveted. "But what?"

"He said if I were truthful with myself, I'd have to admit I was a little bit grateful that I was blind."

"Grateful?" she asked, furrowing her brow. "What does that even mean?"

"My very reaction too," Stew said. "He told me I wanted to suffer for disappointing my wife, for the addiction, for hurting those men at my job."

"That's crazy."

"No, it's not, Brooklyn. He was right. I felt I deserved it. Being blind. Even that beating by those thugs. I thought I deserved every bad thing that happened to me."

She pondered this a moment. Maybe the guy helping him that day was a therapist or something. "What happened then?" she asked.

"He told me my ex, Sarah, forgave me long ago and is happily remarried. He said the men I hurt are fine now and hold no grudge." Stew reached out to take her hand. "He took my hand like this and said, 'Everyone has forgiven you. It's time to forgive yourself.'"

When Brooklyn released his hand a moment later, she asked, "How did he know all these things about your life?"

"I asked him that too."

"And?"

"He said, 'I'm the one you prayed to when you were a little boy, when your father lost his job. I was the one you asked for guidance after you met Sarah and fell in love. And I was the one you spoke to from jail, alone and blind in your cell, asking for mercy.'"

"He said he was God?"

"Yes."

Brooklyn considered his answer, then asked, "How do you know he wasn't just a kind stranger trying to comfort you?"

"He knew everything about me."

"Right. But claiming he's God, come on, Stew. You're an educated man. You know better than that."

"I'd be inclined to agree, except—" Stew reached inside his t-shirt and pulled out a small silver necklace. "How did he know about this? How did he come to have it?"

Brooklyn leaned closer and saw Stew was wearing a sterling silver medal. She squinted her eyes and read the words *ST. LUCIA*. "This medal was a gift from my grandfather at my baptism. He was a very religious man and fond of the less popular saints in the church."

"The only saint I ever heard about was St. Francis, the one who liked animals," Brooklyn said. "What's old Lucia famous for?"

"She's the patron saint of the blind," Stew said.

"Shut up," Brooklyn replied. "Your grandfather gave this to you when? How old?"

"I was a newborn."

"And you weren't blind until—"

"Forty years later."

"That's a heck of a coincidence," Brooklyn said.

"That's not even the crazy part," Stew replied.

"By all means, get to the crazy part," she quipped.

"I wore this medal every day, until the night before I went to jail."

"You gave it to someone, to hold for safekeeping?"

"No. The night before jail, I had a crisis of faith."

"What does that mean?" she asked.

"It means I stood on the Longfellow Bridge in Boston and tossed this medal into the Charles River."

His story didn't make sense. "Then how do you have it now?"

Stew said, "The day the bullies beat me up, the day the kind man helped me to my feet and told me it was time to forgive myself—"

"Yes?"

"He handed me my medal."

"Who?"

"Jesus," he answered.

"But that's impossible."

"Not for him," Stew said.

"Wait, wait . . . Give me a second to think." She stood, walked in a small circle, and snapped her finger. "It's a different medal. Same saint but a different medal."

He smiled and slowly turned the medal over, showing her tiny numbers etched in. "The date of my baptism," he said.

Everything about this man seemed sincere. A reliable witness, her journalist instincts told her. But the story kept getting crazier. "What you're claiming is impossible."

"No, Brooklyn, impossible is what came next. He asked me one last time if I wanted to be healed. I started to cry and told him yes. Then he led me to the river, splashed water across my face, put his palms against my eyes, and said, '*Come back to the light.*'"

"That was it? No mumbo-jumbo prayer?"

"No *mumbo jumbo* anything. I opened my eyes and could see."

Brooklyn was quiet. All of this was too ridiculous to believe. She reminded herself that she was a journalist, and this man's claims had to be fiction. Had to be.

I should have stayed in the darn apple tree, she thought.

Stepping off that ladder is what caused all this.

"I know it's a lot to process," Stew said. "But I'm not insane."

Brooklyn just stared at him.

Stew said, "I was blind and now I see, and Jesus is the reason why."

She sat down on the stoop again. "I don't suppose you have a picture of him or a selfie of you two, after your so-called miracle by the river?"

"No."

"Can you at least *describe* what he looks like, just in case I run into him?"

Stew laughed. "I can do better than that." He hurried into the building and disappeared behind the double glass doors. When he returned a few minutes later, he was holding an 8 x 10 charcoal sketch of a man's face.

"This is him? Where'd you get it?"

"After he healed me, we walked up near the New England Aquarium, and a friend of mine who does sketches of people was there."

"He did this?"

"Free of charge," Stew answered. "I offered it to Jesus, but he wanted me to keep it in case . . ."

"In case what?"

"You'll think I'm being nutty again," he said.

"In for a dime, in for a dollar, Stew."

"He said, 'Hang onto it in case someone comes along looking for me.'"

"Someone like me?" Brooklyn asked.

"I guess."

She took out her camera and snapped a photo of the sketch. "You've certainly surprised me today. I'm not sure what to think about any of this, but . . ."

As she rose to go, Stew said, "God be with you, Brooklyn, wherever the road leads." Then, unexpectedly, he hugged her.

"Thank you," she said. "I'm glad you can see again."

As they released their friendly embrace, Stew said, "Wanna know the last thing Jesus said to me?"

"Sure," Brooklyn answered, her tone likely revealing she didn't believe a word of this story.

He said, "The world is filled with people who have sight, yet walk through life blind to what matters."

"What do you think he meant?" she asked.

Stew pondered a moment, then replied, "Love each other."

CHAPTER 13
I'm the Second One

Gabriel hadn't sat on his front steps in quite some time. He noticed the blue paint was starting to peel.

I'll need to pay someone to scrape and repaint this.

At his age, crawling around on his hands and knees had lost all allure. He didn't want to admit it, but he'd slowed down since Paul died. The loss had taken a piece of his spirit away to a place that wasn't accepting visitors.

Gabriel was outside because he wanted to be there when Edward and Piper returned from this mystery trip. Piper was broken when Paul died, so if Edward could help, Gabriel wanted to be the first to see it.

As the Jeep pulled up, he could tell that something had happened in Gloucester, just by the expression on their faces. Piper and Edward were both grinning.

"What?" he asked after they exited the car.

Piper crossed the distance between them and hugged her father. As he squeezed her back, Edward walked past them and into the house.

Once they broke their embrace, the father and daughter went in. No sign of Edward. After checking the usual places, Gabriel called his name.

From across the home, he replied, "Is this Paul's room?"

They found him standing outside a closed door at the end of the hallway. "Yes," Gabriel said. Since Edward never seemed to do anything without a reason, he opened the door and motioned for him to go in.

The bedroom had remained untouched since Paul joined the Marines and shipped off to war all those years ago. After his death, friends suggested that Gabriel turn it into an office, but he couldn't bring himself to do it. He went to a support group once for parents who had lost a child and found others did the same thing. Putting your child's prize possessions in boxes made the loss real.

"What's this?" Edward asked, picking up a small glass apple from a shelf full of trophies.

"Paul won it at the state fair when he was a kid," Gabriel said. "That game where you toss softballs into a wicker basket."

"I remember that day," Piper said.

"Do you?" Edward asked.

"Yeah. You have to toss three balls in without them bouncing out. It's impossible."

"Except for Paul," Gabriel said. "Paul figured out the trick was to hit the front edge of the basket with your toss."

Piper laughed. "He won three times in a row until the man running the game cut him off."

"That's right! I remember. He won a stuffed bear for you, a tiger for me, and the glass apple for himself."

Edward glanced around the room. "You come in here sometimes, Gabriel."

"I do." He sank onto Paul's old bed and rubbed his hand along the New England Patriots blanket.

Still holding the glass apple, Edward crossed the room and sat down at Paul's desk. "You talk to him," he said as a statement, not a question.

Piper looked at her father, his eyes taking on a sadness she'd seen a hundred times before.

"You tell him you're sorry," Edward continued. "Sorry you weren't there when he needed you on that terrible day."

Gabriel nodded. "I understand war and that young men die." His lips started trembling.

"It's alright, Daddy." She sat beside him on the bed.

"What I can't live with," he murmured, "is the thought . . . the thought . . ."

"The thought that Paul died scared and alone," Edward said gently.

Gabriel raised his eyes to meet Edward's. "Yes. I don't care how old a boy is. A moment like that, he needs his daddy."

"But, Gabriel, he was never alone."

"What do you mean?"

Edward extended his arms to each side. "This house was filled with so much love. Then Paul died, and that joy was replaced by sadness." He gestured toward Piper. "You believed your brother died in vain, but now you know he sacrificed his life to save a brother and ultimately a child."

"What's he talking about?" Gabriel asked Piper. "What brother?"

"Our trip north," she answered. "Edward took me to meet a Marine who knew Paul. He told me how Paul saved his life. And because that man lived, he saved the life of a little girl in Gloucester."

Edward gestured toward Gabriel now. "And you, sweet Gabriel. You think Paul died scared and alone. I assure you he did not."

Gabriel sat frozen in place.

"Who is the small white dog," Edward asked, "an Australian shepherd, with a fluffy tail and face that looks like someone splashed brown paint on it?"

"We don't have a dog," Piper said.

"She's right," Gabriel added.

"It wasn't in this home, Gabriel. In the place you lived before."

Gabriel furrowed his brow. "Laddy? Are you talking about Laddy?"

"Who is Laddy?" Piper asked.

Gabriel rose to his feet, crossed the bedroom, and opened Paul's closet. Above the hangers on a dusty shelf were books and binders. He removed a photo album and returned to Paul's bed.

"What are you looking for, Dad?"

He flipped pages until he found it. "There you are!" He pointed to a photo of Paul when he was five years old, his tiny arms wrapped around a very happy-looking dog. "Laddy. I'd forgotten all about him." He turned to Piper. "You were just a toddler, so you wouldn't remember him."

"Tell her how you got Laddy," Edward said.

Gabriel smiled, remembering. "When your mom and I bought our first home, there was a stray that hung around the neighborhood. No name and no owner. Paul kept feeding the thing, even when we told him not to."

Piper smiled too. "That sounds like Paul."

"So, you adopted him," Edward said.

"Yes, we did. Paul called him Laddy. Old Laddy boy." He ran his finger over Laddy's photograph and saw again the joy on Paul's face.

Why can't they stay this age forever?

"What happened to him?" Piper asked.

He closed the album. "Laddy was very old when we found him, or when he found us. He was with us about a year. Then we lost him."

"It hit Paul hard, didn't it?" Edward asked.

"Yes, it did. He loved that dog." He gently placed the album down on the bed, then pushed it away as if it might bite him. Gabriel knew every time he looked at old photos of those he had lost, his joy in the moment would soon be replaced with an aching sorrow and longing.

Piper asked, "Why did you bring up the dog, Edward?"

"Because the day Paul died, he wasn't alone, Piper. Laddy was there."

"I don't understand," Gabriel said.

Edward sat down on the bed beside them. "When we die, we are never alone. Those we love, who have already passed, come to us, to offer comfort. Reassurance."

"Reassurance of what?" Piper asked.

"That there is a God who loves us and a heaven waiting. And that this world, wonderful as it can be, is just temporary."

Gabriel considered everything Edward was saying, then asked, "So, when my son died, Laddy came to him. That's what you're saying?"

"Yes. Laddy, and Jeremiah, his grandfather."

Gabriel's mind swirled with thoughts.

Is this man crazy? Why is he saying this? How could he possibly know these things?

Piper looked at her father. "You've talked to Edward about Nana and Pa?"

"No. You?"

"No."

They both looked at Edward, waiting for more.

"Your father, Jeremiah, who used to take Paul to Eagles Drug Store on Main Street in Stockbridge to buy penny candy. He was there to assure Paul that everything was okay and to take him to his mother, who was waiting."

Gabriel was stunned, unable to process what he was hearing.

Finally, he looked deeply into Edward's eyes and said, "Who are you? And don't tell me we'll get to that later. Later is right now. Who are you, Edward?"

Edward smiled. "You know. In your heart, you've always known."

"You're a psychic of some kind?"

Edward chuckled "No, Gabriel."

"A prophet?"

"Warmer, but no."

Gabriel looked at Piper. "Does any of this make sense to you?"

She shrugged. "No. But maybe it's not supposed to."

Gabriel turned back to Edward. "Not a prophet or magician. You're not leaving me many options, my friend."

Edward said, "My name, Gabriel. Look closer at my name."

"What about it? Edward. Edward Manuel. Eddie? Manny?"

"Try my first initial."

Gabriel thought for a moment, then said, "Son of a gun."

"What, Daddy?"

"Edward Manuel. E. Manuel. Immanuel."

"I'm still lost," she said.

"It's a word I learned a long time ago in Sunday school. You hear it in Christmas songs all the time."

"Immanuel? What does it mean?"

"It's Hebrew," Gabriel said. "It means *God is with us.*"

Gabriel and Piper both paused to consider those four simple but powerful words.

God is with us. GOD IS WITH US?

Gabriel's immediate thought was, *Well, at least this explains the kid on the bike getting up.*

Piper stared at Edward. "So, you're telling us—"

"Yes."

Gabriel said, "That you are?"

"Yes."

Gabriel and Piper looked at each other.

"Just so we're crystal clear on this," she said, "you're saying, Edward, that you are—"

"GOD!" Gabriel exclaimed. "You know, Father, Son, Holy Spirit."

Edward held up two fingers. "I'm the second one. It's nice to meet you."

CHAPTER 14

The Bright Place

Every afternoon at the *Boston Globe*, Rex Ryerson gathered reporters for a quick update on the stories they were working on. Brooklyn normally skipped the meeting, so when she opened the conference room door, others at the table looked surprised.

"What's wrong?" Rex asked.

"Nothing." She took a seat.

Rex gave her an unconvinced look.

Brooklyn drew in a breath and sighed. "Actually, everything."

"Should we talk in private?" Rex asked.

Brooklyn scanned the faces of her colleagues. "No. I'd like everyone's opinion on this." She folded her hands on the table. "I set out to do a story on scam artists who target tourists in Boston."

"Right," a fellow reporter said. "The violin people and a blind guy."

"The first one was a disaster," Brooklyn said. "I feel like I exposed shame, not grift."

"We had this conversation already," Rex said. "I thought you were tougher than this."

"I am," she shot back. "But that's not the problem."

"What is?" he asked.

"The problem is the second guy we were going to expose, the blind guy, isn't blind."

"Wasn't that the point of the scam?"

"Yes, but . . ." She felt herself getting flustered.

Rex and the dozen others at the long conference table waited.

"The short version is this. The man *could* see, was hurt in an accident, and lost his sight. Then got his sight back."

A colleague asked, "So, there's no scam? When the guy sold the pencils, he *was* blind?"

"Correct."

Rex tossed a yellow legal pad onto the table. "Sounds like we don't have a story, then."

Brooklyn bit her lip and tipped her head to the side. "Well . . ."

"We *do* have a story?" Rex asked.

She shrugged.

"What am I missing here?"

"It's just . . ."

"WHAT?" Rex barked. "SPEAK."

"I know this sounds crazy, but the blind guy swears he was healed by God, and it's a miracle."

There was silence, and then a co-worker asked, "You mean he prayed and got healed?"

"Not quite."

As everyone stared and waited, she added, "He says God showed up one day in Quincy Market, took him to the river and, ya know, healed him."

Several at the table burst into laughter. Rex said, "I don't know why you thought that sounded crazy. Feels like a front-page story to me. God visits Boston and heals a blind guy. The real question is, since he's in town, can he fix the Patriots? They need a new quarterback. Did God happen to bring another Tom Brady with him?"

The laughter grew. Brooklyn smiled and said, "I hear ya, joke away. I laughed myself."

When the laughter drifted to silence, she said, "We can all laugh, but here are the facts. This guy was blind and now he can see, and doctors can't explain it. Call it luck or a miracle. Something strange happened here."

"Do you think he met God?" Rex asked directly.

"No. But I can't explain it."

A college intern named Connie raised her hand to speak.

Rex said, "While I appreciate the manners, young lady, we don't sit on formality here."

Connie, clearly confused, replied, "Sit on what?"

"You can just talk."

With all eyes on her, Connie lowered her hand. "My roommate's sister is friends with Veronica Snow from Channel 5 News in Boston."

Rex said, "A bit off topic. Let's move on."

"Wait, Rex," Brooklyn said. She turned her eyes to the intern. "It's okay. Finish what you were saying."

Connie continued, "Veronica, the TV reporter, was telling my roommate's sister that she thought she saw a miracle recently in Meriam Hill."

"What in Paul Revere's name are you talking about?" Rex barked.

"I'm only bringing it up because Brooklyn was just talking about miracles."

Brooklyn said, "Go on, Connie."

The intern said, "Veronica Snow, from Channel 5, said she went to a street where a little boy got hit by a car, and when she saw the bike twisted like a pretzel, she was sure the kid was dead."

"He wasn't?" Brooklyn asked.

"No, ma'am. He went from unconscious and bleeding, to wide awake and fine in the snap of a finger. Least, that's what the lady from Channel 5 said."

The room went quiet. Brooklyn wasn't certain what to make of this new information.

"The whole neighborhood is talking about it," Connie said. "They're calling him the miracle child."

An editor named Mike joked, "Step right up! Brooklyn is having a sale on miracles today. Buy one, get one free."

More laughter. Rex slapped his hand on the table to gain control. "ENOUGH."

"Meriam Hill?" Brooklyn asked the intern.

"In Lexington. Yes, ma'am."

"Did she say where exactly?"

"Near a pond."

Another reporter chimed in. "I know that area. She's talking about Granny Pond."

Brooklyn looked at Rex. "I'm sure it's nothing, but would you mind if I—"

"Go," her boss said. "But we can't waste time on this. A half-day, then we move on."

As Brooklyn reached the door to go, something possessed her to turn back to the group and say, "Maybe we should go easy mocking the God stuff."

Mike, the joker, said, "I didn't know you were a holy roller."

Brooklyn grinned. "I'm not. But my heart isn't closed to the possibility of something better."

"Better than what?" Mike retorted.

"This." She gestured with both hands toward everyone who had laughed at her expense. "Making fun of people for their faith is a bad look. Just saying."

"Go chase your miracle," Rex said.

She gave him a wink and went out the door.

It didn't take long for Brooklyn to get the boy's address. Helpful neighbors pointed her in the direction of a stately home where the "miracle child" lived. She climbed the steps and rang the doorbell.

When there was no answer, she pushed it again, holding it down longer this time.

Finally, a voice came from the speaker. "Help you?"

"Yes, my name is Brooklyn Sterling. I'm a reporter from the *Globe*. I'm looking for the little boy who was hit by the car."

The voice answered, "I'm his mother, Elsie Lancaster. What's this about?"

"Nothing is wrong, ma'am. I just had a couple of questions about what happened."

A *BUZZ* filled the air, so Brooklyn instinctively gave a pull to the door, opening it.

The voice from the box said, "Stay in the hall. I'll be right down."

Brooklyn did as she was told, waiting in the well-lit hallway. As approaching footsteps echoed down the staircase, she noticed a strange object in the corner.

She inched toward it for a better look as Elsie said, "That's the bike."

"You're kidding me."

What Brooklyn saw looked nothing like a bicycle. The front wheel was bent, and the metal frame twisted beyond repair. The handlebars were squished as if King Kong had crushed them with his fist, and the seat Jayden was sitting on was facing the wrong way.

"Is your son here, Mrs. Lancaster?"

"Not yet," she replied. "His school bus is due any minute."

Brooklyn noticed a pair of empty chairs along the wall and asked, "May we sit?"

Elsie obliged, sitting where she could watch out the window for her son's bus.

"I'm here because someone told me they're calling your boy—I'm sorry, what's his first name?"

"Jayden."

"They're calling Jayden a miracle child."

"And you doubt that?" Elsie asked.

Brooklyn pressed her tongue to the roof of her mouth, thinking of how to respond. "Honestly, I don't know what to think."

Elsie pointed at the bike. "Look at that thing. How does my Jayden walk away with barely a scratch?"

Brooklyn stared at the hunk of metal. "I don't know. Maybe he bounced, just the right way."

Elsie scoffed. "Bounced, are you kidding me? It's all stone and asphalt out there." She pointed toward the street. "Eyewitnesses saw it happen. He should have been dead."

Brooklyn took out her notepad. "I'd like to talk to them."

Elsie said, "The woman across the street is a retired nun. She was praying over him and said his breathing was getting slower and slower." Elsie started to cry.

Brooklyn reached into her pocket and took out a napkin. "It's not much, but it's clean." She handed it to Elsie.

The woman wiped away the tears. "Thank you. I'm sorry about that."

"It's understandable, to almost lose your son. If we ever lost our Evi . . ."

"Evi?"

"Our daughter." For a moment Brooklyn's mind drifted to the terror she'd felt as she watched Evi fall off the ladder. *If Connor hadn't caught her . . .*

Elsie said, "I don't know where my manners are. Did you want some tea or coffee?"

"No, no. I'm fine." She pulled her thoughts back to Elsie's son. "I was just curious about Jayden and what happened."

Elsie glanced out the window. "They say it looked like he was dying until that man touched him."

Brooklyn sat up straighter. "What man?"

"Beats me. He left before anyone could thank him."

"And you're saying he touched your son?"

"That's what they say."

Brooklyn said, "I know you weren't there, but walk me through what witnesses said happened."

Elsie met her eyes. "He came out of nowhere and asked the nun to step back. Leaned in and put his hands on Jayden's chest, whispered something in his ear and that was that."

"That was what?"

Elsie laughed. "Jayden woke up."

"And he was fine?"

Elsie replied, "Took him a minute, from what I was told, but yeah, a couple of scrapes. That's it."

"And you have no clue who this guy was?"

"No. Like I said, he left before anyone could ask. Somebody told me he was in the neighborhood for work."

"What kind of work?"

"I didn't ask."

Brooklyn thought a moment. "Do you know what the man looked like?"

"I told you," Elsie said with an edge to her voice. "I wasn't there. I didn't see him."

Just then, Brooklyn heard air brakes outside, followed by the beeping of a school bus.

"That's Jayden now," Elsie said.

In a matter of seconds, the front door opened, and Jayden bounded in with his backpack flung over his shoulder. "Hey, Mom!" He eyed Brooklyn and then said, "Hi."

"Hello, Jayden. I'm Brooklyn."

"Like the city?"

"Exactly."

"Are you a friend of my mom's?"

Elsie answered, "Brooklyn is a newspaper reporter. She heard about you getting hit by a car and wanted to meet you."

Jayden dropped his backpack and extended his hand like a gentleman. "Nice to meet you."

"You as well," Brooklyn said, shaking his hand. "Your mom was just telling me about the accident. Do you remember anything?

He sat down on the bottom stair. "To be honest, not much."

"Tell her what you do remember, hon."

Jayden took a deep breath. "Sure. Okay. Well, I went fishing for Jumbo, but he wasn't around."

"Jumbo?" Brooklyn asked.

"It's a fish. Doesn't matter. After fishing, I was riding my bike home, went to cross the street, and then woke up on the sidewalk."

"He knows he's not supposed to ride that darn bike across the road," Elsie said sharply.

"I said I was sorry." Jayden cast his eyes to the floor.

Brooklyn intervened. "So, fishing, bike, accident, and you woke up?"

"Yep."

"And nothing else happened?"

Jayden looked at his mom and appeared uncomfortable.

"It's alright, baby, you can tell her."

The boy looked at Brooklyn. "I don't tell the kids at school this part because it's weird and I don't want them thinking I'm a nut job."

Brooklyn, in her most encouraging voice, said, "I promise I won't think anything of the sort."

He looked again at his mom.

"Go ahead," she said.

He took another deep breath. "After I got hit by the car but before I woke up, I was in the bright place."

Brooklyn leaned in. "The bright place?"

"Yeah. The floor, ceiling, walls. Everything was white and bright."

"And did something happen in the bright place?"

"Yeah. A boy about my age, who looked a lot like me, walked up and said, My name is Charlie. I'm your brother. You can come with me, it's alright."

Brooklyn turned to Elsie. "He has a brother?"

Elsie's eyes filled with tears as she reached over to squeeze Jayden's hand. "Before Jayden was born, my husband, Charles, and I had another, um—"

"Take your time," Brooklyn said gently.

Elsie said, "The baby was stillborn."

Brooklyn drew in a hard breath. "I'm so sorry, Elsie."

"There's more," she replied. "We knew we were having a boy, so we chose the name Charles, after my husband. We planned to call him Charlie."

Brooklyn was trying to wrap her mind around this. "Elsie, are you saying . . ."

"I'm not saying anything. I'm just telling you what Jayden saw when he was dying." Elsie pulled Jayden closer to her. "Two years after we lost the baby, Jayden was born."

Brooklyn's mind was spinning. "So, in the bright place, Jayden, this boy who looked like you. He said he was your brother?"

"Charlie. Yes."

"And did you go with him?"

"I was about to when I heard a voice."

"Was it a paramedic?" she asked. "Or maybe a police officer?"

"No, this was the other guy."

Brooklyn hesitated. "The man on the street?"

"Yes," Jayden replied. "He was in the bright place too. He walked up and hugged Charlie like they knew each other. Then he touched my chest, and it felt like he was pulling me back."

"Back where?"

Jayden put his hands out, palms up. "Here. Home."

Brooklyn paused to think.

Jayden said to his mother, "I'm hungry. Can I go grab a snack?"

"Certainly, honey."

"Real quick," Brooklyn said. "One more question, Jayden?"

"Sure."

"Your mom told me earlier that this man whispered something in your ear. Do you remember what he said?"

"Yes."

"Would you mind telling me?"

The child smiled at Brooklyn and said, "Not yet."

Brooklyn was confused. "You don't want to tell me now? Is that what you're saying?"

Jayden laughed. "No. I'm saying, that's what he whispered to me. *Not. Yet.*"

Brooklyn stared at the floor for so long that Elsie asked, "Are you alright?"

She looked up at Jayden again. "I'm sorry, Jayden. I lied. I have one more question."

He waited.

"Is it possible the boy who looked like you and the bright place was all just a dream?"

"IMPOSSIBLE," Elsie answered.

"Why impossible?"

"The loss of my first baby was devastating."

"I can't imagine," Brooklyn replied.

"We NEVER spoke of it," Elsie continued.

Brooklyn nodded. "Okay."

"To anyone. Ever."

"So, what are you saying?" Brooklyn asked.

"I'm saying, Jayden didn't know he had a little brother who died at birth. He certainly didn't know the child's name. It was a secret between us and God. So how does Jayden *dream* that?"

Brooklyn reached into the pocket of her jacket to fish out her smartphone. "This can't be happening," she murmured. "Not twice."

"What?" Elsie asked.

She pulled a photo up on her phone and raised it in front of Jayden's eyes. "Was this the man who hugged Charlie? The man who touched your chest and said, *Not yet*?"

It was the photo of the sketch, the charcoal image of the man who helped Stewart regain his sight.

Jayden's eyes filled with joy as he smiled and nodded. Come to think of it, she'd seen a similar look in Stewart's eyes when he talked about the man. Like gratitude. And love.

"Can I give you a hug?" Brooklyn asked. He nodded again and reached out his arms. "I'm so glad you're alive, Jayden."

He laughed, "Me too." He pointed to the sketch. "Who is he?"

"I'm not sure," Brooklyn replied. "But you're not the only person who says he healed them."

"So, what now?" Elsie asked.

"What now is, I need to find this man. You said he did work on this block, so I'll knock on every door until someone recognizes the picture and hopefully, we can track him down."

Elsie said, "You want help? There are a lot of doors."

"Thanks. I'd love that."

Jayden stood silent, grinning at both women.

"What?" his mother asked.

"You don't have to knock on any doors."

"We don't?" Brooklyn replied. "Why not?"

"When I woke up, after the man helped me, I watched him and an older guy get into a white van."

"Just a plain white van?"

"Nope," he replied. "There was writing on the side."

Both women leaned in anxiously, waiting for Jayden to speak.

"It said, 'The Carpenter's Son.'"

CHAPTER 15

Newbury Street

Edward was waiting for Piper, the moment she got home from work.

"Before you take your jacket off, I need a ride to Newbury Street, in Boston."

Gabriel said, "You need to go shopping? Newbury's expensive. I can think of a dozen places you'll get a better bargain."

Edward smiled at his friend. "I'm not buying, I'm giving."

"Can we ask what?" Gabriel inquired.

Edward winked at his friends and answered, "Salvation."

Piper grabbed her keys. It was 24 miles from their home in Woburn to Newbury Street in Boston. With heavy city traffic, the ride took nearly an hour, plenty of time for her to tell Edward a hard truth. "My dad and I were talking about you, and we came to a conclusion."

"What's that?"

"We think you are a good man, a kind man, and it's obvious you know things about us and my brother, Paul."

"But?"

Piper patted his arm, as if comforting a child. "We don't think you are the Son of God. No offense."

She waited for pushback, but Edward looked out the window and said, "Such a beautiful day."

"Did you hear what I said?"

"I did."

"And?"

"It's a lot to process. I get it."

They drove on for a bit when Piper, trying to humor him, said, "Okay, let's say, for the sake of argument, you are who you claim to be. Why are you here?"

"Broadly or specifically?"

Piper thought a second. "Both."

"Well," he said, "broadly, I guess you could say I'm here to check on things, to see how my Father's children are doing."

"And how are we doing?"

"Not great. If life were a test, I'm not sure mankind would pass."

"Are you talking about wars and genocide, all the awful things people do?"

"Those are the big ones, yes. But I'm also talking about drugs, crime, neglect, hatred, vanity."

"What do you mean, vanity?"

He replied, "Caring more about *likes* on a social media page than *love* for our neighbors." He pointed to Piper's smartphone. "These devices you cling to. I'm not sure they're helping."

"How so?"

Edward shook his head. "You claim they keep you connected, yet never have I seen so many lonely people."

"True," she agreed. "But they do give us a window to the world."

"That's the thing about an open window, Piper. You never know what might climb through when you aren't watching."

She maneuvered around some traffic. "Since none of us is going to toss our phone into the river, do you have a remedy?"

Edward looked at her. "Love. Forgiveness."

The car went silent, then Piper asked, "You also said you were here for a specific reason. What would that be?"

"Specifically, to heal four people, help a dozen others, and bring three of God's children home."

"By home, do you mean to heaven?"

"No, I mean, home."

The car fell quiet again. Then Piper asked the question she really wanted to. "Is there a heaven?"

"Oh, yes. More remarkable than you could imagine."

The voice from the GPS spoke, "Arrived."

As Piper pulled into a parking space, Edward said, "I have two stops in one place. You can tag along or meet me in an hour."

"Do you even have money?"

Edward shrugged.

"Oh, that's right," Piper said, a note of sarcasm in her voice. "You're giving away salvation. Do I need a coupon for that?"

Edward answered, "Only an open heart. Come, and I'll show you."

They strolled down the sidewalk, boutiques with large windows and expensive items flanking them on both sides. Piper pointed across the street. "Paul and I went into that antique store once. Do you see it?"

"Yes, it's very nice."

"Very nice and super expensive," she said. "The minute we were inside, the guy behind the counter hit a button and locked the door behind us."

"Why?"

"We must've looked poor, so he assumed we were there to shoplift."

"What did you do?"

"I wanted to leave, but Paul told the manager to relax. Then he picked up a twelve-hundred-dollar vase and pretended he was about to drop it." She laughed. "I thought the guy was going to have a cow right there in his store."

"I'm sorry," Edward said. "A cow?"

"It's just an expression." She thought about Paul and how much she missed him. "He was always doing things like that. I was embarrassed because of how the man treated us, and Paul just turned the whole thing around."

I wish he was with me, she thought. *Even for a day, an hour, a moment.*

"He will be," Edward said.

She spun toward him. "What?"

"With you again," Edward said.

How does he do that?

Edward gestured toward a shop. "Chapters Bookstore and Café. We're here."

A small A-framed chalkboard sat outside the store's front door with a notice written in red chalk: *God Lie author Shane Harris book signing today.*

Piper read the sign. "Whoa, hold up, Edward. You don't want to go in there."

"Why not?"

"Because this guy is a famous atheist. He writes books with titles like *God Trap*, and *God Joke*. This must be his new one, *God Lie*. Let's move along."

"Why?"

"Because you claimed to be the Son of God and this guy makes fun of people like you."

Edward smiled. "You're trying to protect me?"

"I am," Piper answered with a sigh.

Edward paused at the door. "Can I tell you a secret?"

"Sure."

"All those artist's images of Jesus holding a lamb in his arms. Do you know what I'm talking about?"

"I've seen statues like that," she replied.

"They're beautiful but only half-true."

"What do you mean?"

"Jesus holding a lamb depicts my tenderness, which is accurate, but being a shepherd is very dicey business sometimes."

"Meaning what exactly?"

"Meaning, a shepherd must also protect his flock and wield a staff to ward off the wolves."

Piper quipped, "I didn't know we had wolves in Boston."

Edward smiled wryly. "There are wolves everywhere. Some stand upright, wear nice clothes, and come disguised as friends."

Piper chuckled. "I'm not sure what that means, but let me ask you this."

"Ask away."

"Do you really want to meet this author who mocks everything you stand for?"

Edward turned the door handle. "Absolutely."

"Why?"

"Because ignorance and arrogance often quarter together in comfort, as long as the closed shutters keep the room dark."

"Let's pretend I have a clue what that means," Piper said. "What's your plan?"

Edward smiled broadly. "Open the shutters and let the light in."

With that, he flung open the door and went inside.

There were racks of books, rows of folding chairs, and a small stage where authors would read and sign their work. Despite Shane Harris's being a famous writer and atheist, only a baker's dozen turned out to meet him.

Edward stood next to Piper in the back, listening to the author read aloud.

We must free ourselves from the bonds of superstition and relics of a time when man raged at the sky. Science must be our religion, intelligence and logic our sacraments. We must not die on the altar of fairy dust and spaghetti monsters.

That last line caused Edward to laugh out loud, turning every head in the bookstore. "I'm sorry," he said, putting a hand over his mouth to stifle the next giggle.

Harris, a short man with stubby fingers and slicked-back hair, shot daggers from his eyes in Edward's direction.

"What's so funny?" the author asked.

Edward shook his head. "Nothing. My sincere apologies."

"Just looking at the hair and beard," Harris said, "I'm getting a patchouli and savior of the world vibe."

Edward gave no reaction as a few in the crowd laughed at his expense.

"I take it you believe in God?" Harris asked.

Edward smiled. "More than you could imagine."

Harris, clearly never one to miss an opportunity to eviscerate a *Jesus Freak*, asked, "Where's your invisible friend now?" He pointed at an empty chair. "Is he sitting over here? I wouldn't want someone to squash him accidentally."

Laughter filled the room.

"I tried to warn you," Piper said. "Let's go."

Edward nodded.

Seeing his retreat, Harris shouted, "There you have it, ladies and gents! Another Bible-thumper running from the truth."

With that, Edward stopped and turned around. He looked to his right, where a twentysomething woman was holding a copy of *God Lie*.

"May I?" Edward asked gently, pointing to her copy. The woman handed him the book. He raised it. "You worship science, not God?"

"That's right," Harris answered.

"Thirty-trillion cells in the human body, each complex, with its own function," Edward said. "All a big cosmic accident?"

Harris smirked. "We were just the lucky lottery winners who got to slither out of the swamp."

The comment brought more laughter from his followers.

Edward appeared unfazed. "Is it not true that Physicist Robert H. Dicke, astronomer Fred Hoyle, and even the famous Stephen Hawking all agree the universe is fine-tuned?"

The young lady Edward borrowed the book from asked, "What does that mean?"

Edward turned to her. "Picture an electronic board with a million dials, each turned to a precise point. Can you imagine it?"

The girl nodded.

"If even one dial was off by the tiniest bit, there would be no universe, no life, no you. And what a sad universe it would be without you."

The way Edward said those words, Piper thought, couldn't be misconstrued as a pick-up line. There was something profoundly honoring in it. Loving. The way the girl smiled, it was clear his comment comforted her.

"That proves nothing," Harris retorted, "only that the universe is complex."

Edward said, "So, you agree it's fine-tuned, just no fine-tuner?"

"Correct."

"Would you agree there is intelligence in how it is designed?"

"Of course."

"But no designer, just dumb luck?"

"Correct," Harris snapped.

Edward continued, "You also believe something came from nothing?"

A man sitting in the front row said, "Yeah, we call it the Big Bang."

"Hmm," Edward replied. "And what caused the bang?"

There was silence now.

Edward addressed the man in the front row. "You're sitting in a chair. Did the chair just spontaneously appear in this room?"

"No. It came from a store."

"And before the store a factory," Edward said, "and before the factory a lumber yard and the lumber came from a tree, the tree from a sapling, the sapling from an acorn and the acorn from a . . ."

Everyone was fixated on Edward now.

"What's your point?" the man asked.

"To call believing in a higher power silly but to call believing that something can come from nothing reasonable, possible. I ask, which requires a greater leap of faith?" He pointed to a teenager standing in the corner. "Jacob. Your name is Jacob, right?"

The boy looked surprised. "Me? Yes, I'm Jacob."

"Can you help me a moment?"

"Sure."

Edward reached into his pocket and produced a glass apple.

"Is that my brother's souvenir?" Piper asked.

Edward raised it so all could see. "It is."

"Why do you have it?"

"So I can throw it at Jacob."

Piper was aghast. "You're going to do what?"

"You're going to do what?" Jacob echoed.

"It's fine," Edward said, "trust me. I'm going to throw the glass apple, but I *don't* want you to catch it."

"I'm sorry, did you say *don't* catch it?" the boy asked.

"Correct."

"Edward!" Piper felt equal parts anger and fear. "It will break!"

"It won't. Everything will be fine. Ready, Jacob?"

Jacob fidgeted nervously. "She's right, sir. If I don't catch it, it *will* break."

Piper, fighting tears, said, "Don't, Edward. Please." If she believed in prayer, she might have said one.

Harris called out, "What are you trying to prove?"

"Relax," Edward said. "It's all part of the spaghetti monster show." He raised the apple. "Okay, Jacob. Eyes on me now." With that, he threw the glass apple, which sailed over the heads of several people before Jacob leaped to snatch it mid-flight.

"Great catch," Edward said. "You can give it to her now."

The boy smiled proudly as he walked the glass prize over to Piper.

"Thank you," she said, trembling with relief.

Edward then asked Jacob, "Why did you catch it?"

"I didn't want it to break."

"Who cares?" Edward asked.

"Her." He pointed at Piper. "It seems to mean a lot to her."

"It does," Edward said. "It belonged to her brother. But why help someone you don't know?"

Jacob paused, seemingly searching for an answer.

"You helped her, Jacob, because you are hardwired for good. A moral compass deep in your soul that you chose not to ignore. That's God working inside of you."

"Oh, please," Harris chided.

"What would have happened if you didn't catch it?" Edward asked.

"It would have smashed on the ground."

"Why?"

Jacob thought a moment, then said, "Gravity."

"What does gravity look like, Jacob?"

"I, um . . . It doesn't look like anything."

"I'm confused," Edward said. "If you can't see it, how do you know it's real?"

He shrugged. "I guess we know it's real because of the things it does."

Edward nodded. "Sounds a lot like God."

The sound of a loud slow clap filled the air. "Wonderful presentation," Harris said, still clapping in mockery, "but you proved nothing."

Edward held up the author's book again. "Do you know how many words are in here?"

Harris answered, "Around 60,000."

"Sixty-three thousand, four hundred and seventeen," Edward said.

"So?"

"The word *Lie* appears in here 114 times. *Fraud* 92. *Fortune* 11. *Ego* 9."

Harris smirked. "Congratulations on being able to count. What's your point?"

Edward said, "The word *LOVE* appears none. *GRACE* none. *FORGIVENESS* none. *HOPE,* not once. My point, Shane, is your book offers no hope in a world starved for it." He walked toward the front of the room. "If God exists and stood right before you, would you even be willing to admit it?" He turned to the crowd. "Would any of you?"

A woman raised her hand to get Edward's attention. "It's hard to believe when there's no proof."

Edward replied, "The Gospels, the death on the cross, the good you see performed in God's name every day. Is there truly no proof or do you refuse to see it?"

A man to Edward's left said, "How do you prove someone existed more than 2,000 years ago? You can't. End of story."

"Tell me, then," Edward said, "was Aristotle real?"

"Yes."

"How about Alexander the Great or Julius Caesar?"

"Of course."

"How do we know?" Edward asked.

The man considered, then answered, "Because of eyewitnesses who knew them and wrote about them."

Edward replied, "Sounds a lot like the Bible." He moved closer to the author. "I understand why you're here, why you do this."

"To sell books, duh," Harris replied.

There was another giggle from the crowd.

Edward shook his head. "No."

"No?" Harris said. "Enlighten me."

Edward leaned close and whispered to Shane, "If my father went out to buy milk when I was only four and never returned, and my mother brought men home, each one worse than the last. The hitting, the drinking, the loneliness. Hiding under the stairs with my brown striped blanket."

Shane stared at him, stunned.

"If I were that little boy," Edward continued, "I too would doubt God's love or existence."

Shane found himself unable to move or reply. *How could he know these things?*

"If I were that boy," Edward went on, "I might even grow up and write books denouncing God." He touched Shane's shoulder, then stood up straight. "One last thing," he said, speaking at a volume the audience could hear.

"What's that?" Shane replied, his voice weak.

"Do you believe in unicorns?"

"Of course not."

"Shane, people who don't believe in unicorns don't spend their lives writing books called *The Unicorn Lie* or *The Unicorn Trap.* We don't run around denouncing things we don't believe exist. The sheer weight of your denial of God gives you away, my friend."

Shane looked down.

Edward lowered his voice again. "I did not come here to embarrass you."

"Why, then?"

"To tell you that God has not forgotten you, Shane. When you grow weary of that dark place under the stairs, please know there is always a seat for you at my Father's table."

All eyes were riveted on Edward as he made his way toward the exit. Passing Jacob, he smiled and said, "Nice catch."

Piper greeted him at the door. "That was amazing," she said.

"Just one more thing to do, and then we can go," he replied.

With that, he turned and walked briskly into the small café attached to the bookstore, where a half-dozen tables were filled with people who hadn't attended the book signing. In the center of the room were four White teenage girls in designer clothing from head to toe. They were whispering and laughing at the expense of a teen who sat alone, reading a book. She was a Black girl, small for her age, in jeans and a purple sweater.

Edward crossed the room, paused at the table of mean girls, and gave them a look of authority which immediately silenced them. Then he approached the lone teen's table. "You're Naomi, yes?"

She looked up. "Do I know you?"

"Not in the way you mean," he said, "but I certainly know you."

Naomi put the book down and looked around nervously.

"It's alright," he said. "I promise. Whatcha reading?"

She picked up her book again. "*The Last Battle* by C. S. Lewis. It's part of the Narnia series."

"Ahh," Edward said. "He's a fine writer. Not afraid to speak of faith."

The teen sat silently.

"Speaking of which," Edward said, "that cross I see around your neck. How did you get it?" He pointed at a lovely sterling silver cross hanging from a matching chain.

Naomi clutched it against her heart. "It was a Christmas present from my mother."

"So many wear them as a fashion statement," Edward said. "But not you."

"No, it means a lot to me."

At that moment there was another giggle from the teens at the other table. Naomi glanced over.

Edward followed her gaze. "I wanted to talk to you about that, Naomi. Ignore them. Know in your heart that you are wonderful exactly as you are, and I . . . I mean, God has great plans for you."

Naomi was still clutching her cross. "It's hard sometimes, being different."

"I know, child."

She looked at him. "They make fun of me because I don't have a boyfriend yet, and I study all the time. Even because I go to church."

"I know," Edward said. "And yet you wear the cross on the *outside* of your sweater, knowing it will make you the target of their teasing." He leaned closer. "Listen to me, Naomi. You are braver than any of them."

"You think so?"

"Definitely." He smiled at her. "You want to be a veterinarian someday, yes?"

"How do you know that?"

He pointed to her phone on the table. "Can I have that for a second?"

She hesitated.

"It's okay. I promise I'll give it back."

She handed it over. He placed it between his hands briefly, then gave it back to her. "Open the photos on your social media account."

She hesitated again.

"Trust me. You'll like this."

As Naomi opened the app, he said, "What you are about to see, you can only see once."

She went to her profile picture and saw a young Black woman, maybe 22, in a red cap and gown. An older couple flanked her. Her parents.

"Wait. Is this . . .?"

"You," Edward answered. "Eight years from now graduating from Cornell, with a degree in Veterinary Medicine."

She could only stare in silent wonder.

"Next picture," Edward said.

Naomi swiped her finger, revealing a photo of herself in a white jacket and a stethoscope around her neck.

"I'm a doctor?"

"Yes," he answered. "At a clinic in Vermont where you offer free vet care to poorer families."

Naomi's eyes filled with tears.

"I'd tell you that you meet the man of your dreams, fall in love, and have a wedding at the top of a mountain, but I don't want to give too much away."

"Why are you showing me all this?" she asked.

"So you'll know you're doing great. Ignore the noise. Stay on the path."

She pressed her phone to her chest, right beside her necklace. "Anything else?" she asked.

He pointed to her cross. "Know that when you pray, I'm listening."

She smiled wide and met his eyes.

"Enjoy your book," he said, before walking away.

As he crossed the room, Naomi opened her Instagram account again. Her old photos of a teenage girl trying to find her way through life had returned. She clutched her cross and whispered, "Thank you, Jesus."

When Edward reached Piper by the door, he said, "You're welcome, Naomi."

"Are we all out of salvation?" Piper teased.

Edward pushed open the front door of the bookshop and answered, "Never."

CHAPTER 16

No. Yes. Maybe.

"Connor? Evi?" Brooklyn called out.

"Out on the swing," he answered.

The back porch at their home in Wakefield boasted a romantic wooden swing. That swing and the thought of snuggling together is what had sold them on the house.

He was holding a half-empty bottle of Sam Adams when she stepped outside. "Where's Evi?" she asked.

"With my folks."

Brooklyn could tell by his tone that something was up. "Was that planned?"

"No. I asked them to take her so we could talk."

Brooklyn plopped down next to him. "Are we about to have a fight?"

"No," he said. "Yes. Maybe."

"So . . . what's on the menu?" she asked.

Connor plunged in. "As you know, Evi is turning ten, and she's already two years behind taking her first Holy Communion with the church."

He stopped and waited for a response.

"And?" Brooklyn asked.

"And this is the part where you lecture me about how Evi doesn't need church or religion in her life to be a good person and how God, if he exists, is an absentee landlord."

"Am I that predictable?"

Connor shrugged. "It's not like we haven't had this debate before."

"Fair enough," she replied.

"So?" Connor asked.

Brooklyn got up from the swing. "If Evi wants to go to church and take communion, I'm fine with it."

"You are?"

"Yes."

Connor took a swig of the beer and studied her with measured suspicion. "What's up with you?"

"Nothing. Other than a splitting headache I can't seem to shake."

Connor followed her into the kitchen. She opened the cabinet where they kept a bottle of ibuprofen and shook several into her hand.

"Whoa, how many are you taking?"

"Four."

"Isn't that more than the bottle recommends?"

"I know better than the bottle," she said.

"These headaches started after you fell from the apple tree?"

Brooklyn swallowed the pills, then answered, "Before."

Connor gave her a worried look.

"Stop with the face. It's a headache, Con. That's all."

"Okay." He changed the subject. "Don't take this the wrong way, but why are you suddenly okay with Evi, church, and the God stuff?"

She sank into a chair at the kitchen table. "Maybe because I'm dealing with my own God stuff."

"Whad'ya mean?"

"My scam story."

Connor took a seat across from her. "Tell me."

"Not much to tell. I have two people saying they were healed by the same man, and the man thinks he's God."

"GOD? Like, God, God?"

Brooklyn smiled. "The Big Guy himself."

"Are we talking about the blind guy who isn't blind?" Connor asked.

"Yes. He says a man touched his eyes and cured him."

"And who is the second one?" he asked.

"A kid who got hit by a car."

"How bad?" Connor asked.

"Well, the bike was bent in half, and the boy appeared to be dying. Two minutes later, he's fine."

"How is that possible?"

"Good question," she answered.

"And the same guy helped the kid too?"

"Yes. And that's not even the strange part."

Connor leaned closer. "I can't wait for this."

"While he's dying—the boy, I mean—he sees a dead brother he never knew he had, and then this mystery man pulls him back from heaven."

"A dead brother, wait . . . what?"

"It's a long story, Con. The headline is the kid claims he was dying and a man brought him back to life."

"And you're certain it's the same guy helping both people?"

"It sure looks like it," she said. "I showed the boy a sketch of the man who helped the blind guy."

"And?"

"Bingo was his name-o."

Connor appeared stunned, prompting Brooklyn to say, "How do you like them apples?"

He grimaced, "Not again with the apples."

"Am I saying it too much?"

He replied, "Perhaps a smidge."

After pausing, Connor said, "Anyway. How is this not a front-page story?"

Brooklyn shot him a skeptical look.

"I'm serious! Mystery man performs two—"

"Don't say it. Don't you dare say—"

"Miracles," Connor uttered, against her wishes.

"Because miracles don't exist, Connor, and I can't claim they do in the Sunday *Boston Globe*."

There was a long pause between them.

"So," Connor finally said, "the man claiming he's God . . ."

"Is nuts," she snapped back. "Come on. Join me in the real world."

"Nuts? Right. 'Cause all of us religious types are nuts."

"I never said that."

Connor abruptly got up from the table and went to the laundry room. Brooklyn followed. He took out a pile of recently dried clothes and tossed them onto a small table next to the dryer. "I love it when they're still warm," he said.

"Don't do that," she replied.

"Fold laundry?" he answered sarcastically.

"Play the victim." She took a towel from his hand.

"Nobody's playing anything, Brooke."

"Right. I say there's no such thing as miracles and that this looney tune can't be God, and you immediately shut down."

He grabbed another armful of clothes from the dryer, then slammed it shut. He opened his mouth as if to say something but instead walked out of the room.

"Wait!" Brooklyn called after him.

He kept walking away.

"You made me a promise the day we got engaged," she said.

He turned to face her. "What promise?"

"That we weren't going to be one of those couples that slams things and walks away angry. We talk things out, especially when it's hard, remember?"

He exhaled slowly. "Yeah. I remember." He set the pile of laundry down on the sofa. "I love you, babe, you know I do. And I understand why church isn't your thing and I understand the anger, having your mother leave you at the hospital that way—"

"She's not my mother, don't you dare call her that! Biological mother at best, NOT my mother."

"Biological mother, then," Connor said, correcting himself. "Her leaving right after you were born was hurtful."

"She abandoned me, Connor. Abandoned. Not *left*. Words matter."

"Alright," he said, "abandoned."

"But?" Brooklyn pressed.

"But . . . It led you to a pair of wonderful parents who adopted you and loved you and an amazing life and . . ." His voice trailed off.

"Say the rest, Connor. I know something has been stuck in your throat for years. I can't stand the *thinking* without the *saying*."

He took the towel she was still carrying, put it down on the pile, and took her hand. "Alright. I will. We don't know what was going on with your biological mother when she got pregnant with you. It's safe to assume something difficult and—"

She shoved his hand away. "So if things were tough in your life, you would have left Evi at the hospital when she was born?"

"Of course not," he said. "My point is, if she couldn't care for you or didn't want a baby, she had another option."

"So, I should thank her for carrying me to term, then dumping me?"

"No," he said. "I understand that's a bridge too far, but maybe . . ."

She waited. She'd asked for him to be honest. Maybe she needed to practice receiving it. "It's okay," she said. "Just say it."

He rested his hand on her shoulder. "Maybe not hate her so much."

She stared at him. He had a point, actually. She'd never met the woman who brought her into this world and then left her at the hospital like an overdue library book. She'd carried around that resentment like a stone in her shoe.

She sighed and gave Connor a look that said *I'm sorry* without the need for words. Her silence was her surrender.

"I love you, Brooke."

"And I adore you, Con." She put her hand on top of his. "I love my parents so much."

"I know you do," he replied.

"And the life they gave me . . ."

"Was fantastic," he said.

Brooklyn squeezed his hand. "Still . . . It would have been nice to have siblings." She couldn't remember ever saying that out loud before.

"They never considered adopting more children?" he asked.

"One and done," she answered.

Connor smirked. "It's obvious you were such an awful child, you scared them from having others."

She snatched a towel from the laundry pile and swatted him playfully. "You are such a jerk."

When their laughter faded, he said, "Kidding aside, which would you have wanted, a brother or sister?"

"Either would be great but, truthfully, a sister."

"Older or younger?"

"Younger," she replied. "A little sis I could teach things to and pal around with."

Connor smiled warmly. "You would have been a great big sister."

Leaving the laundry aside, the two of them returned to the swing on the porch. "Can we get back to shop talk for a minute?" he asked as they sat down together.

"Sure."

"Whatever is going on in Boston, Brooke, you have a blind man who can now see and a child walking away from a horrendous crash. Miracle or not, those are compelling stories."

She thought for a moment. "I know. But what do I do about this mystery man who appears to heal people?"

Connor took her hand again. "Find him. Talk to him. If he's a fraud, expose him. And if he changes water into wine . . . front page story."

She chuckled and snuggled up next to him. This swing and the moments they shared on it were some of the best of their marriage. "You always find a way to make me laugh."

He put his arm around her. "I just realized something," he said.

"What?"

"There must be a million people living in Boston. Good luck finding him."

She pulled back to see his face. "Actually, I don't need luck. The kid on the bike got the name of the business he works for."

"Really? What is it?"

"Hang on." She ran back into the house and retrieved her notepad. "I wrote it down," she said, turning the pages quickly. "Here it is. 'The Carpenter's Son.'"

Connor looked like he'd swallowed a bug. "What did you say?"

"The Carpenter's Son. Why? Does that mean something to you?"

"To me? No. To the world, yeah."

She sat down next to him again. "I don't understand."

He paused. "You said this guy claimed to be God?"

"Yes, God or technically Jesus, at least to the blind man. Why?"

"I keep forgetting you never went to church and learned this stuff," he replied.

She bristled. "What stuff?"

He answered, "Jesus was born of Mary, but his—I guess you could say 'adoptive father'—his name was Joseph."

"So?"

"Joseph was a carpenter, Brooke. That made his son, Jesus . . ."

Brooklyn finished the sentence. "The carpenter's son."

She looked down as the hair on her arm started to rise.

"Did you just get chills, oh woman of little faith?" Connor joked.

Brooklyn rubbed the hair back down. "I'm cold. That's all."

Connor wrapped his arm around her. "Whatever you say."

CHAPTER 17
Tishomingo

Edward came into the house to find Gabriel putting away dishes.

"You missed dinner, my friend."

Edward replied, "Thank you, I'm not hungry."

Piper entered the room holding a small stack of mail.

"Dad, do you know an Emily Johnson?"

"Yes, I just finished a job at her house. Why?"

She held up a sealed envelope that looked the size of a greeting card, "Because she sent this, with a note on the front that you should give it to Edward."

"Me?" Edward asked.

Piper handed it to him and he opened it.

"What is it?" Gabriel asked.

"A thank you card with money."

Edward saw both Piper and Gabriel were waiting with curiosity, so he read it aloud.

Dear Edward, thanks to you I found my Nana's pin. Please take this gift and do something fun with it. Sincerely, Emily.

Piper tried to peek into his hand, "How much you get?"

He held up two hundred-dollar bills.

"Wow, you're rich," Gabriel said.

Edward folded the money and tucked it into the front pocket of his jeans.

"I can use this later."

"Planning to hit the bars tonight?" Piper joked.

"Funny you should mention that," he answered.

"What?" Piper asked. "Do you need something?"

"Yes. A ride to jail."

"Why?" she asked.

"I'll explain on the way."

Whether it was luck or design, Piper caught every red light on her way to the Nashua Street Jail in Boston, allowing her and Edward time to chat. "Do you want to tell me why I'm taking you to jail?" she asked.

"Remember that story I told you about all the images of me holding a lamb?"

"*You* holding it?" Piper replied.

"Ah, that's right. You still don't believe I'm the Son of God."

"It's a lot to believe, Edward."

"Understood. But do you remember what I said?"

"Yes," she answered. "You said they only told half the story because a true shepherd is a tough guy who chases off the wolves."

"That's correct. And sometimes the shepherd has to go right into the wolf's den to save the sheep."

"And that's jail?" she asked.

"Today it is, yes."

"Sounds risky."

"Matthew 18:12," he said.

Piper replied, "Since I work in an insurance office and I don't teach Bible study, do you want to translate that for me, pal?"

Edward looked over at her, smiling. "You called me pal."

"So? Is that an insult for a deity such as yourself?"

He laughed. "Heavens, no. I want you to consider me your friend."

"Okay," she said. "You've got it. Now . . . the Bible verse you just quoted?"

Edward answered, "Short version. If you have a hundred sheep and even one gets lost, you go after it."

"And the sheep are in jail?"

He nodded. "And on the streets and in homes and offices and even churches." He looked out his window. "Hey, pull over!"

She checked her mirrors, then eased the Jeep over to the curb, parking in front of a large brick building with a sign reading *Church of the Advent*.

"We're only in Back Bay, Edward. And that's not a jail. It's a house of worship."

"I'm aware," he answered. "We'll call it a bonus stop."

As she got out of the vehicle, her attention turned upward, taking in the deep blue sky and the majestic steeple reaching for the clouds. "Looks like a postcard," she said. Then she glanced at the darkened windows. "I don't think they're open."

"I'm not going in," he replied. He ran his hand along a black wrought iron bench with wooden slats and looked across to a small park with an ornate fountain surrounded by trees ablaze in color.

Piper followed his gaze. *Another postcard view.*

"I don't suppose you have a pillow or blanket in the trunk?" he asked.

"I don't think so, but let me look." She walked around the back of the Jeep and opened the hatch. "Would an old jacket do the trick?" She removed a blue winter coat and handed it to him. "It belonged to Paul. I meant to donate it to Goodwill but couldn't bear to part with it."

He smiled at her. "Perfect. Thank you." Then he went back to the bench, lay down as if he were on a bed, and put the jacket over him like a blanket.

"You suddenly need a nap?"

"Something like that," he replied.

"What about saving the sheep in jail?"

"I will," Edward said.

"And how will you get there, smarty pants?"

Edward grinned. "Some nice policemen are going to give me a ride."

Piper stood there, dumbfounded.

"You can go," he said. "Pick me up at the jail in the morning."

She shook her head. "Can I tell you something?"

"Sure."

"You were strange the day I met you, and you haven't gotten less so in the days since."

Edward nodded in agreement. "I get that a lot."

Piper rolled her eyes. "I'll see you at the jail first light."

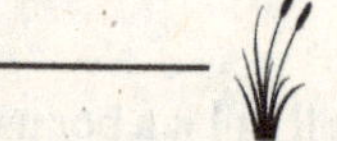

Newsweek magazine once listed the 400 richest neighborhoods in America, and Back Bay, where Edward was now resting, was in the Top 10. Nobody living there could be described as poor.

Edward hadn't been lying there for two minutes when a car slowed down and someone shouted, "You can't sleep here!"

A man walking a dog on the other side of the road also took notice of Edward's shadowy figure on the bench. "We have homeless shelters for that!" he called. When he circled back a few minutes later, he said, "I'm calling the cops."

Rich neighborhoods don't typically wait long once the 9-1-1 call goes out. In Edward's case, no fewer than three people in Back Bay called the police to complain, one describing him as *the bum sleeping outside our church.*

Two patrol cars arrived, and their flashing red lights caught the attention of the church pastor, Father Michael Reilly, who came out of the rectory to survey the ruckus. "What's this, now?" he asked the police.

"Up, please," an officer said.

Edward sat up as instructed.

"Having a rough day?" the priest asked.

"I just wanted to rest a moment on your bench, padre."

Father Reilly looked to the officers. "It's too cold for him to be out here."

Edward held up the large blue coat Piper had given him. "I'm fine with this."

The priest bent forward and said, "Why don't you let these nice officers take you to a warm shelter?"

When Edward didn't respond, an officer flashed the light in his face. "You can't sleep here."

Edward nodded. "If sleeping is the issue, I'm fine to just sit here on the bench awhile. How about that? I promise I won't stay long. May I just sit?"

The officers looked at each other, then at the pastor.

"It is a bench," Edward observed. "Benches are made for sitting. I mean, that's why it's here, right?"

The lone female cop looked at the pastor and said, "Technically, he's not doing anything wrong, but . . . it's your call, Father."

Without hesitation, Father Reilly scrunched up his face as if he smelled rubbish, then shook his head no.

A different officer touched Edward's elbow. "Get up or we'll help you up."

Across the street a crowd had gathered. Despite there being a thousand channels on TV, it would seem the police rousting a man who wasn't doing anything wrong was this evening's entertainment.

As Edward rose to his feet, he looked at the priest and said, "Matthew 25:44."

Reilly's expression indicated he wasn't certain what passage from the Bible this interloper had just referenced. He glanced across the street and called out, "Everything is fine. Go home now."

As the onlookers turned to go, Edward said to the priest, "Your flock?"

Father Reilly turned his face away.

"We have to frisk you." A large policeman, who looked like he could play in the NFL, ran his hands along Edward's pockets, chest, and legs, finding nothing but the two hundred-dollar bills folded in the front pocket. "He's clean. No ID. Just some cash."

The female officer asked in a welcoming tone, "What's your name, friend?"

"You can call me Edward."

"If I ask you a question, Edward, can you be truthful?"

"Completely."

"Have you ever been arrested before?" she asked.

"Yes. A long time ago."

"What did you do?"

"It's a long story."

She paused. "And were you punished for it, Edward?"

He looked down at his hands and wrists. "You could say that."

"And are you in trouble now?" she asked.

"No, officer. Quite the opposite."

She eyed him with compassion. "Well, you seem like a decent guy, Edward, but here's the problem. I can't take you to the shelter until I know who you are. You'll have to come to the jail until we sort you out."

"That's fine. Thank you. And thank you for being kind to me."

As they placed Edward in the back of the squad car, Father Reilly said to no one in particular, "It's for the best. Can't have him freezing out here."

If the priest hoped they would assuage his guilt, the officers did not oblige, looking away instead.

The Nashua Street jail had two options for housing criminals: individual cells for the inmates staying awhile, and a large holding area for short-term guests.

Tonight was a slow one, with only three occupants: a man arrested for a DWI, a domestic violence call, and a young woman dressed provocatively. All three paid little mind to the man with the long brown hair and beard who was being placed in the large cell with them.

When the guard locked the cell door behind him, Edward asked, "Is Sergeant Trask working tonight?"

"Should be here shortly." The guard then took a seat behind a large desk. He'd spend half the night on sports-betting websites and drinking bad coffee, trying to stay awake and make sure the miscreants behaved.

The woman in the cell, more out of her clothes than in, was Lexi Hall, a high-paid escort. Her website advertised Lexi at 200 dollars per hour for *companionship* and there was no shortage of lonely men looking for that. Unfortunately for her, an undercover cop answered the ad, and for the fourth time in a year, she was behind bars like an animal.

There is a silent shame one experiences when put in a cage, and Lexi was feeling it right now. She was so lost in thought she hadn't noticed

Edward pulling a chair right up next to her. "Back up, unless you want a boot to the face," she said.

"You're wearing sneakers," he said in a hushed voice.

Lexi looked down at her feet to see Edward was right. "What do you want?" she barked.

"Just to talk, Alexandria."

Lexi stared at him, her eyes wide. Nobody had called her by her given name since she was a little girl in Herkimer, New York. She stared at him, lost for words.

"It's alright," he began. "I came here tonight just for you."

She'd heard that line before. Plenty of times. "Just for me, huh?"

Edward nodded. "Well, technically I'm here for you and Sergeant Trask when he gets here. But let's start with you."

"I don't know you, man, so move along."

He replied in a gentle voice. "You sell your body to strangers for money."

Lexi gave Edward a hard stare, answering, "A girl's gotta eat, right?"

"She does. But not this way. There was a time when you loved art history. You studied it at college."

"How do you know that?" she asked.

"It was a very nice community college . . . the one with all the C's," Edward said.

"Yes," she responded. "H-CCC. Herkimer County Community College."

Edward continued, "But you met a boy and quit school, and then he met someone else. How am I doing so far?"

"How do you know all this?" Lexi asked a second time.

"We'll get to that part later," Edward replied. "You moved away, eventually landing in Boston. Where you answered an advertisement for modeling."

"Yes," she answered.

"But it wasn't really modeling. It was . . ."

"Escorting," she said.

Edward looked around the police holding cell, then back to her. "And how is that going for you?"

"Up until tonight, pretty good," she snapped back.

Edward frowned., saying, "Alexandria Frances Flynn. You are so much more than this. You know that, don't you?"

Immediately, her eyes filled with tears. Her mother was the only person on the planet who had ever called Lexi by her full name, and it wasn't when she was in trouble. It was when she did something well. That's when she would hear it loud and proud from her mom.

Alexandria Frances Flynn, did you get an A on your math test?

Alexandria Frances Flynn, did you make dinner all by yourself?

If her mother were still alive, one thing was for sure: She wouldn't be in the profession she was in.

She could hear her mother now.

You're so much more than this, Alexandria Frances.

What has become of you, Alexandria Frances?

Don't break my heart, Alexandria Frances.

Tears started falling from her eyes. She hated showing weakness, but she couldn't stop them. Some tears refused to obey.

Edward took both her hands in his. "God loves you more than you could ever know, and he's not the only one thinking of you every day."

Lexi looked at his kind face. "Who would care about me?"

"Your sister, Amy."

The simple mention of her name brought back a flood of happy memories. It had been years since she'd seen her twin sister. After their mother died, Amy and Lexi both scattered like leaves. "I haven't seen Amy in . . ."

"Ten years," Edward said.

"Is she still—"

"Alive?" he said. "Oh, heavens, yes. She lives in Tishomingo, Oklahoma. It's near . . . um . . . well. I guess it's not near anything."

She glanced down at her clothes, suddenly wishing she could cover herself up. "What does she, um . . . do?"

He paused, then said, "She married a great guy named Fred, and they opened a diner. When that went well, they opened a restaurant."

"She's successful, then," Lexi said, feeling a mixture of pride and envy.

"Successful, yes," Edward said, "but not happy."

Lexi sniffed back her tears. "Really? Why not?"

He squeezed her hands. "Because she misses her sister."

Lexi pictured them as little girls again, laughing and playing without a care in the world. If only she could see her again. But with all the trouble she was in, that wasn't likely.

Edward said, "I'll tell you a secret not even her husband or kids know."

Lexi's face lit up. "Wait. Amy has kids?"

"Two boys. Buck and Huck."

She burst out laughing. "BUCK AND HUCK? What great names."

When her laughter subsided, Edward said, "Anyway, the secret I was going to share."

Lexi leaned in. "Go on."

"When she prays at night, after asking God to look after her family, she prays for you, Alexandria. She prays you are alive and okay and will come home to her someday."

"Really?" she asked. It seemed too good to be true.

"It's true," he said. "Every single night. Same prayer."

Lexi started crying again, picturing her twin sister with two little boys.

Edward said, "Did you know that Tishomingo is a two-hour drive from Dallas?"

"What?"

"Dallas, Texas. Lots of colleges there. And several of those schools have art programs, like the one you were in at . . ."

"Herkimer," she said. "It's a nothing town in upstate New York."

Edward looked at her with more kindness than she'd ever seen in any man's eyes. "It can't be nothing if it produced you and Amy."

She glanced down again at the clothes she was wearing and said, "I appreciate what you're telling me, but . . ."

He spoke gently. "You don't think Amy would welcome you if she knew how you ended up? What you do for money?"

Lexi let go of his hands and looked away.

"You're wrong, Alexandria. Wrong by a million prayers. All Amy wants is her sister back."

"So, I just pack up my stuff and run to Tisha . . .?"

"Mingo," he said. "Tishomingo. Yes, that's exactly what you do. You leave here and go home and pack a bag. You look up the Falcon's Nest restaurant in Tishomingo, Oklahoma, and call your sister."

"You make it sound simple."

"The right choice often is."

She patted her pockets and said, "They took all my money. Even if I wanted to go, I couldn't get there."

Edward reached into his pocket. "I knew I brought this for a reason." He pulled out the two hundred-dollar bills. "This will pay for a one-way bus ticket to Dallas and some extra for meals along the way." He placed the cash in her hand.

She looked down at the money. "Who are you and why are you doing this?"

Edward raised her chin. "Look at me, Alexandria."

She did, his kind brown eyes locking with hers.

"Who I am and why I'm doing this is the same answer," he said. Then he whispered, "I'm the one your sister has been praying to, asking me to find you and get you home.

Lexi considered his words. "But, that would make you—"

"Jesus," he said. "Nice to meet you."

Lexi looked around the cell and laughed. "All due respect, I don't think Jesus would be in a place like this, talking to a woman like me."

"Oh, I'd say this is exactly where I need to be."

Lexi just shook her head in disbelief.

Edward grinned. "Someday you'll have to meet my friend Mary Magdalene. She's a saint, highly misunderstood. You'd like her."

Lexi looked back down at the money, closing it tight in her fist.

Edward said, "Ready to go home?"

Lexi couldn't explain why, but a rush of love overtook her, changing her heart. In that instant, she didn't feel like Lexi the prostitute anymore. She was Alexandria, and everything felt different.

She hugged Edward. "Bless you. But they won't just let me leave."

Just then a door on the far wall opened, and an older man in uniform holding a clipboard came in.

Edward said to Lexi, "Give me a moment."

"What have we here?" the man bellowed. His belly spilled over his thick black leather belt as he strolled toward the cell. "My name is—"

"Sergeant Theodore Trask," Edward interrupted. "Your friends call you Teddy."

Trask eyeballed the man with untamed brown hair and beard and joked, "Are we doing a production of Godspell that I don't know about?"

Edward replied, "You have no idea how close you are on that one, Sergeant. Can we chat?"

Trask approached the bars, the clipboard still in hand. Edward met him on the other side.

"You must be Edward, the man on the bench with no ID."

"That's me. And that's Alexandria. I need to talk to you about her."

Trask said, "Why don't we chew the food on our own plates first."

"I'm not sure what that means, but I'd like to make a trade."

The officer quipped, "Since I'm the one on this side of the bars, I'm not sure you're in a position to bargain, *Edward with no ID*."

"You like stories?" Edward asked.

The officer let out a deep breath. "Sure."

"I'm going to tell you a story, and you tell me if it rings true."

Trask folded his arms.

"When you were twelve years old, living in Altoona, Pennsylvania, some friends dared you to steal a baseball bat from a place called *Andy's Sporting Goods*."

Trask's face gave away that it was the truth.

"You got caught and the manager called the police, and unfortunately, a beat cop named Kowalski showed up. How am I doing so far?"

"How do you know this?" Trask hissed through the bars.

Edward said, "He gave you three choices: jail, call your parents, or penance."

Trask's expression went hard. "That's right."

Edward continued, "You didn't want jail or your dad to find out, so you chose penance."

"I did."

"Only you thought penance was scrubbing toilets at the store or mowing a lawn. But it wasn't."

"No," Trask said flatly.

"What did he do to you?" Edward asked.

Trask hesitated, then said, "Kowalski broke the middle finger on my right hand as a reminder not to touch things that aren't mine."

Edward nodded. "You hid the injury from your parents, and it never healed right."

Trask looked down at his right hand and winced when he moved the finger.

"Now, with arthritis, that hand is all but useless," Edward said.

"It's the reason I'm on desk duty," Trask said.

"And the reason you've delayed retiring."

Trask sighed. "I can't fish with it. I used to love skiing, but I can't grip the poles."

Edward said, "You can't even hold your wife's hand properly when you walk together, Teddy."

Trask kept staring at his swollen fingers.

"All that ends tonight," Edward said. "Right now."

Trask looked up. "What do you mean?"

Edward pointed over to Lexi. "I spoke with Alexandria, and if you let her go, no charges, you'll never see her again."

Trask looked at the clipboard and said, "This ain't her first rodeo, Edward, she's a—"

"Changed woman," Edward said. "Look in my eyes and know it's true."

Trask did, then said, "Even so, it's a solid bust, if I look the other way—"

"Teddy," Edward interrupted. "You didn't let me finish."

Trask smiled slightly. "Excuse me. Continue."

"I told you I wanted to make a trade," Edward said.

"If this is a bribe of some sort . . ."

"No, Teddy. A gift. One good deed for another."

Trask looked over at the other officer on duty and saw he was on his smartphone, oblivious to this conversation.

"Let me ask one question," Edward said. "The arthritis. Do you want to be healed?"

Trask squeezed his hands as best he could, his face wincing with pain. "Yes," he answered.

"Give me your hands," Edward said.

Trask paused, looked at Edward's face, and said, "I don't know about this." Corrections officers were taught on day one: never, ever to reach into the cell.

Edward said, "Trust me, Teddy."

In that instant, Trask dropped the clipboard to the stone floor, the noise making the officer at the desk jump from his seat. He saw his sergeant reaching with both hands between the bars toward one of the inmates.

"Whoa, hey, stop!"

Edward took a firm grip on both of Trask's hands. The sergeant would later tell his wife it felt like warm lava was flowing into them.

The desk officer pulled his revolver and pointed it at Edward.

"Let go of him!" he shouted, his hands shaking as he held his gun.

With that, Edward released Trask's hands. Instantly the pain was gone. He shook both hands and started laughing. He turned to the other officer, who was still pointing his gun, and said, "Put that away before you hurt someone."

The desk clerk, shaking and confused, holstered the weapon.

Trask looked through the bars.

Who are you?

He could swear he heard a voice in his head answer.

You know.

He bent down and retrieved his clipboard from the floor. Then he took a pen from his front shirt pocket and ran a bold red line through both Alexandria's and Edward's names.

"Open it up and let them go," Trask instructed.

The desk officer hesitated.

Trask said, "It's my call. Void the arrests. Set them free."

The cell door was opened wide.

Lexi hugged Edward and was so overcome with emotion that she could only leave in tears.

"Before I go," Edward said, "can I ask two small favors, Teddy?"

The sergeant looked down at his healed hands and responded, "Name it."

"I need paper, a pen, and an envelope." Once he had them in hand, he jotted out a short note, sealed the envelope, and gave it back to Teddy.

"The second favor?" the officer asked.

"I'd like to close my eyes a little while to rest." Edward pointed to an empty bed in the cell.

"Most people want to race outta here, but hey, knock yourself out." As Trask went to leave the holding area, he turned to Edward and said, "Why do I get the feeling you orchestrated all of this tonight, from the church bench to this moment?"

Edward answered, "Blessed are the police officers who let me rest."

Trask laughed. "Go ahead. Nap away."

As Edward slept, Lexi ran back to her apartment in Sudbury just long enough to pack a bag and leave a note for her roommates. If thrift in writing was an Olympic sport, she would have scored gold. It simply read, *I'm outta here. Keep or sell my things as recompense for my breaking the lease. I'm going home, Alexandria*

Just 19 words to change a life.

Edward rose with the morning sun and exited the jail just as the city was waking. He smiled when he saw Piper parked outside, asleep behind the wheel. She had never gone home, waiting loyally all night.

At the same moment, a few miles away on a Greyhound bus bound for Dallas, Alexandria settled into her seat and heard music playing across the aisle. It was a country song she'd never heard before, echoing from a small portable radio resting on a seat next to a stranger.

"Excuse me, sir?" she asked. "Who is that singing?"

The man in cowboy boots and Stetson hat raised the brim and answered in a Texas drawl, "Zach Bryan."

"It's pretty," she said. "What's it about?"

The cowboy paused thoughtfully and said, "I guess you could say it's about going home."

The bus started to move, and Alexandria looked out the window. "Tishomingo," she said.

"That's right," the cowboy called over.

"What's right?"

He pointed to the radio. "Tishomingo. That's the name of the song."

"You're kidding me," she said.

The cowboy replied, "Hand to God."

Alexandria turned away and saw her reflection in the bus window. At that moment, she realized the *Lexi* she knew was gone. Somehow the stranger in a jail cell had washed her sins away.

Alexandria began to cry tears of joy.

The cowboy took off his hat and asked with concern, "You alright, miss?"

Alexandria answered, "Yes, sir. Like that cowboy in your song, I'm going home."

CHAPTER 18

Stopping the Bullets

Piper was yawning as she drove Edward home from jail.

"Didn't get much sleep?" he asked.

"This front seat is no substitute for my bed," she said.

"Well, thank you for waiting."

Edward reached out and typed in *117 Chestnut Street, Wakefield* onto the screen of Piper's GPS.

"Are we making a pit stop?" she asked.

"More of a drop-off."

"Anyone I know?"

"Not yet," he replied.

The ride to this mystery destination was quiet, so Piper, looking to fill the void, asked, "At the jail, you helped the people you wanted to help?"

"One healed. One home."

"You healed someone?" Piper asked. "Just now at the jail?"

"His hands," Edward answered.

"So, if I turned the car around and went back, some guy would tell me that you fixed his hands?"

"He would."

Piper lingered on what he was saying, then smiled. "Hey, Edward, remember when I said that I don't believe you are who you say you are?"

"Yes." He paused, then said, "It's getting harder to ignore the truth?"

Piper looked at him, then shifted her eyes back to the road. "Something like that."

Piper felt herself wanting to believe Edward was the Son of God, the "Carpenter's Son." *How amazing would it be to have him living above my garage. All of this feels crazy and wonderful at the same time.*

Edward said, "Can I ask you a question?"

"Sure."

"Why do you work a job you don't enjoy?"

"That question seems kind of random," she answered.

Edward said, "I'm curious."

Piper took a deep breath. "It just happened that way."

"And what would Paul say if he were here?"

"About?"

"You being at a job you hate."

Piper sighed. "He'd be upset with me for settling."

The GPS announced they were two miles away.

"You think I can do better?" she asked sincerely.

"I think you can be whatever you want, Piper. And Paul would help you."

Paul? How would Paul play a role in my life now? He can't drop a line like that and not explain himself.

"Help me? How?"

Edward turned in the seat to face her now. "When people move on from this world, they never completely go. They find a way to nudge you, to remind you of them."

"Like a song on the radio, that kind of thing?" she asked.

"Lots of ways," Edward said. "A dream, for example."

Piper immediately thought of a recurring dream she'd had of her brother. They were kids in elementary school with long hallways and a checkered floor that reminded her of a chessboard.

He was watching her closely. "Something you'd like to share?"

She paused, then said, "Yeah, actually. I've had one about Paul. Lots of times. In the dream, we're young, like seven and nine. Paul takes me by the hand and leads me to the last classroom at the end of this long hallway. The kindergarten room. But it's empty. No kids anywhere. And then Paul walks over to the blackboard and writes my name in big letters in white chalk: Miss Piper Matthews."

"What happens next?" he asked.

"Suddenly, Paul is gone and I'm all grown up, standing at the front of the classroom facing the empty chairs."

ARRIVED, the GPS announced.

She pulled the car to the curb and parked. Then she turned to face Edward. "That's where it ends. And I have no idea what it means."

"What did you want to be when you were little?" he asked.

Instantly, she remembered placing dolls and stuffed animals in rows so she could read to them. "A teacher," she said. "But that was a long time ago."

"Not so long," Edward replied.

"You said people can use dreams to nudge us?"

"Yes."

"So . . . do you think Paul is trying to tell me I should go back to school to become a teacher?"

"What do you think?"

Piper pondered the thought and grinned. Then her mind turned to the daunting task of returning to college at her age and starting over. All the work, the cost.

Edward said, "Close your eyes and see it."

Piper just stared.

"Trust me," he urged.

Piper closed her eyes and imagined herself in college, graduating, and standing in front of a gaggle of five-year-olds. One of them placed an apple on her desk.

It felt real. It *was* real.

"Now open your eyes," Edward said. "And make it so."

As he opened the Jeep door to leave, Piper thanked him.

"For what?" he asked.

"For taking me to Gloucester to meet Paul's friend Luke. For helping my father. For helping me."

Edward squeezed her hand. "You are very special to me."

As her mind wandered, a smile crossed her lips.

"Anything you want to share?" Edward asked.

Sure, she thought. *Why not?* "Just thinking about Luke, actually. He's texted me a couple of times. I like him."

Edward smiled like a Cheshire cat.

"And what are you grinning about?"

"Just thinking of how many great schools in Gloucester need kindergarten teachers."

"Stop," she said, blushing. "I'm not becoming a teacher and moving to Gloucester to be with a man I just met."

Edward opened the car door to exit and said, "You know what they say."

"No," she replied. "What do *they* say, Edward?"

"Announcing your plans is the best way to hear God laugh," he answered, laughing loudly.

As Piper smiled, Edward said, "See you in a couple days."

"Wait—what? Where are you going? Who lives here?"

Edward ignored the questions, saying instead, "When I return, we're going to the fair."

"The fair?" she said. "Like with rides and cotton candy?"

Edward leaned into the open passenger-side window, and said, "Saturday night. Seven o'clock sharp. Bring your dad to the Fall River Festival." He paused. "You should invite Luke. You never know what might happen on the Ferris wheel." With that, he stepped back onto the sidewalk.

Piper felt a pang of sadness, watching Edward walk away. Two weeks ago, she wanted him gone, and now she found herself missing him.

Who is this man? Can he be who he claims to be?

The front door of the house was white with a brass knocker that looked like a lion's head. Edward was just about to use it when the door flung open.

"Hello, Brooklyn," he said, extending his hand. "I hear you've been looking for me."

She stood motionless, mouth open. Here was the spitting image of the sketch Stewart had shown her, the same one the boy on the bike also recognized.

Evi and Connor joined her in the doorway. "Who is it, Mommy?"

Edward looked down at her and smiled. "You can call me Edward, Evi." Then he looked again at Brooklyn. "But we both know that's not my real name."

Brooklyn finally found her words. "What is your real name?"

"Yeshua. Rabbi. I answer to so many."

Connor leaned toward Brooklyn and whispered, "Is this?"

"Yes," Brooklyn replied.

"Who touched the people, and—ya know?"

Edward laughed. "Healed them. Yes. I'm that guy. Nice to meet you, Connor."

Connor pumped Edward's hand. "Won't you come in? I'm sure my wife has a million questions."

They led him to the living room, where the embers in the fireplace glowed red.

"You'll need more wood for that," Edward said.

Connor grabbed a piece of split oak from a metal basket and tossed it on the fire. "Thank you, yes."

Brooklyn motioned for Edward to take a seat. "Just so we're clear. You're the man who touched that boy on the bike, Jayden, and helped Stew with his eyesight?"

"I am," Edward replied. "And rather than *bury the lede*, as you reporters say, I will answer the question you want to ask but are afraid to."

Connor interrupted. "My wife isn't afraid of anything, sir."

Brooklyn touched her husband's shoulder. "It's alright, hon, I can handle this." The two of them sat together on the sofa while Evi warmed herself by the fire.

Edward said, "Go ahead and ask me."

Brooklyn paused, staring at his face. "Who are you? Really?"

Edward met her eyes. "I'm Jesus, the Son of God. Or, God, the Messiah, take your pick."

Connor said to their daughter, "Evi, why don't you go play in your room?"

"He's God?" Evi asked.

Before Edward could answer, Connor said more forcefully, "EVI, room, please."

"Can I use my iPad?" she asked.

"Sure," Brooklyn answered, her mind still reeling from Edward's ridiculous statement.

The Son of God? Messiah? Who says that? Crazy people, that's who.

Edward said to Connor, "Nice catch, by the way, the apple tree."

Connor paused, then replied, "Oh, at the orchard, catching Evi when she fell, yes. Thanks. I did play a little football in college—"

"*Connor*, really?" Brooklyn barked.

"Sorry, babe," he answered with a chuckle.

Brooklyn narrowed her eyes at Edward. "Why are you here?"

"That's a complicated question," he said. "Do you mean, on earth or at your house?"

She threw her hands in the air. "Both. Either."

"Well, I'm here because the boy, Jayden, told you how to find me. I thought I'd save you the trouble."

"You talked to Jayden?" she asked.

"No."

"But you know what he told us?"

"Yes."

"How?" she demanded.

Edward shrugged. "God knows everything."

Brooklyn recoiled at the response. "Of course, and you're God, so . . ." She snapped her finger. "Have you ever considered opening a psychic hotline? You could make a killing, charge five bucks a minute, since you know everything."

"Brooklyn, stop!" Connor said. "There's no need to be disrespectful."

"Brooklyn, STOP?" she sniped back. "Are you kidding me right now, Con! Look at him. He's just a man. Flesh and blood. No offense, Joshua."

"It's Yeshua, but none taken," Edward replied. "Although that was kind of the point of me coming, then and now."

"What was?" she asked.

"Flesh and blood. Becoming man to show you the way."

"And dying for our sins," Connor added.

"That's right," Edward said.

Brooklyn stared at both men, speechless. Her husband was not helping debunk this nonsense.

He's encouraging it.

"You don't believe?" Edward asked her.

"No, I don't."

"Despite what you've seen?"

"Correct."

"Yet you're still searching for answers?"

"I am."

Edward said, "Why don't we do this? You're a reporter with questions, right?"

"That's right."

"You take today and ask me anything you want," he said.

"And then?" Brooklyn asked.

"Then tomorrow, you come with me on a short trip so I can show you something."

She looked at her husband, uncertain how to respond to this offer.

"Give me two days," Edward said, "and I'll change your mind."

"About?"

"Me. Heaven, miracles, angels, the whole boatful."

Brooklyn said, "Don't you mean basketful?"

"No. I like boats."

Connor said, "Because you're a fisher of men, right?"

"Very good, Connor," he said with a wink.

"Okay, okay, enough, you two," Brooklyn blurted.

Edward folded his hands in his lap and leaned forward in his seat. "So, what do you say?"

Connor eyed her with a *What have you got to lose?* face.

Brooklyn mirrored Edward in his forward lean. "Understanding, upfront, that I don't believe you are the Son of God. If I agree to this, how should I refer to you? God? Jesus? Edward?"

"What you call me doesn't matter. What you believe in your heart does."

Connor spoke up. "I have to ask, though, if you're God, why choose the name Edward?"

"My full name is Edward Manuel. E, for short."

"Ah!" Connor tapped his nose. "E Manuel, very clever."

Brooklyn glared at both men. "Let me state for the record, that you two becoming fast friends is starting to annoy me."

Smiling, Edward turned his attention back to Brooklyn. "So? What do you say?"

"Okay. Fine, you've got a deal."

"Good," he replied. "So. Today for you, tomorrow for me."

Brooklyn asked, "Are you a fan of Jonathan Larson?"

"Who?"

"The Broadway composer. You just quoted him." When Edward didn't reply, she said, "I'm not singing it for you."

"Okay." He clapped his hands together once. "Let's get started."

"Don't be so eager," she said. "You're not going to like my questions."

"After my conversation with Job, nothing will surprise me."

She stood. "I don't know what that means, but let's get in the car. You and I are going for a ride."

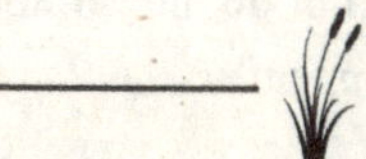

Twenty minutes later, Brooklyn and Edward were at the trauma and cancer wing at Boston Children's Hospital. She intended to unmask his *God charade* on the hospital's sixth floor, where the sickest children clung to life.

The elevator door opened, and the two of them were greeted by an eerie silence.

"Are we allowed to be here?" Edward asked.

She stepped into the hall. "Being a journalist, I have special privileges, and the nurse manager told me we could visit for ten minutes if we didn't disturb anyone." She led Edward to the center of the floor, flanked by rooms on each side.

"You say you're God," she began.

"I am."

"Explain childhood cancer to me." Before Edward could reply, she added, "And while you're at it, explain rape and murder and hurricanes and floods and car crashes that rob children of their parents."

"Is that it?" he asked.

"No," she replied. "Explain the Holocaust, starvation, neglect. And while you're doing all that, enlighten me on why the people on this planet, the ones you created and love so much, keep suffering *WAR, after WAR, after WAR.*"

She stopped and gave Edward a cold, hard look. "If you are who you claim to be, explain how I or anyone else shouldn't view you as nothing more than an absentee landlord who doesn't give a fig if we live or die."

There was a row of chairs along a wall near the nurse's station. "Let's sit together," he said. Once seated, he said in a calm voice, "I could take a year and a day trying to explain my Father's divine plan to you, Brooklyn, but it would be easier to put it to you this way: free will."

"Free will?" she replied with ample snark in her voice. "I give you the Holocaust and you come back with *free will*?"

Edward said, "For my Father's children, you among them, to have free will, free choice in what to do or *not* do, he cannot intervene and stop every bad thing that is going to happen."

"Why not?"

"Two reasons. First, you would not be free. You'd be no different than that copy machine in the corner, performing a task."

Brooklyn glanced over at the copier, then back to Edward. "The second reason?"

"Where would it end? Take Jayden on the bike. I healed him. But you might ask, why not stop him from getting hit by the car in the first place?"

"Right. Why not?"

"So, I should stop a healthy little boy from doing something he loves, riding his bike. Because riding a bike in the street is dangerous, right?" He paused. "Of course it is. As is climbing trees and bouncing on trampolines. Skiing, swimming, sports—we'd have to stop all sports. Is that what you'd have me do to keep children like Jayden safe?"

"Of course not."

Edward continued, "Or maybe, in Jayden's case, I just make it rain. You can't ride your bike in the rain. Of course, that would mean rain every day of that little boy's life, and that would cause the flooding you already mentioned."

There was a certain logic to what he was saying, much as she hated to admit it.

"If God gives you free will," he said, "you must be allowed to make *all* the decisions, good and bad."

"But Jesus," she said—"I mean, Edward. The school shootings? Little children in Connecticut, Texas, Colorado, murdered in their classrooms?"

He looked deep into Brooklyn's eyes. "Do you think for a second it doesn't break the Father's heart to see those children hurt? My heart, to see those families suffer?"

There was silence between them, and then Edward said, "You can only see this one moment in time and place, but the Father sees eternity."

Brooklyn tried to wrap her mind around that concept, to know everything. To see a million miles down the road how things will ultimately turn out. Would she even want that power?

"Brooklyn," he continued, "God loves every person, and the pain they endure, the hardships, difficult as they are in the moment, are but a moment. God knows a place waits for you in heaven where there is no pain, no Holocausts, no slaughter of the innocent."

He took a deep breath. "You want me to stop the bullets? I understand. I'm telling you, if you could see the entire plan God has for each of us, you'd know everything will be okay."

She turned toward him. "How do you expect people to believe that? That, if they just hang in there, all the hardship and hurt of this world . . . that something better is coming?"

"What would you have God do?" he asked. "Send a personal message to eight billion people, a guarantee that there is a heaven waiting?"

"Yes! That's exactly what I want. Send a message that cannot be ignored. SHOW ME. Show us, that this isn't all there is."

Edward slowly pulled up the sleeves of his jacket, revealing nasty wounds on both of his wrists. They weren't bleeding but looked fresh, sore, and tormented. He raised his shirt and showed a jagged wound on his side, as if a spear had pierced his flesh.

"He did, Brooklyn. Two-thousand years ago. God sent his only son to live among his children and show them the truth, the light, and the way."

She stared at the open wounds. "I don't understand what is happening."

"For one moment of your life," he said, "stop doubting and try listening."

He spoke with such authority, yet such tenderness. She'd never heard anyone speak quite like him. "I'll try," she murmured.

He lowered his shirt. "He sent his only son because he loves you. He loves you enough to let his son be nailed to a tree and die for your sins. And then rise again, proving to you that all of this . . ." He raised his arms to his sides, exposing his wrists again. The wounds were gone. "All of this, the cancer and the wars and the heartache, are only temporary, Brooklyn. Eternal life awaits all those who seek it through him."

He gently took her by the hand and said, "Things aren't always as they seem. Come with me."

He led her down the hospital corridor to the ICU and a large glass window. Brooklyn peered into a room and saw two familiar faces: the man and the young girl who were pretending to play the violin outside of Quincy Market. The very couple that Brooklyn ambushed, exposing their fraud.

"I know them," she said.

The father and daughter were next to a hospital bed where a little boy was hooked up to several machines. The child looked very sick.

"That is why they were humiliating themselves in the town square," he said. "He can't work a normal job since his son took ill, and he rarely leaves the boy's side here in the ICU."

Brooklyn felt her throat constrict. "What's wrong with him?"

"He needs a new heart," Edward replied.

The man with the violin, whom she had humiliated only days earlier, looked up and saw her standing with Edward. For reasons she could not comprehend, the worried and exhausted father smiled and waved. Brooklyn thought of another gesture that would have been more appropriate, given how she had treated them, but she managed a half-hearted wave back.

"I didn't know," she said, tears filling her eyes.

"I know," Edward said. "And he knows it too. He's not mad at you."

She wiped away a tear. "He'd have every reason to be."

Edward touched her shoulder. "But he's not. There is only love in his heart."

"His child is dying and there's love in his heart?" Brooklyn asked. "How?"

"Because he knows, from his faith, that no matter what, this isn't how the story ends."

In that instant, Brooklyn admired the man. To have that level of faith in the face of such calamity. Her *so-called* scam artist might be the bravest man on earth.

"Do you know them?" she asked.

Edward nodded. "God knows all his children."

Brooklyn stared at the sick boy. "Can I ask you something?"

"Why don't I just heal him?"

"Yes," she replied. "If you are who you say you are."

"I see we're back to doubting me," he said.

"I'm sorry, I'm just trying to make sense of this."

Edward looked back into the hospital room. "His boy will be healed. But not by me."

Brooklyn was confused.

"He'll be healed by doctors and nurses and all those who have dedicated their lives to helping the sick."

She looked at the medical staff buzzing around with urgency and purpose.

Edward said, "You argued with Connor earlier, telling him there are no miracles."

"I did. How did you know that?"

"What I did for Jayden and Stewart were miracles, but so is this, Brooklyn. Look at them."

She returned her gaze to the doctors and nurses taking care of the sick children.

"These people come here each day," he said, "knowing many of these children won't make it. The emotional toll that takes, to bear that cross, every day, and still come back because you love them and want to make them well."

Brooklyn looked at the ICU nurses. "I guess that is a miracle."

He nodded. "Tell you a secret?"

"Sure."

"Every time you help the sick or less fortunate, God smiles."

She looked back into the room at the pale boy. "You said this boy will be saved?"

"Yes."

"But he needs a new heart," she replied.

"Yes, he does. Four hundred miles from here a car accident has happened, and the heart of a little boy will give this boy a full life."

Brooklyn considered the ripple effect of all of this. "And that poor child who died in the crash?"

"Will be raised up by my Father to walk the streets of paradise and one day be reunited with his family for all eternity."

Edward turned to Brooklyn. "Earlier you wanted me to stop the car from hitting Jayden. Would you have me stop this car crash today? Save that boy and let this man's son die?"

She didn't answer.

"Look at me, please," Edward said more insistently. "Would you like to play God for a moment and choose which child to take?"

She ran her hands through her hair and said, "No. I couldn't . . ."

"I know it's hard," Edward said. "But I take you back to the Cross. The answers you seek to all these hard questions are there, Brooklyn."

She touched her bare neckline. "My parents gave me a cross once, but I never wore it. Not once."

Edward nodded. "I know."

Brooklyn could picture the cross still, sitting undisturbed in a jewelry box on her dresser. Eventually she closed the box so she didn't have to look at it. Why did just looking at it haunt her?

"You say you were the man on that cross, all those years ago?"

"Yes," he whispered.

For the first time in her life, Brooklyn considered the gravity of the sacrifice Jesus made.

"And you could have spared yourself and chosen not to die that way?"

"Yes," he replied.

"You never doubted this plan? This suicide mission, from the man you refer to as father?"

"I was human, Brooklyn. Of course I had my doubts. But I had faith that my death was not the end, but the beginning."

Brooklyn looked again at the medical staff, busy trying to save lives. "I brought you here to shock you," she said. "To expose you as a fraud. I'm starting to wonder if it's me who is the fraud."

"You're not, Brooklyn, far from it. And you're asking questions that have been put to my Father since the beginning of time."

He then said, "Look at me, child."

Brooklyn met his kind brown eyes.

"Everything is connected in ways we cannot see. 1 Corinthians 12:21."

"I don't read the Bible, Edward. If you know everything, you certainly know that."

Edward then paraphrased Scripture. "*The eye cannot say to the hand, I have no need of thee. Nor the head to the foot, I have no need of thee. All serve a purpose. We are all one body. If one part suffers, all parts suffer. When one rejoices, we all rejoice."*

Brooklyn chuckled. "Sounds like a half-time speech a coach might give when the team is losing."

"Yes," Edward responded with a smile. "I suppose it does."

"And are we losing, Edward? God's imperfect little creations?"

He answered, "The game isn't over yet."

Brooklyn then asked sincerely, "Why are you here? I mean, really . . . here?"

"I get that question a lot."

"Oh, yeah? What do you say?"

"I say that specifically, I'm here to heal four people, help a dozen others, and get three people home."

Brooklyn smiled wryly. "I don't suppose you'd like to give me a list of these people so I can interview them and confirm you're not fibbing."

"Always the journalist," he answered. "No, I'm not handing out lists, but I can tell you that *you* are going to help me."

"Me? How?"

Edward started walking back toward the elevators. "Don't worry. You'll know it when you see it."

She followed him and punched the down button. "Do you know I've never prayed in my entire life."

"I do," he answered.

"Not even once."

"I'm aware."

"I wouldn't have a clue how to do it, even if I wanted to," she added.

"Can I give you a tip?" Edward asked.

"Sure," Brooklyn replied.

"You don't need to be kneeling in church to do it," he said.

"Is that so?"

"Sure," he said. "One of the best prayers I ever heard came from a woman at the end of her rope, lying on a dirty floor, sick as a dog, wanting to end her life."

"Sounds sad."

There was a *ding* and the elevator doors opened.

"Quite the opposite," he replied. "It was one of the most beautiful prayers I've ever heard."

She looked at him. "How so?"

He held the door open for her. "At precisely the moment anyone else would have been selfish, the prayer wasn't for her."

Brooklyn pressed the first-floor button. "Do you think it's strange that in my whole life, I've never asked God for a single thing?"

Just as the doors shut, Edward answered, "Perhaps you're saving it for something big."

CHAPTER 19
Soul with a Body

After her visit with Edward at the hospital, sleep did not come easy for Brooklyn.

"Do you want to talk about it?" Connor asked as he poured their morning coffee.

She sat motionless at the kitchen table. "I've never been more confused in my life."

"About?"

"Connor, he can't be who he says he is. That's insane."

He set their coffee mugs on the table and sat down across from her. "So, how do you explain him knowing things he shouldn't and healing people?"

"I can't," she replied. "And then he . . ." Her voice drifted off. She didn't even want to say it out loud.

"He what?" Connor asked.

Brooklyn raised her hands. "He showed me these awful wounds on his wrists and side, and then they were gone."

"What do you mean *gone?*"

She answered, "Just what I said. He showed me these horrific wounds on his body and a moment later they were healed."

Connor rubbed his chin.

Whenever her husband did that, he was trying to solve a puzzle and had just found the missing piece. "What is it?" she asked.

"His side and wrists?" Connor asked.

"Yes."

"The Crucifixion," he explained. "He was trying to prove to you who he is."

"But how could he make them appear and then be gone?"

"I don't know, Brooke. Maybe we should consider that he's telling us the truth."

"I'm losing my mind." She covered her face with her hands.

"What if he is?" Connor asked. "The real deal. The Lamb of God."

Brooklyn scoffed. "Careful. I think I hear 12 years of Catholic school leaking out."

Connor retorted, "*You* be careful. I think I hear an atheist afraid to face the truth."

Brooklyn went silent. She had no stomach for a fight.

Connor reached to touch her hand. "I love you; you know that."

"I do."

"Can I say something, and you think before you react?" he asked.

"Oh boy. This ought to hurt."

"It won't, I promise," he said.

"Go ahead," Brooklyn replied.

"Working in the news business you're exposed to all kinds of misery. True?"

"True," she answered.

Connor said, "Not always, but sometimes I think you find that misery useful."

Brooklyn shook her head. "Useful how?"

"I think you use that misery as a convenient way to dismiss the possibility of a higher power."

"Meaning?"

"Meaning, if there's a God, why would he allow so much suffering?"

Brooklyn considered his words and answered, "If it makes you feel better, I had the same conversation with Edward at the hospital."

"And?"

"He gave me chapter and verse about free will and God loving us, despite the suffering."

Connor picked up his coffee mug and took a slow sip. "What else did he say?"

"That I refuse to see miracles."

"What does that mean?" he asked.

"He quoted something from the Bible, Corenthius or something, about us all being connected and in service to one another."

Connor smiled. "I think you mean Corinthians."

"Yeah, okay." She paused. "I didn't even tell you the worst part. That man and his daughter, the ones I confronted with the fake violins, were there."

"Where?"

"The hospital. The man's son is sick in the ICU. That's why they were begging for pennies in the town square."

"Oh, gosh," Connor said. "Did Edward know they'd be there?"

She answered, "It would appear there is nothing Edward doesn't know."

Brooklyn fiddled with her coffee mug. "I'm at a loss on what to do."

"What do you mean?" he asked.

"I have this crazy story about miracles and a guy who claims he's Jesus. I'd prefer writing about politicians stealing money."

"Easier to understand?" he asked.

"A lot easier," she replied.

"You plan to see him again today, right?" Connor asked.

"Yes, this morning."

Evi walked into the kitchen as if on cue and said, "That nice man who says he's God is back."

Brooklyn peeked her head around the corner and saw Edward sitting on the front porch, waiting.

Connor hugged her and said, "You'd better get dressed."

A few moments later, Brooklyn came outside wearing a white cable sweater and jeans, her hair tied back in a ponytail. Edward was in a black navy peacoat and khaki pants, with faded brown boots.

"You two look like you're going hiking," Connor observed. "Hope it's not Golgotha."

Edward turned his head slowly to Connor, giving him a look that said *really?*

Connor turned red. "Bad joke. Apologies."

"I don't get it," Brooklyn said.

Edward smiled and answered, "You had to be there."

With that, Brooklyn and the carpenter's son set off for the Mass Turnpike and a trip west.

Lenox, Massachusetts, is a small town in Berkshire County with a population of barely 5,000. That number swells each summer when the tourists arrive. Today, late fall, it was a ghost town as the trees freed themselves of their leaves, bracing for the harsh winter that felt just over the hill.

Tucked among the tall pines of Lenox, sitting high on a cliff, is the Hallowed House Addiction Center, an in-person treatment facility helping lost souls wrestle with addiction and behavioral problems. Driving into town on Route 20, you couldn't miss the structure, its large front windows resembling eyes peering down like a hawk perched on a branch.

After they parked, Edward pulled open the large cherrywood doors and guided Brooklyn into the front hallway of the rehab facility.

"May I help you?" a receptionist asked.

Edward smiled. "We are just here to see your wall of fame."

In the reception area was a slate wall covered with framed photos of doctors, nurses, and staff who dedicated their lives to helping the broken.

"Why are we here?" Brooklyn asked.

Edward pointed at the third photo from the top left. "To meet her."

It was a woman in her late twenties with dark brown hair, wearing a nurse's hat and matching white blouse. Below her photograph, it read *In Memoriam.*

"I don't understand," Brooklyn said. "You want me to meet a dead nurse?"

Edward whispered, "Look at her eyes."

Brooklyn did, at first staring blankly at the woman's face, then focusing more closely on the woman's deep-green eyes. There was something strangely familiar about them and for good reason. They were identical to Brooklyn's.

"You see it now," Edward said.

Brooklyn took in the rest of the woman's features and realized that while the hairstyle was different, and the nurse carried a bit more weight, she could have been her sister.

She turned to Edward. "Is she?"

"Your biological mother?" he replied. "Yes."

The receptionist came out from behind the desk. "This is a private facility. Do you have a purpose here?"

Edward answered, "We all have a purpose. We need only open our hearts to it."

Brooklyn took Edward by the arm and said under her breath, "I think if you give her any more fortune-cookie answers she's calling the cops on us."

Edward gestured to the receptionist. "We're going now. Thank you."

Outside the facility were a half dozen benches scattered among the trees. All the leaves had fallen, turning the green grass into a red and orange carpet. Brooklyn took a seat next to Edward on one of the benches, waiting for answers.

"Her name was Mary Elizabeth Flanagan," he said. "She was nineteen years old when she began dating a man she thought cared for her."

"Sounds like he didn't," Brooklyn said.

"No. He was a playboy, skilled in charming women. Many women."

"Including my biological mother?"

"Yes," Edward said. "And when he learned she was pregnant he abandoned her. Abandoned you."

As Brooklyn tried to wrap her brain around this, Edward added, "He also gave your mother an addiction to drugs. He was quite insistent she take them with him."

Brooklyn pictured the face of the woman in the photograph. "Are you saying she never did drugs before she met this man?"

"Never."

"Go on," she said.

"She lived in Brooklyn, in a small flat above a pet store where she worked part-time. She attended a small Catholic church on the same block, Saint Augustine, and was friends with a nun there, Sister Catherine."

Brooklyn urged him further. "Keep going."

"After getting pregnant with you and being abandoned, she struggled with her addiction and stole from the pet store where she worked, to support her habit."

Brooklyn started feeling sorry for this woman she'd always despised. "Was she arrested?"

"No," Edward answered. "The pet store owner knew she had a drug problem, so instead of calling the police, he called Sister Catherine."

"That was kind of him."

Edward looked deep into her eyes. "Mary thought about ending the pregnancy and running away."

"Why didn't she?"

"Sister Catherine told her the one good thing in her life was the baby she was carrying. You."

As she sat silent, Edward added, "But she was little more than a child herself, Brooklyn, and in the grip of those terrible drugs."

"Is that why she gave me up?" Brooklyn asked, her voice cracking.

"Yes. The nuns at Catholic Charities promised that her baby would be placed in a loving home with no addiction, no violence, no abandonment, ever again." He looked into Brooklyn's eyes again. "She wanted to be certain *your* life was not *her* life."

An older maintenance man wearing green overalls and carrying a rake walked by and waved hello.

Brooklyn instinctively waved back as the man shuffled on.

"Did your parents ever tell you how you got your name?" Edward asked.

"No. They just told me I had it when they adopted me."

Edward smiled wide.

"What?"

He answered, "The only joy your mother ever knew was growing up in Brooklyn. When she saw your face, before she handed you over to the sisters, she asked the nuns if she could give you the best part of her life."

"Which was Brooklyn," she said.

"Yes."

Edward fell quiet, giving Brooklyn a chance to process the truth.

She began thinking about the woman in the photograph, young, pregnant, and alone. She must have felt so lost. So scared. "All my life I thought I was abandoned," she said.

"Heavens, no! You were saved."

Brooklyn chuckled and said, "And Irish apparently. Flanagan?"

"Yes," he said.

She perked up. "Did you know I met Connor in an Irish bar?"

"I did. First Corinthians, remember?"

"From our chat at the hospital?" she asked.

"That's right. And what did I tell you?"

"That all things are connected?"

Edward nodded.

"And then you went on about how my head is attached to somebody's knee and your foot is connected to my elbow and whatnot," Brooklyn joked.

It gave Edward a hearty laugh.

She glanced over at the sign outside of Hallowed House. "How did she end up here as a nurse?"

Edward explained, "Catholic Charities in Brooklyn had a program where church members could be placed in rehab. Mary was sent here, to Hallowed House, to kick her addiction."

"Then what became of her?" she asked.

"The nuns in a nearby parish made room for her at their provincial house, and she was given a scholarship at Williams College to study nursing."

Brooklyn, "And then?"

"She did her clinical work, right here at the place that had helped her back to good health, and when she graduated, she was offered a job."

"Did she die young?" she asked.

"In her thirties," Edward answered. "Breast cancer. But not before falling in love with a nice man here in Lenox."

"No kids?" Brooklyn asked.

"Oh, yes. Two."

"Wait! So I have siblings or half-siblings?"

"Yes. All grown up now, just like you."

"It would have been nice to know them," she said. She looked off at the beautiful mountains, her mind drifting away.

"What are you thinking?" Edward asked after a while.

"I'm happy for her," Brooklyn said. "Happy that she found love and had a good life here. But . . ."

"But what?" he asked gently.

"I guess hearing all this makes me wonder if she ever thought of me. The baby she left behind." Her eyes stung with tears.

Edward took her hand. "Every. Single. Day," he said. "More than once, she contacted the hospital, trying to track down the couple who adopted you, but back then, the rules were different."

"Right," Brooklyn said. "All the records would have been sealed."

Edward squeezed her hand. "Can I tell you something, kiddo?"

"Sure."

"All your life you have felt *less than*, because of how your story began."

She stared at him. She'd never thought of it that way before, but what he said was true. Deeply true.

"The truth is, Brooklyn, there is no shame in your history. Only love. Do you see that now?"

She closed her eyes, thinking of her birth mother, perhaps sitting on *this* very bench long ago.

The ice that surrounded Brooklyn's heart all these years seemed to melt away in that instant.

"Mary?" a voice called. It was the maintenance man who passed by earlier.

Brooklyn opened her eyes. "Are you speaking to me?"

The man stared a moment, then said, "I'm so sorry, miss. I think I'm losing my mind."

"Malcolm," Edward said, "you are not confused. This is Mary's daughter."

The old man leaned on the rake. "Mary Flanagan, who worked here?"

"Yes."

Malcolm looked closer and said, "Oh, my." He then turned to Edward. "Do I know you, sir?"

"Not in the way you mean," Edward answered.

Malcolm removed his ballcap and scratched his head, his expression one of confusion.

"Don't mind him, Malcolm," Brooklyn said with a friendly grin. "He says that to everyone."

Still holding the rake, Malcolm fixed his gaze on Brooklyn's face. "You have her eyes."

"You knew my mother?"

"More than knew," he answered. "She saved my life."

Edward leaned back on the bench. "Tell her the story."

The old man explained that when Mary Flanagan was a young nurse at the rehab center, he was a very reluctant patient. "I wanted to quit, to leave this place every day," he explained. "And your mom would say, 'Malcolm Hughes, you listen to me now. Give me one more day. Then if you want to leave tomorrow, I'll personally drive you out of town.'"

"And you ended up staying," Edward added.

"That's right."

"And now you work here?" Brooklyn asked.

"Just like your mom did," Malcolm answered.

A stiff breeze swept by them suddenly, making the fallen leaves swirl and fly.

Malcolm said, "Well, they aren't going to rake themselves. God bless you, young lady."

With that, the old man returned to his chores, and Brooklyn and Edward climbed into the car to go home.

She stared up through the car's moonroof at the bright sky and said, "I feel like a weight has been lifted from something deep inside me. I can't describe it."

Edward said, "I think the word you're looking for is *soul*."

As she put the car in drive, she said half-jokingly, "Those are real? Souls?"

"Oh, yes!"

She thought a moment. "So, I'm a body with a soul."

"No," Edward answered. "You've got it backward. You are a soul with a body. One temporary. The other eternal."

As she eased the car down the long circular driveway, Brooklyn said, "You're the Son of God, huh?"

"Yes."

"And the carpenter's son?" she asked.

"Indeed."

After seeing a sign for the Mass Pike ahead, Brooklyn then, "Can I ask where you've been my entire life?"

Edward asked, "What do you mean?"

"I mean, if I were God, I'd shout it from the rooftops."

Edward paused, then said, "Has Connor ever come up from behind you and placed his hands on your shoulders to tell you something?"

"Sure."

"Did he whisper in your ear or shout?" Edward asked.

Brooklyn considered his point. "You're saying you've been right behind me all these years?"

Edward said, "Behind. Supportive. Waiting."

"For what?" she asked.

"For you to turn around."

CHAPTER 20

Goodbye

"Have you heard of the Fall River Festival?" Edward asked Brooklyn on their drive home from Berkshire County.

"Of course. It's like a big party for people in Boston, Cape Cod, Rhode Island. Rides, games, food."

"Right," he said. "It's happening tonight, and I want some of the people I've met to come meet me there."

"Why?" Brooklyn asked.

"Two reasons," he replied. "The first is . . . fun."

"Fun?"

"Yes, fun. A relationship with Jesus, whether it's worship at church, or doing good deeds and sharing memories with those we love, all of that can be fun."

"And the other reason?"

Edward looked over at her. "To say goodbye."

"For how long?" she asked, feeling an unexpected twinge of sadness.

"Until we see each other again."

Even though she'd just met him and was conflicted over who he might truly be, Brooklyn's heart sank at the thought of the world being without him.

Her world without him.

"Could you be more vague?" she asked, jokingly.

Edward smiled slightly, then said, "Before we all have fun together, I need you to drop me off somewhere."

A short time later, Brooklyn pulled her car in front of the Church of the Advent in Back Bay. "Saying hello to your heavenly father?" she asked as she looked up at the church.

"Something like that," he answered, getting out of the vehicle. He patted the roof as he shut the car door. "See you at seven at the festival in Fall River. Meet me by the Ferris wheel. Remember, seven sharp."

Father Michael Reilly was about to start the second reading at the Saturday evening vigil mass when the front doors opened, causing the setting sun to burst in and send a bright orange beam up the center aisle. The pews were packed, but it was more a demonstration of convenience than devotion. Parishioners preferred to keep their Sundays free, favoring football over faith. This was a New England Patriots town, after all, making Saturday the church day.

The beam of light caused heads to turn, revealing Edward's silhouette in the doorway. As he stepped forward, a gust of wind closed the doors behind him with a BANG, reminiscent of a father slamming his fist at the table to get a child's attention.

Edward didn't appear upset, however. He stood calm as a cup of water, looking directly at Father Reilly, who was still at the center of the altar.

"Don't let me stop you," Edward called out.

Father Reilly stared in stunned silence. He recognized that face, that voice. The homeless guy on the bench. "Can I help you?" he asked, when he found his voice again.

Edward began walking toward the altar, reciting the very Scripture they were reading from the Book of Matthew. "The King will say to those on his right, come, you who are blessed by my father. For I was hungry, and you gave me something to eat. I was thirsty and you gave me something to drink."

He reached the front of the church and turned his attention away from the altar and toward the congregation. "I was a stranger and you invited me in."

Some of the parishioners who had gathered to watch the police take away a homeless man who'd sought refuge on their bench shifted uncomfortably in their seats.

Edward looked into their eyes and repeated the verse. "I was a stranger and you invited me in." With one more sweeping glance around the sanctuary, he added, "Yeah. Not so much."

He stepped onto the altar, raised his hand, and laid it upon the priest's shoulder. Reilly immediately sat down.

Edward looked out at the congregation and said, "And those who call themselves righteous will look to each other and say, 'Wait a second. When did we ever turn you away, Lord?'" He chuckled. "Do you really need me to answer that question?"

Parishioners silently looked to their left and right, as if seeing who might dare respond. None did.

Edward continued quoting the book of Matthew. "If you did not do it for the least of these, you did not do it for me."

He reached over to the table at the center of the altar and picked up the Bible, raising it above his head for all to see.

"This is the Word of God, and it's good that you are here today to listen," Edward called out. "But words without action or meaning are just words."

He pointed at a large statue of the Virgin Mary. "My Holy Mother would tell you, no more does standing in a hospital make you a doctor, than sitting in a church secure your place in heaven."

Reilly kept his head down. Most of them did.

"On the day of judgment," Edward said, "my Father won't ask what psalm you memorized. He'll ask what you did. He'll ask who you helped."

With that, he handed the Bible to Father Reilly and patted him on the back. "I leave them to your loving heart and guiding hands," Edward said.

Father Reilly locked eyes with Edward and nodded. He would do better. He needed to do better. *God help me do better.*

Edward stepped down from the altar and made his way to the center aisle of the church, walking slowly. The only person in the entire building not watching his every step was an 11-year-old boy named Finnegan Tarp.

Young Finnegan was fixated on one of the stations of the cross mounted on the wall next to his pew. The fourteen stations depicted Jesus's final and painful steps toward Calvary and his crucifixion. Finnegan appeared mesmerized by the ninth station, which showed a small statue of Jesus falling under the weight of the cross for the third time.

Edward approached the boy and asked, "What do you think, Finn?"

The boy looked from Edward back to the image of Jesus and answered, "Looks painful."

"It was," Edward replied. "Would you get up?"

Without missing a beat, Finnegan answered, "Nope."

"Do you know why I did?"

The child responded, "Why *you* did?"

"Yes."

"You?" Finnegan asked a second time.

Edward pointed at the statue and said, "Me."

Finnegan focused on the pained face of Jesus crumpled under the cross. "Ask me the question again."

Edward said, "Why, despite all that pain and suffering, when I knew what was coming . . . why, Finnegan, did I get up?"

Finnegan met Edward's eyes and answered, "For me."

Edward put his hand on the boy's shoulder. "Say it louder."

The boy exclaimed, "YOU DID IT FOR ME."

Edward smiled. "Perhaps you should be standing at that altar."

Finnegan looked toward the front of the church where Father Reilly stood. "You think?"

Edward replied, "Little League first. Priesthood later." Then he tousled the boy's curly brown hair.

With that, he made his way back to the church doors, pushing them open and letting the sunset bathe the center aisle once again.

Father Reilly called out, "Rabbi?"

Edward turned toward him.

"Is there anything else we should know?" the priest asked.

With every parishioner hanging on his response, Edward said, "When in doubt, remember they're called the Ten Commandments, not the Ten Suggestions."

At seven p.m. sharp, many of the people Edward had met during his time in Boston were gathered by the Ferris wheel at the Fall River Festival. Gabriel and Piper were there, along with Brooklyn, Connor, and Evi. Stewart, the blind man whom Edward healed, was talking to Jayden, the boy on the bike.

"I'm sorry I'm late," a voice called out.

Piper's face lit up when she saw Luke. He hugged Piper, causing Gabriel to smile and make a silly face only Piper could see.

She mouthed the words STOP IT, to her grinning father.

Edward gathered them around and said, "I'm so glad all of you are here. Thank you for coming. I wanted to have an evening of fun together before I say goodbye."

As a chorus of sorrow and questions erupted, Gabriel pulled Edward into a hug. "I'm sorry to hear that. For selfish reasons, if I'm being honest."

"There isn't a selfish bone in your body, Gabriel," he replied. "Besides, I bet the right person to replace me is right under your nose."

Stewart approached, extending both of his hands to grip Edward's. "In case I don't have a chance to say it later, thank you."

Edward smiled. "See good things, do good things."

"I will. I promise."

Edward laid his hand on Jayden's shoulder. "Did you catch that fish yet?"

"Not yet, sir."

Edward looked him in the eye. "Did you know some of my best friends were fishermen?"

"Really? Did they catch many?"

"With my help," Edward said, "they caught millions."

"Wow!" Jayden exclaimed.

Connor approached. "I know we just met, but I'm going to miss you too."

Edward leaned in close and whispered, "You are a good man, and I know you believe in me."

"I do."

Edward took hold of his arm and said, "A moment alone, if you don't mind."

Connor stepped aside from the others as Edward said, "I need you to do me a favor."

"Anything."

"Take Brooklyn to the doctor as soon as possible."

Connor searched Edward's face for an explanation.

"The headaches are not just headaches, Connor."

"Is she okay?" he asked, panic in his voice.

Edward grabbed Connor's forearm again. "She's going to be fine. Just take her soon."

"I will," he said, choking up.

Edward saw. "She'll be okay, I promise."

When they rejoined the others, Piper said, "Before we scatter, I have a question, Edward. You told me on the day we went to Newbury Street that you were here to do several specific things. You said you would heal four people, help some others, and get three people home."

Brooklyn said, "Yeah, you told me the same thing."

"Yes, I did," Edward said.

Piper pointed at the people she'd just met in the group. "You healed Jayden and Stewart. That's two."

Edward answered, "I also helped a police officer who was in terrible pain."

"Okay," Brooklyn said. "And who did you get home?"

"A young lady named Alexandria. She's home now with her sister."

"And the others?" Connor asked.

"And the others," Edward said, "will reveal themselves at the appropriate time."

Brooklyn said to her husband, "That's what you call a dodge."

Everyone laughed.

"If we're done playing twenty questions," Edward said, "I would like us to enjoy the festival."

Gabriel, who had been watching quietly, spoke up. "Can I ask one more, please?"

"Of course, my friend," Edward replied.

"The day we met, when you walked into our lives. Why didn't you just tell me who you were?"

Edward patted his chest. "You mean, that I was—"

"Jesus," Gabriel said.

Edward pondered the question, then said, "Have you ever given a dog medicine?"

"Sure."

"Did you hand him the pill and say, 'Here, swallow this, it's good for you?'"

"No, sir. We'd hide it in a piece of baloney or maybe a treat."

"Why?" Edward asked.

"'Cause even though it was good for him, the dog would reject it."

Edward addressed the group. "If I walked up and said, 'Hello, my name is Jesus, and I'm the Son of God,' would any of you have believed me?"

Everyone smiled, understanding his point.

"I was the medicine sent to make you better, Gabriel."

"And you hid the truth until we got to know you?"

"Correct. And do you know what God's only Son wants right now?"

"Fried dough," Evi called out.

Edward took the child by the hand. "You lead the way."

"Hold up," Luke said. "Let me take a group photo."

Brooklyn handed him her phone, and he snapped one perfect shot of all of them beneath the Ferris wheel, with Edward in the center, his arms draped around Jayden and Evi.

Darkness fell fast as the friends spread out to enjoy the festival. The lights from the rides illuminated the night, making it even more magical.

Luke asked Piper to take a ride with him on the Ferris wheel, and just as Edward had hinted, the ride stopped at the very top, causing the young couple to sway in the cold autumn breeze.

"You cold?" he asked.

Piper answered, "I'll be okay."

Without hesitation, Luke took his denim jacket off and wrapped it around her. The chivalrous gesture caused her to act without thinking, planting a warm kiss directly on his soft lips. It would be the first of a million to come.

Edward spent time with everyone over the next two hours, sharing stories and messages of hope that each would take away as a treasure when the evening was done.

Evi had the greatest story to share, watching Edward play three-card Monte with a slippery carnival barker who had been taking money from tourists all night.

The man placed three cards face down on the table, two of them black aces and the third the queen of hearts. He'd then mix them quickly and when the cards stopped you guessed where the queen was hiding. Each wager cost five dollars, and if someone guessed correctly, they won a large stuffed bear. You could see by the wad of cash in the carny's hand and the number of bears hanging above his head, very few went home with the prize.

Edward sidled up to the tent and stood next in line to be fleeced.

"Follow the lady, easy as can be," the charlatan tempted. "Win a bear, one, two, three."

The carnival worker was rail-thin with bloodshot eyes, wearing a straw hat that failed to cover his bald dome. Under his palm he hid an extra black ace, so no matter what card the customer chose, he'd swap out the ace, making certain they never saw that queen.

Edward asked Evi, "Do you know what the eighth commandment is?"

She shrugged. "Beats me."

Edward looked at the unscrupulous carny and said, "Thou shall not steal." He then announced to anyone listening, "Let's play!"

"I don't see money on the table," the carny said. "No money, no play. No play means get on your way."

Evi took his hand. "We should go."

"Listen to your kid," the man said, "before I move you along myself."

Edward ignored him. "Evi, can I borrow five dollars?"

"I don't have any money."

"Sure you do. Check your right pocket."

Evi reached into her jacket and sure enough, pulled out a crisp five-dollar bill. "Where did that come from?"

Edward took it from her hand and slapped it down on the counter. "Ready."

The man smiled like a hyena who'd just seen a vulnerable fawn wander into his path. He began flipping the cards, slowly at first, and then at blinding speed.

Evi watched nervously. "Oh, Edward, I lost it. I lost the queen. He's too fast."

The man kept going, moving his hands so quickly that a crowd gathered and started to hoot and howl at the display of dexterity. As sweat dripped from the carny's brow, he realized his customer wasn't watching the cards at all. Edward was staring him right in the face, smiling.

What is this weirdo doing? Is he trying to rattle me? It doesn't matter, I have the hidden ace. He can't win. He CAN'T win.

Finally, after a lavish flurry, the card shark stopped and placed the three cards face down on the table. "Which one is the queen? Choose."

Edward answered, "All of them."

The man replied, "No, sir. Two aces. One queen. Pick the queen."

"It doesn't matter," Edward said. "Evi, point at any card."

"Me?"

"You. Any card you pick will be the queen."

The crowd grew larger, watching with anticipation.

Edward looked at the carny. "I promise, they're all queens. Even the one you're hiding in your hand."

The scam artist pulled his hands close to his waist as people moved closer to see what Edward was talking about.

"If he won't show us," Edward said, "you do it, Evi. Turn over a card."

Evi flipped the center card on the table. Queen of hearts.

The scam artist, clearly wanting all of this to be over, shouted, "LOOKS LIKE WE HAVE A WINNER." He then said under his breath to Edward, "Take your prize and go."

"Show us another card, Evi," Edward said.

Evi turned over the one to the left, then the right. Both the queen of hearts.

The carny stared in disbelief. *Impossible.* "You made your point, now go."

Edward reached out and grasped the carny's right hand, forcing him to turn it over and reveal the ace of clubs he was hiding. Only when he flipped the man's hand, it too was the queen of hearts.

The worker threw the card as if it were a scorpion that might sting. "How did you do that?"

Edward leaned closer. "Give Evi one of the stuffed bears. Donate the money you stole from people tonight to a good cause, and don't do this anymore, Andrew."

"How do you know my name?" he asked.

"Andrew Broomfield of Peoria, Illinois," Edward said. "Named after your uncle Andy, who is your mom's favorite brother, who walked with a limp he got after a skiing accident. Your best friends growing up were a boy named T.J. and Jimmy Sullivan, although everyone called him Sully." Edward paused. "Shall I go on?"

Shock spread across the man's face. "Who are you?"

"God sees all, Andrew," Edward answered. "Oh, the bear, please."

Andrew sheepishly handed Evi a large pink bear and said to Edward, "I'm sorry."

Edward took hold of both his hands. "You are forgiven. Now, sin no more."

As Evi and Edward walked away from the tent with her prize, she looked up and said, "You really are him, aren't you?"

"I am."

"Can I call you Jesus?"

Edward smiled warmly. "Do you know, of every person I've met in Boston, you are the first one who wanted to call me by my real name."

Evi lit up. "So? Can I?"

"Any time you want," Edward said as they slowly made their way back to the Ferris wheel to meet up with the others and say goodbye.

One by one, they left the festival, leaving just Evi, Connor, and Brooklyn with the guest of honor.

"Can we chat a moment alone?" Edward asked Brooklyn.

"Sure." They took a seat on a bench, giving them a perfect view of the upcoming fireworks show.

"Do you like fireworks?" she asked.

"I like any light that obliterates the darkness." He paused, then said, "Before I go, I need you to listen to me."

"Okay."

"I have three very important things to say."

"Sounds serious," she said.

"It is." He turned toward her. "First, Connor is going to take you to the doctor's tomorrow. Don't be afraid. I promise you, everything will be okay."

"What's wrong with me?"

Instead of answering, he said, "Number two, I want you to write an article for the *Boston Globe* about what you have witnessed, telling people who I am and what I've done. People may be skeptical, even mock you, but don't listen to them. Believe your heart, Brooklyn."

She stared at her feet. "I'm not sure I like this conversation, Edward."

"Why?"

"First, you tell me I'm sick, and now you want me to write something that invites ridicule."

"And . . ."

Brooklyn replied, "I hate to break it to you, but a lot of people don't believe in God or miracles."

"Don't you think it's time they should?"

As she pondered Edward's question, he pressed on. "Third thing. After the article comes out, you'll be invited to speak about my miracles. I want you to go."

"Where? Why? You're not making sense, Edward."

"Listen to me. This is very important. During that trip, your faith will be put to the test. If you believe in me, you'll save a life and help get someone home."

"What do you mean? Who?" And how in the world was she supposed to save a life? "You're talking in riddles, Edward."

Edward gently turned her chin so that she was facing him. "Repeat back to me the three things I just said."

Brooklyn stared at him in silence.

"This is important, Brooklyn."

She let out a deep breath. "Fine. Connor takes me to the doctor. I write an article about you and your miracles. And the last one, I go make a speech someplace, save somebody's life, and help them get home."

"Perfect."

"No, it's not perfect! I'm worried and confused."

"God loves you, Brooklyn. Don't be afraid."

As she continued looking into his eyes, she could hear his voice inside her head, saying, *Surrender your doubt. Trust in God. There is nothing to fear.*

"It's about to start," Edward said. He gestured for Brooklyn to look up toward the stars.

Boom. Bang. Boom.

High above, bright orange, red, and yellow fireworks splashed across the darkness as if an artist were throwing paint against a black canvas.

Brooklyn found herself staring at them and getting emotional, her heart and soul pulsing with each flash of light. Life was indeed beautiful, and she was so blessed. For the family she had now, for the parents who adopted her, for the biological mother who saved her life.

As the fireworks came to a spectacular conclusion, Brooklyn turned and said, "Oh Edward, did you see—"

Her smile dropped; all words fell away. Brooklyn was alone on the bench. The carpenter's son was gone.

CHAPTER 21

The Fourth Miracle

The following morning was strange for everyone who'd met and spent time with Edward. He was gone, but the emptiness one might expect in their heart was filled with gratitude instead.

On the south side of Boston, Stewart Phillips dropped by the shelter to help Pastor Rip pass out breakfast, regaling anyone who would listen with stories of the kind stranger who granted him not just sight, but permission to forgive himself.

In Meriam Hill, Jayden Lancaster surprised his mother by making the beds and tidying up the house before giving her a small trinket he'd won at the festival: a glass diamond heart on a plastic chain. She loved it.

In Woburn, at the home of Gabriel and Piper, breakfast was tranquil. "Can I tell you something, Dad?"

"Of course."

"A couple of things, actually. First, I want to start going back to church with you."

"That's wonderful," Gabriel replied. "And the other?"

"Call me crazy, but I don't think this is over."

Gabriel put down his fork, giving Piper his full attention. "What do you mean?"

She shrugged. "Edward dropping into our lives, then poof, he's gone. I feel like the puzzle isn't quite finished."

"How so?" he asked.

"I haven't a clue. It's just something I feel inside."

Gabriel looked at the half-empty cereal box on the counter and remembered Edward's Bible passage with the little nuggets of Cap'n Crunch. "Can I tell you something?"

"Sure."

"I have no doubt he was the Son of God."

"Was it the miracles?"

"No," he replied. "I mean, yes, of course, but something else. He made you see the world differently, like we all served a higher purpose."

Piper smiled, her eyes distant.

"What?" Gabriel asked.

"He freaked me out when he was talking to the deer, remember?" She giggled.

Gabriel laughed along, adding, "I'm gonna miss him. In fact, *The Carpenter's Son* woodworking business is once again short a son."

Piper bit her lip and looked away.

"Something on your mind?" Gabriel asked.

"I was waiting to tell you, but Luke, Paul's friend . . . my friend—"

"*More* than a friend, you mean?" He grinned at her.

"Yes, Daddy. My *more* than a friend told me he's handy with tools. He also considered moving closer to Boston to be with me while I return to school."

"Wait! Stop the presses! Did you say, school?"

"Yes. College. I was talking to Edward before he left, and I think I'd make a good teacher."

"So do I," Gabriel said proudly. "A great one, in fact."

Piper said, "As for Luke moving closer . . ."

"An apprentice, perhaps?"

"If you'll have him."

Without hesitation, he answered, "Of course I will."

Piper came around the kitchen table to hug her father. "Thank you, Dad."

"For?"

"Everything."

In Wakefield, Connor and Brooklyn sat silently together in the living room.

"You said the doctor would see you first thing this morning?" he asked.

"Yes."

"What did you tell them?"

"Well, I didn't tell them that the Son of God urged me to make an emergency appointment, just that I've been having terrible headaches and we're concerned."

"Hey, Con?" she said.

"Yeah, hon."

"I'm scared," Brooklyn admitted, her voice shaky.

"What did Edward tell you?" he asked.

"That I'd be okay."

He reached out and took Brooklyn's hand, "Believe it, then."

Connor pulled her closer, hugging her tight as he whispered, "Go shower, and we'll face this together."

Brooklyn's visit with her primary care physician took less than an hour, as the doctor ordered her to go immediately to Boston's largest hospital, Mass General, for a CT scan.

Shortly after the test, a doctor entered a private waiting area holding a printout of an X-ray image. Brooklyn didn't need a medical degree to read the results on the face of the doctor.

"You'd be terrible at poker," Connor said to the physician.

Brooklyn asked, "What? Just say it."

"You have a small but dangerous pituitary adenoma behind the nasal cavity at the base of your brain. It's the size of a dime and is the reason for your headaches."

As Brooklyn's stomach turned sour, Connor asked, "So, how do we . . . I mean, what's the next—"

"Slow down," the doctor said. "There's lots of good news you didn't let me get to."

Brooklyn, still processing that something dangerous was growing inside her head, managed to say, "Good news?"

The doctor continued, "Ninety-nine out of a hundred of these tumors are *not* cancer."

"NOT cancer," Connor repeated. He exhaled slowly.

"Correct. But we can't leave it in there. With your permission, I'd like to run a blood screen, clear you for surgery, and get it out of there first thing in the morning."

"So, I'm staying?" Brooklyn asked.

"That's awfully quick, doc," Connor said.

"If you want to go home and process this, a few more days won't matter."

"NO," she shot back. "I want it out."

"But it's probably not cancer, right?" Connor asked.

"Correct," the doctor replied. "No guarantee, but almost certainly not."

Brooklyn said, "Thank you, doctor. I'm staying for the surgery."

An hour later, Brooklyn was changed into a gown and resting comfortably in a hospital room bed. There was a television mounted on the wall, but entertainment was the last thing on her mind. Brooklyn welcomed the silence, her mind circling back to her last conversation with Edward.

He knew I was sick. Why am I surprised? He knew everything.

After school, Evi stopped by the hospital with Connor for a quick visit. The moment she walked into the room, her eyes darted to the medical machines attached to her mother.

"I promise I'm going to be okay, sweetie," Brooklyn assured her.

What should have been terror and tears from a child Evi's age was the opposite.

"I know you will, Mommy. Edward told Daddy you'll be okay, so I'm not worried."

Tears filled Connor's eyes as he hugged their daughter.

"Don't you start," Brooklyn joked.

He squeezed Evi and said, "The youngest and smallest among us has the biggest faith."

Brooklyn opened her arms, so Evi broke away from her father and hugged her. "Do me a favor and take care of your dad. He gets nervous when I'm not home."

Evi kissed her mom on the cheek. "Will do."

Connor hugged her next. "I'll see you in the morning before surgery. Love you."

That was all it took for the dam to break, and tears started flowing from Brooklyn's eyes as well. "Love you too. Now *go* before I make the both of you sleep with me in this tiny bed."

After the door closed, Brooklyn felt more alone than she ever had in her life. She'd heard what the doctor said, how 99 out of 100 had nothing to worry about. But what if she were the one? She was too young to have cancer, certainly too young to leave Connor and Evi.

The room was dead quiet, except for the rhythmic low beep of the EKG machine monitoring Brooklyn's heart. She closed her eyes and did something she'd never done before.

Brooklyn bowed her head and prayed.

Dear God,

I'm sorry it has taken me all these years to talk to you. I guess I wasn't sure if anyone was really listening. Something happened to me recently. I don't mean this illness—I'm talking about a man I met. He was kind and did things to help others. Things that I can't explain.

My husband once asked me what I would do if I ever had to confront my lack of faith. If I saw actual evidence that you exist, would I believe or shut my eyes to it? If you asked me that question a month ago, I'm pretty sure I would have laughed at the notion. But now, tonight . . . I think, for the first time, I believe.

The man I'm talking about, who changed me, changed my heart, was your Son. He told us to call him Edward, but we all knew his real name. I think we were too afraid to say it out loud, for fear it wouldn't be true. But it was true, wasn't it God? You sent him here . . . twice. Once to pay for our sins, and this time. Why you chose us to be the lucky ones to meet him, I'll never understand.

I know what I'm doing right now, praying, must seem disingenuous. The gall this lady has, right? Waiting until I'm in trouble and only hours from surgery to finally talk to you. I wouldn't blame you if you told me to take a hike. What kind of friend only reaches out when they need a favor? A lousy one, that's who.

The tears in Brooklyn's eyes began rolling down her cheeks now, her voice shaking with fear.

But I am praying, and I need a big one now, God. I'm not asking you to take away the tumor. I'll do the surgery and recovery. I'm just asking if it could not be cancer. It's not for me that I ask, but Evi. She needs her mommy, and I need to see her grow up and dance at her wedding.

I imagine lots of people try to bargain with you at moments like this. Promise to change or be a better person if you do this one big favor. But that's the thing, God, I don't have to. I already am a changed person, because of your son. Because of Ed . . . I mean, Jesus. He changed me, and no matter what happens tomorrow, I'm grateful for that.

Brooklyn paused now, uncertain what was left to say.

Well, I guess that's it. I've never prayed before, so I'm not sure how you end one of these things. Thank you for listening, God. Thank you for my life.

As Brooklyn wiped the tears from her face, she heard a familiar voice say, "Amen."

She looked up. Edward moved from the shadows in the corner of the room into the light, revealing his kind face and knowing eyes.

"You end a prayer by saying *Amen*," he said. "You must have seen someone do that in a movie before."

"You came!" she exclaimed, her heart swelling with emotion.

"I told you that your first prayer would be for something big."

Brooklyn looked at the machines hooked up to her body. "I guess this qualifies."

He smiled at her. "I also told you everything will be alright."

"And will it?" She heard the uncertainty in her voice.

He crossed the room and stood beside her bed. "This is one of those good news, bad news situations."

"Oh, God," Brooklyn replied. "What's the bad news?"

Edward put his hand on her shoulder. "It is cancer. You, unfortunately, are the one in a hundred."

It felt like a punch to the stomach. Brooklyn forgot to breathe. Her mind was now littered with questions she never thought she'd face. *Why me? What about Evi? My God, how would Connor carry on without me? We were supposed to grow old together. This was not part of the plan.*

"So, how could there be good news?"

"Let me tell you a story," he said. "There was a woman who had been bleeding for twelve years. She sought out Jesus, thinking, if she could just touch my garment, my robe, she'd be healed."

"Did it work?" Brooklyn asked.

He smiled at her again. "You could read all about it in the Bible, the book of Matthew. But I'll go ahead and give you the ending. Her bleeding stopped the moment she reached out for me. And I told her, 'Take heart, daughter, your faith has healed you.'"

Brooklyn considered the story, then asked, "And is that me? Am I the daughter who is sick?"

"Yes," he answered. "Take heart, my daughter, Brooklyn. Your faith has healed you."

Brooklyn began to cry, realizing in her heart that her cynicism about God had vanished.

He kept his hand on her shoulder. "It wasn't your prayer alone that brought me to you tonight. It is your faith."

My faith? Me? I'm the one who didn't believe. Yet, he's right. She felt it stir inside of her like a lion breaking free of his cage. *I do believe in God. I'm tired of trying to explain away the things I don't understand. There is an answer. God is the answer.*

Brooklyn looked down and saw her tears staining the front of the hospital gown.

She wiped away her tears. "You told us that you came to Boston to heal four people."

"Yes, I did."

She counted on her fingers. "Stewart the blind man, Jayden on the bike, the police officer, and now me."

Edward replied, "And now you."

"I was the fourth miracle."

He placed his hands on Brooklyn's head. "Close your eyes a moment."

She did, and immediately she felt an intense warmth well up behind her eyes where the headaches had been. Just when she felt the heat might cause her pain, it vanished.

Edward removed his hands and announced, "Right as rain."

As the carpenter's son slowly moved toward the door, Brooklyn asked, "Do you have to go?"

He paused, then said, "Yes. But two important things."

She sat up in bed, already feeling different, better. "I'm listening."

"First," he said, "tell the doctors to do another CT scan *before* cutting you open."

"Of course. And number two?"

Edward answered, "Don't forget what I asked you to do."

Brooklyn named the three things aloud. "Write an article about you. Go visit a place that's going to ask me to speak. And keep an eye out for someone who needs help getting home."

"Very good," he said. "Now close your eyes and think of a favorite memory with Connor and Evi."

Brooklyn did, her mind immediately taking her to a weekend getaway in Rockport, north of Boston.

"Where did you stay?" he asked.

"A bed and breakfast on Andrews Point."

"What did you do there?"

Her eyes still closed, Brooklyn replied, "Walk, swim, everything."

"And what else?"

She scanned her memory. "There was a candy shop we loved. The Fudgery."

"What else do you see?" he asked.

"Birds," she answered. "Big seagulls circling above Evi's head as she throws them bread on the shore."

She could see it as if it happened yesterday. She could hear the gulls squawking in the sky.

"Evi is laughing. 'Do you see them, Mommy? Daddy, look at the birds.' The cold surf is crashing at their feet, making them numb, but they don't care. It's a perfect day. Is there anything better than the sound of a child's laughter in the sunlight?"

Finally, she said, "Is this part of your miracle with me, these memories?"

There was no answer.

"Edward?" she called out.

She opened her eyes, and he was gone.

CHAPTER 22
Worth It

Brooklyn had held six jobs in her life: babysitter, cashier, cafeteria worker, and three different reporter positions. Six jobs, and she'd never once come close to quitting, until this moment.

A month had passed since she'd left the hospital tumor-free. Connor still joked that the fifth miracle was her persuading the medical staff to run another CT scan. The doctors and nurses were still talking about this miracle woman who stumbled in sick and danced out healed. To those who worshiped at the altar of science, it made no sense.

Her boss at the newspaper was having a hard time swallowing the story as well, and, much to Brooklyn's dismay, he had no intention of running it in the Sunday *Globe.*

"He's not the Son of God," Rex barked. "He didn't heal those people, and I'm not going to watch one of my most talented journalists flush her career down the toilet!"

"Those people?" Brooklyn shot back. "By *those people,* I hope you know you're including me."

Rex gave her a hard stare from behind his desk. "Can you really not see the reality here?"

"What reality?"

"Reporters who write stories about aliens, the Loch Ness monster, and Jesus coming back work for the *National Enquirer*, not the Pulitzer Prize-winning *Boston Globe*."

"You're worried about being mocked?" she asked. "I'm touched."

"I'm worried that you're *not* worried, Brooklyn. Listen. This kind of story . . . you ring this bell once and then they run you out of town."

"Hear me out, Rex. Please."

He waved her off. "We're done."

"But I have interviews with the people he healed, others who met him, all offering written and eyewitness testimony to what this man could do." She sat down across from him. "We've run dozens of stories with less corroboration than I have on this man, on this story."

"It can't be true," he replied sharply.

She reached into a brown folder and yanked out a copy of her CT scan. "Tell that to my CT scan, which shows a tumor, Rex. A tumor that is now gone, AFTER he healed me."

He blew out a loud sigh. "I can't run a story in the *Globe* that Jesus came down from heaven to spend a couple of weeks kicking around Boston with some lovable, gray-haired carpenter and his daughter and decided to heal a few people because he was bored."

"*Not* because he was bored. Because he's the Son of God and wanted to alleviate suffering."

Rex shook his head in disbelief. "You were *never* like this."

"No kidding," she replied. "If you're saying I'm a changed person, well . . . guilty as charged."

She glanced through his office window to the newsroom, where colleagues were no doubt pretending to work while eavesdropping on this combustible conversation.

She lowered her voice. "For God's sake, Rex. Look outside, and all you see is story after story on poverty and crime and racism and hatred. Is it any wonder Jesus might come here to check on us and spread a little kindness? Is it really that hard to believe in miracles?"

"Yes. Hundred percent."

She stood and turned toward the door. "If you look at the facts and the notes that I have backing everything up and still refuse to run this story . . . well, I have to question your journalistic integrity."

"And if you really think this man is Jesus Christ," he retorted, "I have to question your sanity."

"If you mean that, Rex, maybe I don't need to be here." She couldn't hide the hurt in her voice as she opened the door to leave.

"Hold on," Rex said.

Brooklyn halted but did not turn to face him.

"I can't run it as a news story," he said, causing her to turn sharply and give him a snide look. "But I can run it as a commentary about your experience with this man. A firsthand account of what appears to be a series of miracles happening in Boston."

"What are you saying?"

"What I'm saying is the *Boston Globe* cannot tell its readers this man, this *carpenter's son*, is Jesus."

She waited.

"But *you* can, if that's truly what you believe."

"It's not what I believe, Rex. It's what is."

Rex's compromise was a solution, but Brooklyn wanted one thing more. "Make me a promise," she said.

"I'm already on a limb here. What now?"

"When you read it. If it's good, I mean *really* good, promise you won't bury it in the newspaper where no one will see it."

Rex crossed his office and shook her hand firmly. "Brooklyn, you have my word. If it's great, I'll give you front page, Sunday edition."

She felt a swell of confidence as she let go of Rex's hand. She'd write the best piece she'd ever written. Jesus would help her.

"Know this," he said, looking her square in the face. "When they come for you, and trust me, they'll come for you, I'll be standing right by your side to defend it and you."

Brooklyn hugged her boss and whispered, "God bless you."

It took her four days to write her article. Since *Edward* was the name *the carpenter's son* chose during his visit, that is how Brooklyn referred to him throughout her story. She did not pull her punches, however, making it clear that in her mind and in the minds of Piper, Gabriel, Stew, Jayden, and others, Edward was in fact Jesus, the Son of God.

She printed the four-thousand-word essay, long by journalistic standards, and handed it to Rex. Then she sat outside his office, waiting for a verdict. Normally, when Rex read something for the first time, he'd wield a red sharpie and slash across the pages making edits and corrections on the fly. In this case, he turned pages slowly until he reached the end.

She watched as he took off his reading glasses and put them down. Then he retrieved a small bottle of bourbon from a desk drawer, poured himself a shot into a paper cup, and tossed it back, looking like a soldier who had just gone to battle.

She kept hoping he'd look in her direction and welcome her in. Instead, he rose from the desk and went to a shelf with a litany of awards and dusty old books. As she watched, Rex picked up the only framed picture on the shelf: a black-and-white photo Brooklyn had seen but had never been curious enough to ask about. He touched the glass. Then he turned toward the window and motioned for her to come in.

When she entered, she noticed tears in his eyes.

He turned the photo in her direction, revealing a couple all dressed up as if going to a wedding. "This is my mother and father," he said. "For the first time ever, I actually believe I'm going to see them again." His voice cracked. "Because of your story, Brooklyn."

Her eyes stung with tears. At that moment, Rex reminded her of a little boy who missed his mom and dad. She couldn't help but think, *We never stop being children when it comes to our parents.*

"I think you will see them again, Rex. And I believe Edward would tell you it's a certainty."

He cleared his throat. "A deal's a deal, Brooklyn. Your story blew me away, so, front page, Sunday *Globe*."

As much as Brooklyn was filled with joy, there was also a sudden rush of apprehension. "Are you going to get in trouble if you run this?"

"Don't worry about that."

"I don't mean the *letters to the editor* kind of trouble, Rex."

"I know."

"I'm talking about the publisher, *your boss,* kind of trouble," she said.

"And I said, don't worry about it," he replied more firmly.

Brooklyn gave a thoughtful pause, then said, "I don't want you fired because of me, you hear me?"

He looked out his window down onto the busy street. "Let your light shine before others, so that they may see your good works and give glory to the Father in heaven."

Brooklyn's jaw dropped. "Is that from the Bible?"

"New Testament," Rex answered.

"Since when do you quote the Bible?"

He smiled. "Since I grew up Catholic and had a brother for a priest."

"Wait. What? I had no clue."

He set the photo back on the shelf. "I suspect there's a lot you don't know about me," he said. Then he sat back down at his desk. "Thank you for writing this."

"Thanks for giving me the opportunity, Rex." She turned to leave.

"Don't forget," he said. "If they come for you, they have to go through me."

Brooklyn smiled wryly. "And if they call me nuts and decide to fire us both?"

Rex replied, "Worth it."

CHAPTER 23

Proof of Life

Rex's fears were not unfounded, but his worry was quickly extinguished when the phone calls, letters, and emails *loving* the story far outweighed the negative by a hundred-to-one ratio. The account of God's true existence appeared to quench a thirst many didn't realize they possessed. It also sold a record number of newspapers, which the publisher loved.

USA Today picked up the piece, so the lore of Edward's miracles and grace were now being read and shared all over the country. It was exactly as Edward had predicted, the good news spreading far and wide.

Three weeks after the story received national attention, Brooklyn received a call from a Jesuit priest from Auriesville, New York. Father Giacomo Francesco invited Brooklyn to visit the famous Auriesville Shrine and speak about her *walk in faith*.

"All due respect, father, my religious conversion, or whatever this is, has happened only recently. Surely there is someone more worthy."

"Nonsense," the priest said. "Jesus chose you, and that's good enough for us."

Edward's instructions came to mind again. *Go visit a place that invites you to speak.* She thanked the priest for his invitation and accepted it.

When the day came to visit the Auriesville Shrine, Brooklyn's speech lasted barely a half hour. She walked them through the miracles and the gentle preaching that Edward disguised as everyday conversation. Mostly, she spoke about his kindness.

When she finished, many of the priests, nuns, and lay people wanted to meet her and know what it was like to spend time with Jesus. "Yes, he's the King of Kings," she told them. "But he's also your friend. That's how he mostly presented himself. As the best kind of friend."

By the time she got on the road back home, it was later than she'd expected. She set her phone app to guide her, and the app directed her east to Albany, south toward Catskill, and then across the Rip Van Winkle Bridge toward Massachusetts.

She never made it across the span, however. That's where traffic stopped, and Brooklyn got out of the car and met Sandy, clinging precariously to the edge.

Now the two of them sat together in the backseat of Brooklyn's car, where Brooklyn had been trying to follow Edward's final instruction: *Help save a life and help her find her way home.*

"I know all this sounds crazy, Sandy," she said after sharing her story, "but this is why I believe in God. It's why, whatever troubles you're facing, trust me, it's nothing Jesus can't fix."

Sandy, who had listened carefully without interrupting, now shook her head. "Brooklyn, I'm happy for you that you had this, what's the word, *transformation* of faith. But my situation is far worse, there is no redemption for me."

"Why?"

Sandy looked up at the ceiling of the car and balled her hands into a fist. It was as if she was trying to control her rage.

"Sandy?"

"I hurt people, do you understand? A child is dead because of me."

"What do you mean, *a child is dead* because of you?"

Sandy leaned forward placing her face into both her hands, sobbing.

"Sandy? What child?" she asked a second time.

As the crying continued, Brooklyn tried to comfort her, "Listen to me. I know we just met but I can tell . . . what I mean to say is . . . Sandy, I can tell whatever happened you are not a malicious person."

As the sobs began to dissipate, Brooklyn added, "And whatever you did, I know if you ask forgiveness, God will grant it."

Sandy gained control of her tears, prompting Brooklyn to ask, "Can you tell me what happened?"

She wiped her eyes and answered, "I was back home in Boston."

"Boston?" Brooklyn asked. "You're not from here in New York?"

She shook her head. "I lived in a small town outside of Boston, and my marriage was a mess, because of the alcohol."

"Your drinking or his?" Brooklyn asked.

"Mine," she replied.

"Go on."

"I had a drinking problem, but the morning it happened I swear I was sober, but with two DWI's in my past, there was no way the police were going to believe me," Sandy said.

Brooklyn leaned closer, "The morning what happened?"

"I was late for work, not an uncommon occurrence for me, and was speeding through a neighborhood."

"And?" Brooklyn asked.

"I couldn't be late. One more time late and he said he'd fire me."

"Go on."

"Losing my job on top of the drinking, my husband would leave me for sure."

Brooklyn touched her hand, "Sandy, please get to what happened."

Sandy went quiet, her eyes looking off as they filled with tears.

"I swear to God, I didn't see him. Even when I hit him. I didn't see him," she said.

Sandy put her hands over her ears, "And the sound. Sometimes at night when I can't sleep, I hear it over and over again."

"You hit someone?" Brooklyn asked.

"I killed someone," she answered.

"Who?"

"I don't know his name."

Brooklyn waited for more.

"So young, too young . . ." she added.

She looked up to Brooklyn's eyes then, "I still see his face, as clear as that day. That precious little boy, broken and bleeding on the sidewalk because of me."

"Were you arrested?"

Her eyes went wide, "ME? No. I did what cowards do. I ran."

"Here to New York?" Brooklyn asked. "With your husband?"

"Yes, to the first part, and no to the rest," she responded. "He was done with me."

After a pause, she added, "I guess *for better or for worse* was a bit too much for him."

"I'm so sorry," Brooklyn said.

"I don't blame him; I'd be done with me too."

Brooklyn was at a loss for words. Surely this was the person Edward wanted her to help get home, but home to what? A broken marriage and a homicide charge?

Brooklyn then asked, "The police never tracked you here?"

"I hid out with my cousin in Catskill, different last name."

"Wouldn't your husband tell them where you'd be?" Brooklyn asked.

"No, not Frank," she insisted. "He loved me too much to want me sitting in a jail cell."

Sandy looked off into the darkness and added, "He was done with the marriage but not with caring for me."

"So, you just ran, then?" Brooklyn asked.

"When I heard the sirens coming, yes," Sandy answered. "By the time they got around the pond I was gone."

Brooklyn heard what Sandy said but didn't process it right away.

Finally, she asked, "Pond?"

"What?" Sandy asked.

"You said something about the cops coming around the pond."

"Yes, in Meriam Hill," she said. "That's a small area in Lexington."

Brooklyn's jaw dropped open, her mind shifting in all directions.

It can't be.

"Sandy, when was this accident?"

"Last fall," she replied.

"In Meriam, on a road by a pond, you hit and killed a little boy?"

Sandy sniffled, then replied, "Not *little little*, more like twelve or thirteen, I'd say."

Brooklyn almost smirked, raising her hand to cover her mouth.

"What is wrong with you?" Sandy asked. "This is not funny."

"I'm sorry, Sandy."

Then her tone growing with excitement, "SANDY. That's your name right? *Sandy, Sandy, Sandy.*"

"Are you having a nervous breakdown or something?" Sandy asked.

"What's your real name?" Brooklyn asked.

"What?"

"Your real, God given name that your parents called you. You're not really Sandy."

"You're scaring me now, Brooklyn."

"Listen to what I'm asking you, please," Brooklyn continued. "What is your legal first name?"

"Cassandra," she replied.

Brooklyn added, "Cassandra Marshall."

"How did you know that?"

Brooklyn slapped her knees with both hands with excitement, "Son of a gun, he knew. HE KNEW."

"Who knew what?" she asked.

"Edward. He knew you'd be on this bridge tonight and he is using me to get you home. Can't you see it?"

Sandy shook her head, clearly not following.

Brooklyn reached out with both hands, taking Sandy by the shoulders, "He's not dead, do you hear me? The boy you hit, he's alive and well."

Sandy's eyes were filled with confusion.

"Yes, he is," she replied. "I saw it."

"NO, he is NOT."

Sandy could see the overwhelming confidence in Brooklyn's face, but this made no sense.

"I was there. I watched that little boy die," she insisted.

"You thought you did," Brooklyn replied. "And then you left before Edward arrived."

"What are you talking about?" Sandy asked.

"You heard the sirens and ran. Then Edward laid his hands on the child and brought him back."

Sandy looked away with confusion, her mind clearly racing.

"The miracles you mentioned . . ." Sandy said. "In your story about why you believe in God."

"YES."

"You're saying?

"Yes, Sandy. Yes."

There was silence, when Brooklyn said, "His name is Jayden Lancaster. I met him. I spoke with him. Heck, I went to the fair with him and watched him eat fried dough and ride the roller coaster."

"When?" Sandy asked.

"Weeks after you hit him with your car."

"I'm not trying to be cross, but what you're saying sounds crazy, Brooklyn," Sandy said.

"Why?"

"Because people don't come back from the dead," Sandy answered.

Brooklyn took a deep breath, meeting Sandy's eyes.

"Jesus did. And the day you hit Jayden, he brought him back as well."

Sandy shook her head again in disbelief.

"You don't believe me?" Brooklyn asked.

"I know what I saw."

"Do you want proof he's alive?"

Brooklyn didn't wait for an answer, instead taking out her phone and swiping through several photos before, "Here it is."

She held up the phone, showing the photograph taken of the entire group the night of the festival in Fall River.

"Jayden is right there next to Edward," Brooklyn said. "His arm is around him. *Look*."

Brooklyn could tell by Sandy's expression that she recognized the boy's face immediately. She took the phone from Brooklyn's hand, moved her eyes closer to the screen, and started to cry.

Sandy then touched Jayden's face with her finger, asking, "When was this taken?"

"Look at the time stamp. It was at least a week *after* you hit him."

Sandy checked the date, and it was nine days after she struck Jayden. She continued to stare, her hands shaking as she held the phone.

"That kid is alive, Sandy," Brooklyn repeated.

Her eyes glistened with tears as she looked at Brooklyn, asking, "You promise this is true?"

Brooklyn answered, "I swear to you, he's fine. There's nothing we break that God can't fix."

Brooklyn looked up and let out a loud laugh.

"What?" Sandy asked.

"I'm starting to talk like him now," she answered.

Bang, bang.

The sound made both women jump.

Trooper Mills tapped hard on the car window, "I have to make a decision here, ladies. Are we going to jail or the hospital?"

Brooklyn lowered the window, answering, "The hospital."

She turned her attention back to Sandy and added, "Then home to Boston."

As the ladies got out of the car, Brooklyn said, "Can I ask, are you still drinking?"

"No," Sandy replied. "I stopped after I hit the boy. I started attending meetings to help me stay on the path."

Trooper Mills moved closer, gently taking Sandy by the elbow.

"Go with this kind officer to the hospital to talk to someone about what you've been dealing with," Brooklyn said.

"Okay."

"Stay in the AA meetings and continue healing," Brooklyn added.

"I will."

Brooklyn turned to the officer now, "Trooper Mills, do you have a pen and paper."

Mills went into his inside pocket and retrieved both.

"Thank you," Brooklyn said. "I'm writing down my address and phone number, Sandy."

She pushed the paper into her hand, "When you're released from the hospital, I want you to come back to Boston."

"Home?" Sandy questioned.

"Yes," Brooklyn confirmed. "If you can't fix things with your husband, Connor and I have a spare bedroom that you can use until you're back on your feet."

Trooper Mills turned to Brooklyn, "That's very kind of you."

"It's not me, it's Jesus," Brooklyn replied.

"Ah, yes," the trooper said. "You mentioned earlier that you and J.C. were pals. How's that working out?"

Brooklyn joked, "Ya know, Trooper Mills, at first I had no use for the guy, but now he's like a pair of old leather boots you put on and then get caught in the rain."

Mills cracked a smile, "I have no idea what that means."

Brooklyn continued, "The moisture from the rain causes the boots to shrink, and then no matter how hard you pull, you can't get the darn things off your feet. It's like they . . . *he* . . . is a part of you."

"Did you just compare Jesus to a pair of old boots?" Mills asked, fully grinning now.

Brooklyn giggled, "I guess I did. But in a good way. Trust me, Jesus would get it."

Mills rubbed his arms to stave off the chill and said, "Well, much thanks to you and Jesus for helping tonight."

He then turned to Sandy, "I'm glad you are safe, miss. I promise, the people at the hospital are going to help you."

After she was placed in the backseat of the police cruiser, Sandy pressed her nose against the glass and mouthed the words, *Thank you.*

Brooklyn silently answered right back, *God bless you.*

CHAPTER 24
Three Zebras

"You were late," Connor said.

Brooklyn was sitting by the kitchen window in their home watching two squirrels chasing each other around a maple tree. They reminded her of a young couple when they meet and fall in love. You can never tell who is chasing whom.

"Earth to Brooklyn, is anyone home?"

'I'm sorry, what?"

"I said you were late getting home last night."

"Yeah, about that," she said. "Grab us both a cup of coffee. I have a story to share."

For the next half hour, she told him about the bridge, Sandy, and the mess she had made of her life one sunny fall morning: the accident, the drinking, the broken marriage, the running away, and the shame.

"She was literally hanging off the side of the bridge?" Connor asked, eyes wide. When Brooklyn nodded, he said, "You saved her, Brooke. You saved her life."

"Well," she said, "Edward did, or God. He put me on that bridge."

Connor hugged her. "I'm proud of you."

There was a comfortable silence then, the kind soulmates share that need not be troubled by words. Brooklyn loved that about their relationship, how moments of nothing could mean everything.

After a while Connor said, "Something else is going on . . . you seem different."

She gazed at him. "I guess I wouldn't make a good poker player, would I?" At least, not with him.

"What is it?" he asked.

"I don't know, Con. I always viewed religion and faith as quicksand and did my best to avoid them."

"And now?"

"And now . . . that's a good question. And now . . ."

"Hey," he replied. "It's me. Just say it."

Brooklyn hesitated, then said, "One of the reasons I never believed in God was the suffering and evil in the world."

Connor nodded. "I think lots of people struggle with that."

"Yeah. True. Edward explained that it's the unfortunate byproduct of free will."

"What do you think he meant?" he asked.

"That if we're free to live our lives and make our choices, sometimes they'll be the wrong ones."

Connor put his coffee mug down. "Go on."

She said, "I've been thinking about how the darkness of this world really does bring out the light. I know that sounds like something you'd read in a Hallmark card, but it's true."

"Give me an example," Connor said.

"Sure. Take the children's hospital where I brought Edward to embarrass him. I wanted to point at a toddler with tubes coming out of his veins and no hair from the chemo and say, 'Look at this, Edward. There is your omnipotent God at work. Explain child cancer.' I wanted to paint him into a corner."

Connor said, "I'm guessing that's not what happened."

"No. For every sick child, he pointed out five hospital workers who dedicated their lives to save that one fragile life."

She thought, *Billions of people in the world, and they'd fight to save just one. Every single one of them matters. No matter how sick. No matter the odds.*

Her eyes began to tear. "Can you imagine spending weeks trying to save a baby, losing it, hugging the sobbing parents, and then coming back the next day to do it all over again?"

He shook his head. "No. I couldn't."

"But *they* do, saving the ones they can, mourning the ones they can't, and, God knows, losing a piece of their hearts in the bargain." She planted her elbows on the table. Brooklyn leaned towards him. "Think about it.

My newspaper writes about fires, floods, and car accidents, and standing right there in plain sight are the EMS workers, the Red Cross volunteers, and the firefighters who will run *into* danger to save a stranger. That's amazing."

"Yeah," he said, "it is. But it doesn't explain why you seem, I don't know, sad this morning, especially since you helped Sandy."

She sighed. "I guess I'm thinking about how I've behaved whenever you've brought up your faith."

Connor responded, "It's *my* faith, hon, and it works for me. I never judged you or tried to push what I believe on you."

"I know that, and I love you for it," she replied. "Still, knowing what I know now, knowing Edward, Jesus, I feel like a fool."

"But you're not, hon. Everyone struggles with faith, and if they say they don't, they're lying. Or fooling themselves."

"Okay," she said. "I hear you. But can I tell you something, and you *not* defend me or insist it isn't my fault?"

Connor folded his hands.

"Just let me sit here and be wrong for once," she said. "Can you do that, please?"

Connor nodded slowly. "Yeah, okay. Sure."

She took his hand. "I'm sorry I've given you such a hard time over Evi's going to church or first Holy Communion or the million other ways you were trying to bring her closer to God."

He looked like he wanted to soothe her, then caught himself. "Apology not needed, but apology accepted."

"Good, thank you."

Connor said, "Have you thought about what you want to do next?"

"What do you mean? Today?"

"Well, today for starters. Then at work. Do you want to keep writing the column?"

Brooklyn turned her eyes back to the window and noticed the squirrels were gone. "They must have had a lunch date."

"Who?"

"Nothing. I was talking about the silly squirrels."

Connor waited silently for an answer to his question.

"Oh, you asked what I want to do?"

"Yes."

"Today, I was thinking we wake up Evi and get pancakes at the diner," she said.

"Love that," he answered. "And work?"

She scrunched her face. "Would you think I was nuts if I wrote a book about Edward? Take my newspaper article and add all the stuff there wasn't room for."

Connor said, "I think that's a great idea. And you just got the perfect ending—saving the woman on the bridge."

"I guess."

"You guess? It completes the story perfectly," Connor said.

"That's the thing, though," Brooklyn replied. "It doesn't complete everything."

"What do you mean?"

She took a sip of coffee, then answered, "Edward said he was here to heal four people, help others, and get three people home.

"Right."

"He was very specific," Brooklyn said.

"So?" he asked.

"Name them, please."

Connor began counting people off. "He healed Stew, Jayden, the guy at the jail, and you. That's four."

"Keep going."

Connor said, "Lord knows he helped a bunch of people in a variety of ways, and he got people home."

"Count them," she insisted. "The ones he got home."

"Okay. Let me think. He told us at the festival how he helped the lady at the jail get back to her sister, and with your help, he's getting Sandy back to Boston, so, that's two."

Brooklyn nodded. "Exactly. Two. Not three."

Connor thought a moment. "What about Stew? Did he go home?"

"Nope. He's from Boston and never left."

Connor said, "It's probably someone we don't know, then."

"I guess," Brooklyn said.

"But you don't believe that?"

"Probably I don't. No. Loose ends."

"You've always hated them," he said.

"'Cause that's what always trips you," Brooklyn explained. "In journalism and in life."

Connor smiled. "Maybe Edward screwed up. He said three but meant two."

"Yeah, that makes sense, Con. Because God can't count."

He raised his eyebrows. "This might not be the first time. For all we know there may have been three zebras on Noah's ark."

Brooklyn picked up a napkin from the table and raised it, pretending she was going to swat him.

Ding, Dong. The doorbell chimed.

"Saved by the bell," Brooklyn said with a grin.

Before they could move, Evi ran from her bedroom toward the front door to see who it was.

"No running, young lady," Brooklyn called out. "If you slip, you'll regret it."

Evi ignored her mother's warning, and when she tried to stop, her socks slid along the hardwood floor, sending her crashing into the front door.

Bam!

"What was that bang?" Connor called out.

"Just me," Evi called out. "I'm okay." She then peeked through a window and said, "It's some old guy."

Connor eased past his daughter and opened the door to find a man with a receding hairline, in jeans and a flannel shirt, standing on his front step.

"Help you?" Connor asked.

"Is everyone okay?" the man asked. "It sounded like someone hit the door."

Connor answered, "My human bowling ball here. She's fine."

The man was holding a simple white envelope. "Is there a Brooklyn here?"

"I'm Brooklyn," she said as she joined them at the door.

The man held out the envelope. "This is for you."

"What's this about?" he asked the man, as Brooklyn inspected the envelope.

"I honestly have no clue," the man said. "I'm just returning a favor."

"What favor?" She shook the envelope.

It's light. Feels empty.

The man hesitated.

"My wife asked, 'What favor?'" Connor repeated.

"This'll probably sound nuts," he said, "but I was a cop for many years, just retired, in fact. A few months back a man came into the jail, and he did me a kindness."

Brooklyn's jaw dropped. "Oh my God, you're the cop Edward healed! It was arthritis in your hands, right?"

The man smiled wide. "Yes, ma'am, that's me. Teddy Trask." He raised both hands and wiggled his fingers around effortlessly. "See? They're good as new."

"That's wonderful!" Brooklyn exclaimed. "I'm so happy for you."

"Thanks," he replied. He gestured toward the envelope. "So, anyway, Edward wrote a note at the jail, stuck it in there, gave me this address, and told me to deliver it on this *exact* date."

Brooklyn raised her eyebrows. "Did he say why?"

"No. He was just insistent it needed to be today."

She extended her hand to shake Teddy's. "Well, thank you for delivering it."

Teddy looked at their clasped hands. "That Edward is something, isn't he?"

"He's the Son of God," Evi said.

Connor put his arm around his daughter. "That's right, Evi."

Teddy's face lit up. "Wait. Did you say *Evi*?"

"Yes, I'm Evi." She stood up a little straighter.

Trask pointed at the three of them now. "Evi, Brooklyn, and that would make you . . . Kenny?"

"Connor," he corrected him.

"Oh, holy cow," Trask said, looking again at Brooklyn. "You're the one who wrote the article for the *Globe* about Edward and the miracles."

Brooklyn answered, "Guilty as charged."

Teddy scratched his balding scalp. "Can't believe I didn't make that connection until now."

"Well," she said, "according to Edward everything is connected in ways we don't always see."

Trask smiled. "He did talk that way, didn't he?"

"He sure did," Connor said.

Teddy put his hands in his pockets. "Well, my part is finished. It was nice meeting you all."

As he turned to leave, Evi said, "God bless you."

Trask turned back, his eyes filling with emotion. "And God bless you too, Evi. God bless all of you."

After he left, Brooklyn retrieved a brass letter opener she kept in the top drawer of the antique desk in the den. She wasn't going to risk tearing anything that had Edward's handwriting. With one careful *swoosh,* she opened the envelope, then removed a single piece of white paper, folded once, with an address printed inside. Brooklyn flipped it over, hoping to find more, even shaking out the empty envelope to no avail.

"That's it?" Connor asked. "An address with no name?"

"Guess so."

"Do we know anyone at that address?" he asked.

Brooklyn shrugged. "Don't think so. It isn't far from here, though."

"Whad'ya wanna do?" Connor asked, as if the three of them didn't already know the answer.

Evi said, "I'll get the car keys."

CHAPTER 25

He Meant Me

A ten-minute drive took them to a house only two towns away. "Does it look familiar?" Connor asked as he pulled up in front.

"Not one bit," Brooklyn answered. "You?"

"No."

Before the two of them could exit the car, Evi flung open the back door, ran toward the front steps, and rang the doorbell.

"*EVI,*" Connor called out. "Wait for us."

Before they could scold her further, the door opened, and an attractive woman in her twenties appeared. For a moment both sides just stared with confusion.

"It's Piper, right?" Brooklyn asked. "We met at the fair."

Gabriel stepped into view. "Well, isn't this a surprise! Come in, come in. Any friends of Edward's are friends of ours."

Evi skipped in after him.

"How did you find us?" Piper asked as they all went inside. "I don't recall giving you the address."

"You didn't," Connor said.

"The cop did!" Evi exclaimed.

"What cop?" Piper asked.

Brooklyn rested her hand on her daughter's head. "This is a strange one to tell. Are we interrupting you?"

"No, not at all," Gabriel said. "We've got a few minutes. Come sit down."

After they all sat down together in the living room, Brooklyn began, "Did you know that Edward healed a police officer at the jail?"

"Yes," Piper answered. "I'm the one who drove him home after that."

"Plus, you wrote about it in the *Boston Globe*," Gabriel added.

"That's right," Connor confirmed.

"On our drive back from Berkshire County, Edward shared his encounter with the officer," Brooklyn said. "I included it as one of his miracles."

Brooklyn continued, "Anyway, that cop, whom we never met, showed up this morning out of the blue at our home and handed us an envelope with an address inside. No name, just an address. Yours."

Piper raised her eyebrows.

Connor said, "The guy said he got it from Edward, and he was told to deliver it today."

"Why today?" Piper asked.

"That's the million-dollar question," Brooklyn replied.

After a moment's silence, Connor said, "Maybe Edward just wanted us to stay in touch with each other."

Brooklyn was unconvinced. "But why specifically today? If he wanted us together, why not have us exchange information the night of the festival? And why send a note with no name to go with the address?"

Gabriel answered, "I guess that's Edward. Always keeping you guessing." He chuckled. "He once left me a message using Cap'n Crunch cereal."

"What?" Brooklyn asked.

Gabriel held up three fingers. "Scout's honor."

"Did you eat the message?" Evi asked.

"Of course, I did," Gabriel answered. "I was hungry."

Everyone laughed.

Evi said, "Well, I'm thirsty."

Before Brooklyn could apologize for her daughter's directness, Piper replied, "I can take care of that. Do you want to come to the kitchen with me, Evi? We'll get drinks for everyone." A few minutes later, they returned carrying a tray of mugs.

With juice for Evi and coffee for the adults, the two families shared about their time with Edward. The conversation for the next half hour flowed easily as if they'd been friends for years.

Gabriel then checked his watch. "I'm so sorry, but I need to get going." He looked at Piper. "Why don't you stay with our guests? I'll be fine on my own."

Piper sprang up. "The mass. Geez. I'm sorry, Dad. With all the excitement of this visit, I almost forgot." She turned to their guests. "I hate to rush you out, but we have to go."

Brooklyn rose from her chair, still clutching her coffee mug. "It's our fault for dropping in unannounced. I hope we didn't inconvenience you."

Gabriel answered, "Nonsense. It was great being with you."

Connor reached for his coat. "Where do you go for mass?"

"Cathedral of the Holy Cross," Gabriel said. "It's for my late wife."

Piper touched her father's shoulder. "Dad has a mass said in mom's honor every year on her birthday."

"And that's today?" Connor asked.

"Yes," Gabriel replied. "We like to get there early to light a candle."

"Wait a minute," Brooklyn said. "*Today* is your late wife's birthday?"

He nodded.

"Well, this just got weirder," she said.

"What do you mean?" Piper asked.

"Your mom's birthday falls on the exact day Edward wants a note delivered to us, with your address. That's a bit of a coincidence, don't you think?"

"Could be a fluke," Connor said.

Brooklyn scoffed. "With Edward? No way. I always felt like Edward was playing chess while the rest of us were stuck on checkers."

"What do you mean?" Gabriel asked.

"Putting us together *today* of all days? It smacks of . . . I can't find the right word."

"Serendipity," Piper said.

"Exactly," Brooklyn replied.

Connor helped Evi into her coat. "If you don't mind me asking, Gabriel, when did you lose your wife?"

He paused, then said quietly, "A long time ago. The kids were very young."

Brooklyn saw the pain in his eyes. "I'm so sorry. I'm sure she was wonderful."

"She was. And beautiful."

Piper said, "You should show them her picture, Dad."

Gabriel glanced nervously at his watch.

"It's okay," she said. "We have time."

He walked over to a shelf and took down an 8 by 10 brown frame, then used his sleeve to clear the dust on the glass. "Here we are," he said as he held out the photo for them to see. It was a picture of Gabriel, his wife, and their two young children. "This was taken a couple of years before we lost her," he said, his voice shaky.

"What a gorgeous family," Connor said.

Evi pointed at the baby in the photo and said to Piper, "Is that you?"

"It sure is," Piper said. "We all start pint-sized."

Brooklyn was still as a statue, her eyes fixed, face frozen. Silent.

"That's something, eh, Brooke?" Connor nudged her to remember her manners and stop staring.

She inched her nose closer to the photo. Then, with a gasp, she dropped her ceramic coffee mug onto the hardwood floor.

CRASH.

The mug broke to bits. "I'm so sorry," she said, as Connor knelt to pick up the pieces. "It's just . . ." She pointed to the face of Gabriel's late wife. "Mary," she said.

Gabriel looked astonished. "That's right."

"Mary Elizabeth Flanagan," Brooklyn continued, her eyes tearing up.

"How did you know that?" Gabriel asked.

Brooklyn reached for a chair to steady herself. "I'm sorry, Gabriel. I know you're in a hurry, but can I just ask how you two met?"

Still holding up the photo, he said, "I worked for a small woodworking shop, and we got a job at a health clinic in Lenox."

"The Hallowed House Addiction Center," Brooklyn said.

"Gosh, I think that *was* the name. How'd you guess that?"

Brooklyn replied, "Please. Continue your story."

"Anyway, I noticed Mary right away, but she was always busy, being a nurse and all, and I didn't think she knew I existed. Then a few weeks later, the church had a dance and a bunch of us went. She asked me to dance, and from that day forward we were together."

Brooklyn said quietly, "Until you lost her to breast cancer."

Piper stared at her. "My father asked you earlier how you know all this?"

Evi pointed to the photo. "Look, Mommy! She has green eyes just like yours."

Piper leaned forward to examine it. "She has more than just your eyes! If you change the hair and narrow the face, she could be your sister."

Gabriel turned the photo around so he could look at it. "She does look a lot like you."

"More accurately," Brooklyn said, "I look like her."

"Let me see it again, Dad." Piper took the frame from him, her eyes darting back and forth between Brooklyn's face and her mother's, as if comparing every hair, freckle, and eyelash. "Who are you?" she finally asked.

Brooklyn gripped the back of the chair. "Evidently, I'm your sister. Half-sister, to be exact."

"Wait. What?" Connor said. He set the broken mug pieces down on the serving tray.

Brooklyn turned toward him. "The day Edward took me to Berkshire County. Remember, I told you he showed me a photo of my biological mother?"

"Are you saying?"

"Yes," Brooklyn answered.

"So," Piper said, "your mother is . . ."

"Yes." She reached for Piper's and Gabriel's hands. "Mary Francis Flanagan Matthews."

There was a long pause. Then Brooklyn, measuring her words, asked, "She never spoke to you about a baby?"

Gabriel looked down, like a little boy caught in a fib.

"Daddy?" Piper asked. "Did she?" When he hesitated, Piper said, "We've still got time. Please."

Gabriel looked at his daughter. "You were just babies yourselves when we lost your mom, and I never told you because . . . I didn't want you to think less of her."

"I could never, Daddy. Please, just tell me."

Brooklyn released their hands. This was between them now.

Gabriel clutched the photo to his chest. "She was young. Barely eighteen. She told me she got mixed up with the wrong man and drugs. He got her addicted, pregnant. Then left her." He paused. "She didn't feel right . . . um . . . ending things, so she had the baby and gave the little girl up for adoption. She wanted her daughter to have the life she couldn't give her."

Piper eyed him with deep tenderness. "Why would I ever think less of her for that? It sounds like she did the brave thing. The hard thing."

Gabriel took his daughter's hand. "She did. And she dedicated her life to helping others who found themselves in the same dark place. Helping them back to life."

"It only makes me love her more, Daddy."

Brooklyn waited a moment, then said, "All my life I've wished I had a little sister."

Piper looked at her and smiled. "Now you do."

"Now I do," Brooklyn answered, with love in her eyes.

"And a brother," Gabriel said. "Don't forget Paul."

"Yes," Brooklyn said, "Paul. Does he live in Boston?"

Gabriel touched his son's face in the photo, answering, "Paul was a Marine. We lost him in the war."

"I'm so sorry, Gabriel."

After a silent pause, Brooklyn added, "I wish I could have known him."

Piper nodded. "I think the most important thing you need to know about Paul is that when he had the chance to run and save his life or stay and save others, Paul stayed."

Brooklyn, seeing the love and pride in Piper's eyes, said, "I'm sure if Edward were here, he'd quote us some passage from the Bible about that."

Connor said, "Heck, I can do that. John 15:13. One of Jesus's greatest hits."

Gabriel nodded. "That's the perfect one to describe Paul."

Brooklyn asked, "What's John 15:13?"

Gabriel smiled at Connor, and they quoted it from memory together in one voice. *"Greater love hath no man than this, that he lay his life down for his friends."*

Connor nodded, and a warm smile spread across Gabriel's face.

Piper said, "Looking at you now, Brooklyn, I can't believe we didn't make the connection when we all met at the festival. Or from old photos of Mom."

"Remember," Connor said, "it was dark, and we only spent a few minutes together with Edward."

"That's true," Gabriel said. "I didn't see the resemblance until now."

Brooklyn brought both hands to her cheeks and said, "Oh, my God."

"What?" Connor asked.

"I just realized something! Edward promised to bring three people home."

Connor counted them off. "The young lady at the jail. The woman on the bridge and—"

"Me," Brooklyn said. "He meant me." She looked at Piper and Gabriel. "Home to a family I always wanted but never knew I had."

Piper hugged her new big sister.

"What woman on a bridge?" Gabriel asked.

Brooklyn smiled. "Oh, that's a story you've got to hear—"

Ding, Ding, Ding.

All heads turned to see what that noise was.

Evi was banging a spoon on the edge of a coffee mug. "Hold up! Does this mean I have aunts and uncles?"

Everyone laughed.

Piper reached out and put her arm around her. "Yes, you do."

Gabriel looked at his watch again. "I wish we could stay, especially after this amazing revelation, but I don't want to miss Mary's mass."

Piper looked at Brooklyn, Connor, and Evi. "What are you three doing right now?"

Brooklyn locked fingers with her husband and daughter. "Going to church to pray for our mother, Mary."

CHAPTER 26

I'm Already There

The mass for Mary was held at the Cathedral of the Holy Cross in Boston's South End. Afterwards, Brooklyn, Connor, and Evi lingered on the gray stone steps out front with their newfound family while the sound of church bells rained down from the belfry above. With a reluctant goodbye, they all agreed to gather again soon to share stories and try to catch up on a lifetime of memories.

Once in the car, Brooklyn took off her beige Burberry jacket and bunched it up to form a small pillow.

"I see somebody's tired," Connor said.

"Yeah. I am. Do you mind if I grab a catnap on the way home?"

"Saving Sandy on the bridge and meeting your new family wear you out?" he teased.

She placed the rolled-up jacket against the car window and rested her head against it. "Maybe a little."

"Dream sweet things," Connor said, as she closed her eyes.

With the gentle rocking of the car, it didn't take long for her to drift off to sleep.

Lost in dreamland, she heard a voice calling from the darkness, "*Brooklyn, open your eyes.*"

At first, she thought it might be Connor telling her they had arrived home, but this felt different.

Brooklyn, open your eyes now.

When she did, she was struck by a white light. Brooklyn thought she was still in the car, blinded by another vehicle's headlights, but that didn't make sense because it was daytime.

"It takes a moment to adjust," the voice assured her.

Slowly the light eased, as if someone lowered a dimming switch, and Brooklyn found herself not in the car, but standing beneath an apple tree. She was holding her Burberry jacket and instinctively put it on.

As she buttoned the front, she realized Edward was standing before her, wearing a crisp white robe, his long brown hair resting gently on his shoulders. For the first time since she laid eyes on him months earlier, he looked every bit the image of Jesus Christ.

"Edward?" she asked, sounding only half-convinced he was there.

"I think we're past using that name, don't you?" he replied.

"Jesus," she offered then.

"There you go," he said, grinning.

"Is this a dream?"

"What do you think?" Jesus replied.

Brooklyn said, "Feels like a dream except for—"

"The light?"

"Yes. It reminds me of what Jayden called the *bright place*."

Jesus picked an apple from the tree. "You mean the day he was hit by the car? The day I brought him back."

Brooklyn surveyed her bright white surroundings. "Yes." She paused then, wanting to say something but guarding her words.

"What?" Jesus asked.

"If this isn't a dream," she began.

"I assure you, it's not," he said.

Brooklyn said, "Does that mean . . ."

"What?" Jesus asked a second time.

"I hope you aren't planning to take me anywhere, especially after I *just* met my new family."

Jesus handed Brooklyn the apple. "Heavens, no. But I am here to give you a choice."

"Of what? Apples?" She raised the fruit in her hand.

"No," he replied with a smile. "The apple is for later. Look around. Don't you recognize this place?"

Brooklyn casually placed the apple in her jacket pocket, turned, and realized she was flanked by dozens of trees standing neatly in rows. "An apple orchard?"

"*The* apple orchard," Jesus corrected. "The one where the branch broke, and you fell."

Brooklyn rubbed the back of her head. "I remember."

"Before that day and before we met, you seemed happy with your life," Jesus said.

"I was. For the most part."

Jesus continued, "I thought I'd offer you a chance to go back to it."

"What do you mean?"

He took a seat on a bench beneath a tree. "I mean, go back to your life before."

"Before what?" Brooklyn asked. "I'm not following."

"Before me," he answered. "It would be as if we never met."

"That's not possible."

"Sure, it is. I snap my finger, and you wake up on the ground after falling out of the apple tree. Our time together, our conversations, all a dream."

"It's *not* possible," she said more emphatically.

"Why?"

"Because I don't want it," Brooklyn answered sharply.

"Why, Brooklyn?"

"I just don't," she barked back. "Can't we just leave it there?"

Jesus moved closer. "Don't get upset. Just tell me why?"

"Because . . ." she began, then stopped herself.

Jesus waited patiently.

"Now that I have you in my heart, I can't live without you."

Jesus embraced her. "And the student becomes the teacher," he whispered.

At that moment, Brooklyn heard barking. She turned and saw a handsome man in his early twenties tossing a stick to a small white dog. The two were playing, the man laughing with unbridled joy.

"Who is that?" she asked.

The Savior was silent, his eyes urging her to watch. When the man bent over to pick up the stick, a pair of military dog tags dangled from his neck.

"Wait," she said. "Is that Paul?"

"Yes, it is. And Laddy, his faithful friend."

Brooklyn watched them play for a moment. Paul seemed oblivious that they were there.

"So, our pets do go to heaven?"

Jesus answered, "Would it be heaven without them?"

When Brooklyn looked back, Paul and the dog had moved beyond the trees and faded out of sight. "Is this why you brought me here? To make me an offer I'd never take and to see a brother I never knew?"

"No," Jesus said, "I want you to meet someone."

"Who?"

"Her." He pointed toward a wall of white mist that surrounded the apple trees.

At first, Brooklyn saw nothing, and then a figure took shape in the mist.

It was a woman, dressed head to toe in lavender, the blouse matching her pants. She was a few years younger than Brooklyn, yet her face was undeniably familiar.

As she approached, Brooklyn looked at Jesus and said, "Is that?"

"Yes," he answered.

"But I'm not ready for this. I don't know what to say."

He put his hand on her shoulder. "Look to your heart."

Brooklyn was now face to face with a woman who could have been her twin.

"She won't speak first," Jesus said. "It has to be you."

The woman waited, as pretty and patient as a butterfly resting on a flower.

"Hello," Brooklyn said.

In a mild, welcoming voice, she responded, "Hello, Brooklyn."

"What should I call you?" Brooklyn asked.

"You already have a mom who raised you, so Mary would be fine."

Even though she had seen two photos of her biological mother, this younger version of Mary looked different than Brooklyn had imagined. Her skin smooth, hair dark, no wrinkles or signs of the difficult life Brooklyn knew she'd had.

Jesus said, "You're the best version of yourself here."

"So this is heaven?"

"No. More of a waiting room."

Brooklyn turned her attention back to Mary. "I have a confession to make," she began.

"What's that?" Mary replied.

"I dreamt for years of this moment and all the terrible things I'd say to you."

"I know you did," Mary replied.

"But now," Brooklyn continued, "the only words that come are . . . I'm sorry."

"There's nothing to be sorry for."

Brooklyn looked down, conflicted. "There is, though. I judged what you did, not knowing your reasons why. I was wrong."

"Everything happened the way it was meant to," Mary answered. "Can you see that now?"

Brooklyn nodded, thinking of her beautiful life.

"May I make a confession now?" Mary asked.

"Sure."

"I've waited a long time to say something to you," Mary continued.

Brooklyn waited, breathless.

"I'm so proud of you, Brooklyn, the person you've become."

Mary reached her hand out, and Brooklyn took it in hers.

Brooklyn's eyes began to well up as she looked down at their clasped hands. "Thank you for the choices you made, regarding me," Brooklyn said.

Mary replied, "Tell you a secret?"

"Sure."

"The moment I felt you stir inside me, there was no choice."

Brooklyn smiled.

"What are you thinking?" Mary asked.

"I was remembering the first time I felt Evi toss and turn in my tummy. I woke Connor from a sound sleep, and we sat up in bed for two hours, our hands pressed to my skin."

"So, you understand?"

"I do."

Mommy!

Brooklyn heard a child's voice call. She looked around, but no one else was there.

"Did you hear that?" she asked Mary.

Mommy, we're here.

Mary let go of Brooklyn's hand. "You have to go now."

Jesus approached and took Mary gently by the arm. She whispered something to him. He nodded and answered, "You're welcome." With that, he started to lead her away.

"Wait," Brooklyn blurted out.

Mary responded, "Goodbye, Brooklyn."

"Don't go yet. Please."

"It's time," Jesus said, as he and Mary walked into the mist.

"But I have so many questions!" Brooklyn called after them.

Mommy, wake up.

Brooklyn looked around again, but no child was in sight.

Who is that? Who is calling me?

"WAIT," Brooklyn shouted to Mary and Jesus. "Answer one question."

The pair paused and looked back.

"Tell me what heaven is like?"

Jesus replied, "It's like the best day of your life, over and over again with everyone you adore, in the presence of God."

Mary nodded and added, "In a word, it's love."

The two of them turned to go.

"Mary," Brooklyn called.

The mist was rising above her waist now.

"MARY," she yelled louder.

There was no response. She was losing her.

Then, as loud as Brooklyn could, she called, "*MOTHER.*"

Mary raised her hand, seeming to halt the advance of the rising mist. "Yes, sweetheart?"

"What should I tell Gabriel and Piper?"

As the mist engulfed her, Mary answered, *Tell them,*

I hear every prayer.

I share every joy.

I catch every tear.

Until we are together in God's holy kingdom. I love you.

Promise me you'll tell them.

Promise me, daughter.

Mary was gone.

As Brooklyn stared at the mist, she whispered, "I promise."

Jesus was still there, looking at Brooklyn.

"Thank you," she said, "for giving me a chance to meet her."

Jesus smiled like a person with the answer to every question. "What's that smile about?" Brooklyn asked.

Jesus said, "Do you know what Mary whispered to me before she left?"

"No. I couldn't hear her."

"She said, 'Thank you for answering my prayer.'"

"Her prayer?" Brooklyn asked.

"One of the greatest prayers I've ever received."

Brooklyn suddenly remembered her conversation with Edward in the hallway of the hospital about prayer. He'd told her that someone didn't need to be kneeling in a church to talk to God.

"What did I tell you that day?" Jesus asked.

"You said one of the best prayers you ever heard was from a woman lying on a dirty floor at the end of her rope."

"That's right," Jesus said.

Brooklyn looked back toward the thick mist where Mary had vanished a moment before.

"My mother?"

"Your mother," Jesus replied. "Two weeks into rehab, struggling to release the demon of drug addiction."

Brooklyn swallowed hard, tamping down her welling emotion. "And what did she ask for in that prayer?"

"Two things involving you."

"Please tell me," Brooklyn said.

Jesus continued, "That her baby be safe and that someday she would get to see her again."

The mist began to rise once more.

Brooke, wake up.

Mommy, please come back to us.

"It's time," Jesus said. "Time to go home."

The bright light returned, hurting Brooklyn's eyes again. She could feel herself being pulled away.

"Jesus," she called.

He was far away.

"*JESUS, WAIT,*" she called a second time.

Brooklyn closed her eyes to the blinding light, lowered her voice, and said, "I just wanted to say thank you."

"For what, child?" he asked, his voice no longer distant.

Brooklyn opened her eyes slightly. Jesus was right in front of her, surrounded by that blinding white light.

"For taking my place on the cross."

Jesus smiled. "You were right, Brooklyn."

"About what?"

"You *are* changed and you could *never* go back to the way life was before."

As Brooklyn closed her eyes, Jesus reached out to touch her shoulder and said, "Now . . . wake up!"

Brooklyn opened her eyes and found Connor's hand shaking her shoulder where Jesus had just touched her. The bright light was gone.

"My God, you scared us," Connor said.

Evi was leaning over the backseat of the car. "Where did you go, Mommy? We couldn't wake you up!"

Brooklyn looked around. They were parked in the driveway outside their home.

"I was in heaven," she said. "Or, close to it."

"Dreaming, you mean?" Connor asked.

"No, Con, heaven. It was our favorite apple orchard, and I saw Jesus, my mother, Mary, and my half-brother, Paul. It was all so bright."

"Dreams can be pretty convincing," Connor said.

"Trust me, *this* was not *that*."

She got out of the car. The chill in the air made her immediately put her jacket back on.

Evi took her hand and swung their arms back and forth as they walked along the stone walkway toward their home. "So?" Evi asked, looking up into her mother's face.

"So, what, buttercup?"

"What's heaven like, silly goose?"

Brooklyn stopped and looked at her daughter and husband, overwhelmed by gratitude for the love and meaning both brought to her life. "I asked Jesus that very question, and he told me that heaven is like living the best day of your life over and over again with the people you love, in the presence of God."

Evi asked, "What does that mean, though?"

Brooklyn kissed Connor and Evi, one after the other, then stepped onto their front porch. "It means, when it comes to heaven, I'm already there." Connor saw a look of absolute contentment in his wife's face. She was indeed a changed woman.

Knowing the front door was locked, Evi said, "Keys, please."

"Do I have 'em?" Brooklyn thrust both hands into her coat pockets.

Connor raised the keychain. "I drove, remember?" As he unlocked the front door, he said to Brooklyn, "You're *sure* you weren't dreaming?"

With both hands still in her pockets, Brooklyn's eyes suddenly went wide, and a smile spread across her face.

"What?" Evi asked, now grinning herself.

"Am I sure I saw Jesus and that there's a heaven waiting for each of us?" Brooklyn said.

As her husband and daughter waited with anticipation, Brooklyn slowly pulled her hands out of her pockets, turning over her right hand to reveal a shiny red apple clutched between her fingers.

Brooklyn stared at the apple and said, "I am."

She tossed it to Connor, then in an exaggerated and slow rhythm said, "How . . . do . . . you . . . like . . . them . . ."

"DON'T SAY IT!" he shouted, while laughing.

"Kiss me then, as if the kiss had to last forever."

Connor drew her into his arms, the apple falling effortlessly from his hands.

There was but one thought as Evi looked up at her parents' embrace.

Heaven.

ACKNOWLEDGMENTS

Because this novel was such a personal story of faith, it was supremely important for me to share a positive Christian message with you, the reader. Writing and editing the story took me more than a year, and the finished product in your hand would not be possible without the help of many people. Author and editor Sharon Brown was instrumental in helping me find my voice and sharpen my focus. From Paraclete Press, Robert Edmonson, Lillian Miao, Michelle Rich, and Lexa Hale are just a few of the many fine Christians who shared my vision for what this story could be.

Also, thank you, the reader, for taking this journey of faith with me. If *The Carpenter's Son* helped bring you closer to Jesus, then my many hours at the keyboard will certainly be worth it.

Lastly, I want to thank God for helping me write it. Many a time, I sat still at my computer, uncertain of which path in the forest this story might take me. I would close my eyes, say a silent prayer, and the light in my mind would guide my steps. Trust me, there was a co-pilot along for this journey.

ABOUT PARACLETE PRESS

Paraclete Press is the publishing arm of the Cape Cod Benedictine community, the Community of Jesus. Presenting a full expression of Christian belief and practice, we reflect the ecumenical charism of the Community and its dedication to sacred music, the fine arts, and the written word.

Learn more about us at our website:

www.paracletepress.com

or phone us toll-free at 1.800.451.5006

SCAN TO READ MORE

YOU MAY ALSO BE INTERESTED IN